Merle E. Taff

DOUGLAS STUART MOORE

DOUGLAS MOORE was born in Cutchogue, New York, in 1893. He studied at Yale with Horatio Parker and D. S. Smith and then, after a tour in the navy, he studied with d'Indy at the Schola Cantorum in Paris, and with Nadia Boulanger. He was later a student of Ernest Bloch in Cleveland. In 1924 he won the Pulitzer Traveling Scholarship, and in 1933 received a Guggenheim Fellowship.

In 1940 Moore succeeded Daniel Gregory Mason as head of Columbia's music department and was appointed MacDowell Professor of Music in 1945. From 1946 to 1952 he was president of the National Institute of Arts and Letters; he was president of the American Academy from 1960 to 1962 and is currently a member of its board of directors. He has received the degree of Doctor of Music from the Cincinnati Conservatory and Syracuse and Yale universities. He has appeared as guest conductor with several leading American orchestras. His Symphony in A major received Honorable Mention by the New York Critics Circle in 1947.

His works have had numerous performances all over the world. *The Devil and Daniel Webster,* his earliest opera, was first performed on May 18, 1939, with Fritz Reiner conducting. *Giants in the Earth* won him the Pulitzer Prize in Music in 1951. He won the New York Critics Circle Award in Opera in 1958, for *The Ballad of Baby Doe,* which was commissioned by the Koussevitzky Foundation and was first performed in Central City, Colorado, July 7, 1956. Five years later it was performed in Europe. His most recent opera, *Wings of the Dove,* had its first performance at the New York City Center in 1961.

Besides the present volume, Douglas Moore is the author of *Listening to Music.*

Books by Douglas Moore

A GUIDE TO MUSICAL STYLES
From Madrigal to Modern Music, Revised Edition

LISTENING TO MUSIC

A GUIDE TO
Musical Styles

FROM MADRIGAL TO MODERN MUSIC

Revised Edition

by DOUGLAS MOORE

MACDOWELL PROFESSOR OF MUSIC EMERITUS, COLUMBIA UNIVERSITY

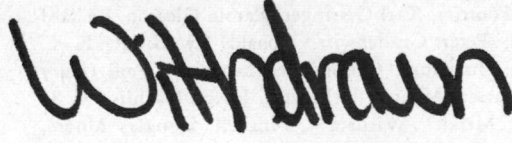

The Norton Library

W · W · NORTON & COMPANY · INC ·

NEW YORK

W. W. Norton & Company, Inc. is the publisher of current or forthcoming books on music by Gerald Abraham, William Austin, Anthony Baines, Sol Berkowitz, Friedrich Blume, Howard Boatwright, Nadia Boulanger, Nathan Broder, Manfred Bukofzer, John Castellini, John Clough, Doda Conrad, Aaron Copland, Hans David, Paul Des Marais, Otto Erich Deutsch, Frederick Dorian, Alfred Einstein, Gabriel Fontrier, Karl Geiringer, Harold Gleason, Richard Franko Goldman, Peter Gradenwitz, Donald Jay Grout, F. L. Harrison, A. J. B. Hutchings, Charles Ives, Leo Kraft, Paul Henry Lang, Jens Peter Larsen, Maurice Lieberman, Joseph Machlis, W. T. Marrocco, Arthur Mendel, William J. Mitchell, Douglas Moore, Carl Parrish, John F. Ohl, Vincent Persichetti, Marc Pincherle, Walter Piston, Gustave Reese, Curt Sachs, Adolfo Salazar, Arnold Schoenberg, Denis Stevens, Oliver Strunk, Francis Toye, Donald R. Wakeling, Bruno Walter, and J. A. Westrup.

CONTENTS

8   Contents

PREFACE

Let it be understood at once that this book is neither a history of music nor a comprehensive survey of the literature. It is an attempt to transport the reader into the spirit of each of several great periods—Renaissance, Baroque, Classic, Romantic, and Modern—so that he feels its quality, understands its enthusiasms, its technical resources and limitations, and its habits of thought and style.

There is first a general introduction to each period in which these factors are considered and the principal composers are listed. Then from each period at least one example of every important type of composition is examined more closely, to see what musical elements go into it, how it is put together, and how it fits into the artistic temper of the age. The compositions thus selected are all chosen with a view to their being available on records, so that they can be played as often as may be necessary to grasp their meaning. In so far as possible they are characteristic examples of each musical type, not average compositions by any means, but representative of the best that the period has to offer. This sampling of the music of the past should give the reader a background of musical understanding, so that when he encounters a composition from one period or another he will feel at home in the style, will have an idea of what to expect, will not be disappointed if he is not blasted out of his seat by a baroque concerto grosso, nor surprised when a contemporary string quartet begins with a fugue. If he can thus develop his musical assurance and broaden his taste he will enjoy his musical experiences more, and, if he cares to go on, he will be well prepared to undertake the study of the history of music which would logically follow.

The composers who are to be discussed are considered only in the light of their compositions. Little will be said of their lives or personalities, except as these are expressed in the works examined. For such information the reader will be referred to biographical and historical material in the bibliography at the end of the book. Our explorations will be confined as much as possible to the music alone.

In selecting the works for study the choice has not been easy. No two musicians could possibly agree on the best fugue of Bach, the best Beethoven quartet or symphony, or the one indispensable Wagner opera. Many favorites will have been omitted, for which omissions apologies are tendered herewith. Nor will it be found that every composer mentioned is represented. No attempt has been made to deal with works which illustrate the transition from one period to another. As far as possible, each period is represented at its height by compositions which mark its culminating achievements, and by the works which are performed most frequently today. If, however, the list of suggested compositions stimulates an appetite for more, so much the better. The literature of music is now so well covered by phonograph recordings that no one would think of confining his explorations to any list as brief as may be included in this book.

The omission of the age of classical antiquity and of the medieval period seems indicated in a work of this type because the music is rarely encountered by the average listener, and, with the exception of Plain Chant, recordings are seldom available.

In the explanations and analyses of compositions the use of technical terms has been limited to what is absolutely necessary to an understanding of design. It would be impossible, because of the space it would take, to explain each term in the text as it occurs. The writer has assumed that the reader before embarking upon this study will have had some previous experience with musical design and nomenclature. For the benefit of those whose knowledge of terminology is not sufficiently inclusive, a dictionary of musical terms with thumbnail explanations will be found on page 321.

The assembling of the material of this book and its present arrangement would have been impossible without the assistance of a number of friends and colleagues. Professor Paul H. Láng with his aid and encouragement and suggested revisions has generously contributed to the result, and I wish not only to thank him but to acknowledge the importance and extent of his distinguished collaboration. To Professor George Dickinson of Vassar, Professor Albert Elkus of California, and Professor Roy D. Welch of Princeton I am indebted for most helpful suggestions in selection of works for inclusion in the text. Mr. Willard Rhodes of Columbia University has generously provided the articles on the Scarlatti sonatas and the *Seventh Symphony* of Beethoven. I wish to thank Professor William J. Mitchell for the extraction and copying of the themes quoted in the text. Mr. Richard Angell, Miss Barbara Lewis, and Mr. Reinhard Pauly have also rendered invaluable assistance for which I am deeply grateful.

Permission to quote musical examples from copyrighted works is hereby acknowledged with thanks to the following publishers and agents: for Stravinsky's *Le Sacre du Printemps,* and Prokofiev's *Third Concerto for piano and orchestra,* opus 26, the Galaxy Music Corporation, New York, sole agents in the United States for Editions Russe de Musique, Paris, and A. Gutheil, Paris; for Bloch's *Concerto Grosso,* C. C. Birchard and Company, Boston, Massachusetts; for Sibelius's *Fifth Symphony* and Hindemith's *Quar-*

tet, opus 22, the Associated Music Publishers, Inc., New York; for themes from Debussy's *Nocturnes*, Jean Joubert, Paris, and Elkan-Vogel Co. Inc., Philadelphia, Pennsylvania, copyright owners.

1 PROLOGUE

EVERY great work of art from the past has two meanings, one of them contemporary, the other historical. If a poem, a painting, or a piece of music has no contemporary meaning, it belongs to history alone, and will be chiefly of interest to the scholar. When we approach such a work as Milton's *Paradise Lost,* Michelangelo's "Last Judgment," or Bach's *St. Matthew Passion* we forget all about history, for it communicates with us directly in terms of our own thoughts and feelings. In other words, it has contemporary significance. The sonorous lines of Milton's poetry, the strength and beauty of his imagery, the rugged force of Michelangelo's figures and the sweep of his design, the dramatic and expressive quality of Bach's music, the gorgeousness of its sound, all these have nothing to do with history. Not that these works do not have historical meaning, for they fairly bristle with it; no one will say that we cannot understand them more clearly when we have grasped their historical implications. But the truth remains that the history of art becomes important to the individual only after the art itself has awakened his interest and has involved, at least partially, his affections.

Music is especially contemporary in significance because it is a thing which exists only in sound, a complex phenomenon of tone combinations organized by a rhythmic pattern in time rather than in space. It parades past the senses, leaving no trace save in the listener's mind. Unless he can read musical notation, the listener has no way of apperceiving the music as a whole other than by re-creating it in his own imagination. This requires careful attention, the ability to recognize features of the design as they are revealed, the power of relating these to the whole, and a good memory. Repeated hearings of the same music are the best aid to understanding it. "I like what I know" is both as trite and as true as "I know what I like," for the ability to re-create a piece of music in the imagination brings with it enormous satisfaction which is enjoyed by everyone, consciously or unconsciously. This process is the largest part of the understanding of music.

How pointless, then, is the study of music history when one cannot recognize the simplest patterns of an unfamiliar piece of music or cannot follow the unfolding curve of a melody without being hopelessly confused. With only the scantiest experience and practically no training in the apperception of music, one is asked to embark upon a historical survey of something that he scarcely understands at all, and to fill his mind with dates, lists of composers and compositions, tendencies, trends, and style evolutions when his rebellious ears fail to tell him the difference between a fugue and a sonata, except that one is mercifully shorter than the other.

The most logical way to approach the literature of music as a study is to build up a technique of listening to it. Listen to a piece of simple music over and over again until the details of its design are clear and you know what it is all about. Try thinking through a song with which you are familiar and see if you can follow each detail in your imagination. The mistake which the average auditor makes is failing to realize that he must really pay attention if he wants to hear music intelligently. And yet if after a course in beginning French someone makes a remark to you in French, you listen to the words carefully, sort them out in your mind, and thus arrive at the meaning.

As you become more familiar with the sound of the language and with its constructions, the process of understanding it grows less painful. You finally arrive at that happy competency when you hardly have to think at all in order to understand. It becomes second nature. Music works the same way but few people realize it; they listen sporadically, but are impatient when results arrive slowly, and are apt to decide that music in the larger forms is impossible to understand, and that even in the case of short pieces they only want to hear familiar music.

The individual who trains himself to concentrate in listening—and it is rather a surprise to find how easy it is and how much pleasure is derived along the way—soon discovers that musical design consists of patterns which recur according to some plan, with contrasting material to give variety. He learns to recognize musical ideas, which consist of arrangements of rhythm, successions of tones in the form of melody, and combinations of tones in the form of harmony. He applies this newly found technique to various pieces which interest him, and discovers that there are certain conventional designs in music which follow a more or less predictable curve. The simplest pattern, that of the *folk song,* can be divided up into a series of phrases of equal length which often repeat and are varied by other phrases not too dissimilar. Generally in a folk song only one key or tonality is employed. A larger design, known as *song form,* combines two such units with the symmetrical plan of ABA, sometimes employing contrasting keys. The A and B may be entirely different, or certain features from the one may be incorporated into the other to give a design of greater subtlety. A plan of alternately repeated and varied sections with a recurrent refrain is the *rondo.* A succession of sections of approximately equal length, in which the music of the beginning section is repeated with alteration and elaboration in each succeeding section, is the *theme and variations.*

From this point on the patterns become more difficult and complex. Keeping track of a simple melody and accompaniment is one thing, but, when the melodies begin to double up so that two or more independent lines are going on simultaneously, sorting them out is a harder task. But even this type of music, which is known as *polyphony,* has certain habits for which the listener may be prepared. Sometimes the melodies thus combined are first heard separately; more often they are imitations of each other. The device of the *canon,* which, like the round, superimposes a melody upon itself, leads to *canonic imitation,* in which features of the same melody are combined in individual melodies more freely than in the canon. The *fugue,* of formidable reputation, is easy to follow when the plan is understood, because it is based upon a short central subject, first heard alone, and then woven into a texture in which it is constantly reappearing in one of the two or more melodic voices which are engaged in the operations.

The designs which are found in the symphony are the most extended, and for the inexperienced listener the most difficult to understand. In the first place, the style of arrangement which we find in the symphony, the sonata, and chamber music does not follow the idea of simple melodic phrase succession which is characteristic of the song, rondo, and theme and variations. Furthermore, there is a definite plan of key succession and a wider use of key contrast not only between movements but within a single movement. Melodies used in symphonic style are called *themes,* and they often have short, characteristic features known as *motives* which lend themselves well to varied repetition in the melodic design. The texture is more polyphonic as these themes and motives are spun out in a continually changing pattern of construction. This varied repetition of short musical ideas is known as *development.* Sometimes it is easy to follow, as in the first movement of Beethoven's *Fifth Symphony,* when the four-note rhythmic motive, with which it begins, reappears in the design as clearly and even more often than in a fugue. At other times the plan of development is less apparent and more subtle. But in every piece of music, no matter how complex, there is much simple repetition, and if one can grasp the idea which is to be repeated, which usually appears early in the proceedings, there is much pleasure and reassurance to the ear in recognizing it when it returns.

The listener who learns to follow simple patterns with comparative ease is apt to be discouraged when he finds that he gets lost so quickly in a symphony. Let him be comforted; the same thing happens in some degree to everyone, no matter how trained or experienced. Our powers of concentrated attention are too limited for sustained accurate listening. Even the professional usually enjoys familiar music more than music heard for the first time, because the effort in listening is so much less. But, with training and concentrated attention, the path to familiarity is much shorter and the ability to grasp the meaning of the great works of the literature is immeasurably increased.

We have agreed that the contemporary aspect of art is of more immediate importance than the historical. But although we may admit that every piece of music which is interesting enough to be played or sung today has contemporary meaning and lives in our own epoch, the bulk of the music which we hear is not modern in its origin. Because of the part which familiarity plays in the popularity of a piece of music, new music has a definite handicap to overcome, and contemporary music, whatever one may think of its importance, must take time to establish itself. This is not true of our taste in reading. We study the masterpieces of the past as a part of our education, but most of us read contemporary literature for enjoyment. The only contemporary music which is universally enjoyed is our "popular" music, which is carefully planned so as to be quickly grasped and is dinned into our ears as often as possible so as to establish its popularity.

Music of the recent past, say, the nineteenth century, has the advantage of being both generally familiar and near enough to our own times so that the thought and idiom are readily understandable. As we recede into the past through the times of Beethoven and Mozart to the age of Handel and Bach and earlier, we find the conventions and customs of the art stranger and less immediately appealing. *St. Matthew Passion*, great as it is, has certain features that may strike us less favorably than, let us say, Wagner's *Die Walküre* or Verdi's *Aïda:* its orchestration, for instance, and the elaborate and "untuneful" quality of the melodies of its beautiful arias.

We run into difficulties also in instrumental music. Suppose we undertake the study of musical design as suggested above and attempt to apply the knowledge we have gained of the sonata (the plan usually studied is that of Haydn and Mozart) to a sonata of Handel. We discover to our confusion that practically nothing we have learned about the sonata is applicable save that it is a work in several movements. There is no exposition, development, or recapitulation. Instead of concentrated themes, there is usually some kind of figuration which is woven into a melodic texture without much contrast. Movements based on short themes are more in the style of the fugue than of the sonata. There are no crescendos and no dramatic climaxes. And yet this is not a primitive essay toward the style of Haydn and Mozart, the work of a "forerunner," but a fully realized, mature work of art, which follows the stylistic precepts of an earlier age, most enjoyable when viewed in the light of its artistic setting. If we happen upon a work called *Sonata pian e forte* by Gabrieli, an Italian composer of the late Renaissance, we find the plan again entirely different. Here is a one-movement work written for separate choirs of instruments, which alternate and combine in the relationship known as antiphony. Its effect is quite different from that of the classic or the baroque sonata, but when we recover from our surprise we find it attractive and opulent in its sonorities.

We must be careful, therefore, in assuming that a given musical design is the same in one age as in another. The practice of identifying designs can be carried to absurd lengths. The chief value in being able to place a label on a given design is that it proves to us that we have heard the inner evidence, but one must beware of clutching at the bare bones of the structure while the real musical essence goes by unnoticed. Therein lies the richness of the music. But, although we are under no compulsion to place each piece in its formal or historical pigeonhole, some knowledge of the background of thought and style of the great periods of music is a help to enjoyment and understanding of a wider range of the literature of music.

Interest in the music of the various periods of history is probably more diversified today than ever before. The bulk of what we hear may still be from the nineteenth century, but the music of earlier times is performed a great deal. Who would have thought up to a few years ago that college glee clubs would be singing Renaissance motets and madrigals, that harpsichord recitals would be popular on the radio, that Bach would be a box-office attraction at symphony concerts, or that festivals would be devoted to the music of Mozart? The ambitious listener finds himself confronted with many new problems if he wants to be prepared for all contingencies.

So, while reaffirming the principle that the contemporary aspect of music comes first, and that unless we can listen to a piece of music intelligently the study of the history of music is more or less futile, let us examine five of the great periods of music—Renaissance, Baroque, Classic, Romantic, and Modern—from which the compositions which we hear today are chiefly recruited.

Before embarking upon the music of the Renaissance

this much should be said about the antique and medieval periods which preceded it. The music of antiquity played an important part in the life of the times. We know a great deal about its history and its underlying theories from the writings of philosophers and historians who were familiar with it, but unfortunately such records of it as may have existed have remained for the most part undiscovered. It is doubtful if in spite of the activity of the scholars it will ever be more than a speculative study, based on a handful of fragments.

The music of the medieval period, on the other hand, is gradually emerging from obscurity into a full-fledged body of musical literature, and we shall hear more and more of it as time goes on and scholars continue to decipher its archaic notation and make it available in modern scores. The first part of this period was dominated by the church and only such music as it approved has been preserved. Scholars are of the opinion today that the secular music of the time had a more "modern" sound than the music of the church, which for many years was based upon Plain Chant, itself a product of Eastern as well as Western sources. This theory is carried out by the first secular music that is widely known, the songs of the troubadours, trouvères, and minnesingers.

Music of the medieval period consists of the Plain Chant (Gregorian Chant), which is still the fundamental liturgical music of the Catholic Church, and an extensive polyphonic literature of sacred and secular choral music, including other various types of designs, devices, and forms known as organum, discant, fauxbourdon, motet, chanson, and ballad. The study of these types, so important in the evolution of musical style, still may be said to belong to the scholarly sphere of the history of music and therefore will not be undertaken here.

2 *THE RENAISSANCE*

Introduction

THE Renaissance period in music, which corresponds approximately to the same epoch in the other arts, may be said to extend roughly from the institution of certain reforms representing the "modern" spirit, which took place in the fourteenth century, to the end of the sixteenth century. This great epoch of art and letters, which included such men as Giotto, Botticelli, Donatello, Leonardo da Vinci, Michelangelo, and Raphael in art, and Petrarch, Boccaccio, Ronsard, Chaucer, Marlowe, Spenser, and Shakespeare in literature, may appear at first glance to be somewhat disappointing in its music. Several explanations may be advanced for this. Music, unlike painting and sculpture, exists only when performed. Renaissance art is familiar to everyone, evidences and examples of it surround us on every side, but in spite of the recent revival of interest in the music we hear relatively little of it performed, and indeed the bulk of the literature is still unpublished.

During the eighteenth and nineteenth centuries the great emphasis upon instrumental music brought about a decline of interest in choral works. The music of the Renaissance, in which the instrumental was subordinate to the choral, was largely forgotten and unperformed. Unfamiliarity with the notation of the medieval and Renaissance periods, lack of understanding as to the principles of rhythm, meter, and harmonic style, ignorance of the proper method of performance, all these mitigated against a true appraisal of the artistic value of the music. Only in recent years, as a result of the discoveries of scholars of the late nineteenth and beginning of the twentieth centuries, has there been a revival of this music and an opportunity to hear it, and it is still not performed enough for the large music public to become accustomed to its unfamiliar style. The most impressive Renaissance music is the music of the church, and to ears accustomed to the regular pulsations of instrumental rhythm and the tonal splendors of the modern opera and symphony this unaccented choral singing in seemingly undramatic, short compositions, often devoid of any instrumental accompaniment, sounds strange and remote.

The artists of the Renaissance, however, had no feeling of the inadequacy of their music. Contemporaries, among them the greatest literary figures led by Shakespeare, expressed unstinted admiration for the music of their times. Such a man as Orlando di Lasso, skillful composer of all types of music, sacred and secular, whose career was equally brilliant in Flanders, France, Italy, and Germany and who wrote to texts in five languages, must be assigned a place beside the greatest artists of the Renaissance, and it is only now, as his music and his style become increasingly familiar, that his true greatness is understood and acknowledged.

The perfection of music printing in the early sixteenth century made much wider distribution possible, and the fame of composers and performers spread beyond their own locality. The practice of inviting distinguished musicians to foreign courts to compose and to perform was established at this time. Wandering musicians were attracted to the flourishing towns and found employment as civic instrumentalists, as performers for banquets, festivals, and workers' guilds. There were many new patrons for the art in the transalpine countries, among the newly arisen aristocracy of mercantile or of military origin. Castiglione in his famous treatise *The Courtier,* written in 1514, considered musical training an indispensable attribute of the cultured man. Above all, this widespread interest brought about an especial demand for music by amateur performers everywhere. Music was highly respected and universally performed.

The church, which hitherto had supported and controlled all Western music, continued to be its most influential patron and inspired all the greatest artists. But, instead of sternly forbidding all popular elements as represented by the music of the people, it gradually admitted an infusion of secular feeling to the profit and enrichment of musical style. Popular melodies were often incorporated into the polyphonic texture of the Mass, influencing melodic and harmonic structure. Such popes as Julius II actually encouraged the cultivation of sumptuous art music, even in the church.

The most characteristic feature of the musical style of the Renaissance is its polyphony. Ever since the preceding medieval period counterpoint based upon the combination of independent melodies, or upon canonic imitation of one voice by another, had been established as the basis for church composition. As secular influence made itself felt, a tendency toward a more harmonic style, with emphasis on the topmost voice and less independence of the supporting melodic lines, is evident. Simultaneously with this, the modern key feeling of the major and minor scales tends to replace harmony based upon the old church modes. Despite this leaning toward a style more nearly resembling that of our own age, the impression of Renaissance music remains tonally rather vague to the listener accustomed to modern dissonance and frequent modulation. The polyphonic style, because of the overlapping of independent voices, seems lacking in rhythmic color. The church music is definitely mystical, not sensuous or dramatic in the modern sense. The secular music is usually more "modern" in effect, often indeed prophetic of the opera and instrumental style to come, but here also the compositions are short and the instrumental accompaniments disappointing in dynamics and in volume. However, acquaintance with Renaissance music, especially in the case of the choral literature, soon leads to an appreciation of the beauty and grandeur of the Mass and the motet, and to a keen enjoyment of the charm, gusto, and delicate craftsmanship of the chanson and the madrigal.

The instruments of the Renaissance were many and varied, and instrumental skill was highly developed. The most popular instrument of the age was the lute, a many-stringed, plucked instrument appearing in many sizes and shapes. Much of the extensive literature for the lute is still unknown because its notation was indicated by fingerboard positions, known as tablature, rather than on the customary staff, and there were many different systems. Keyboard instruments of the harpsichord and clavichord type, known in England as the virginal, were popular all over the Continent in the sixteenth century. Various wood-wind and brass instruments were in use, but particularly favored by the amateur was the recorder, a mouthpiece flute easy to play and built in different sizes to cover the several ranges of the human voice. Also constructed in different sizes was the viol, the predecessor of the violin, which differs from the latter in smaller sonority, greater number of strings, and in various details of design. The first example of standard instrumental ensemble, the so-called Chest of Viols, which consisted of a set of three—bass, tenor, and treble—appeared in England at this time.

Ensemble music was written during the later Renaissance for these instruments, but in general they were regarded as interchangeable with voices, and with minor exceptions there was no standard ensemble such as later developed in the orchestra or the string quartet. In the earlier periods of the Renaissance instrumental forms were merely transcriptions of choral pieces with little instrumental coloring or attempt to realize the virtuoso possibilities of the instruments. As we advance in the sixteenth century these transcriptions acquire an instrumental character and, under various names—*ricercar, canzone, fancy,* etc.—embark upon an independent career, gradually abandoning the practice of indicating upon the manuscript *per cantar e sonar,* meaning to be sung or played, a symbol which is often found in music of the period. In the second half of the sixteenth century a definite feeling for instrumental coloring appears, and lute and keyboard virtuosi, as evidenced by the music, attain a mastery of their instruments.

The mere listing of the details of Renaissance music cannot convey the true flavor of the period, which even at this distance, with the horizon leveled off by the passing of the years, seems to have been a very exciting time. Discoveries were not limited to science and to geography: the individual was discovering himself, his own possibilities, and the new resources of enjoyment upon every side. The fact that music was no longer merely a part of the church service, to which one listened respectfully but did not really share, and now was becoming a part of his life, enlivening the holidays and coming informally into the home, must have been a grateful discovery to the Renaissance man. For this was a great time for the musical amateur. He could sit around a table and indulge with some kindred spirits in a madrigal or a chanson, or without much difficulty he could learn to play the recorder or the lute and join in an improvised orchestra. Later ages may find the average man relinquishing his rights in participation, preferring to sit quietly and listen to the virtuoso performer, abashed by the thought of daring to compete with him, or in a state of more advanced listlessness turning on the radio for a denatured musical enjoyment, mostly going on somewhere else; the man of the Renaissance found in music a companionable and entertaining relationship and this spirit is reflected in the compositions of the period.

Some Composers of the later Renaissance

Franco-Flemish School

Josquin Desprès, c. 1450–1521	Italy and France. Greatest master of the turn of the century
Willaert, c. 1480–1562	Founder of the Venetian School at St. Marks
Orlando di Lasso, 1532(?)–1594	Chiefly at Munich

Roman School

Palestrina, c. 1525–1594	Composer of Papal Chapel
Marenzio, c. 1553–1599	Famous composer of madrigals

Spanish

Victoria, 1540–1611	The greatest of Palestrina's Spanish colleagues

Venetian

A. Gabrieli, 1510–1586	St. Marks, Venice
G. Gabrieli (nephew), 1557–1612	St. Marks, Venice

English

William Byrd, 1543–1623	Chapel Royal, London
Orlando Gibbons, 1583–1625	Chapel Royal, London
Morley, 1557–1604(?)	Famous composer of madrigals

Choral Types of the Renaissance

THE MASS

That portion of the Roman Catholic Mass, which from the late Middle Ages was customarily set to music in the polyphonic style, consists of five principal divisions with various subdivisions: (1) the *Kyrie* (Lord Have

Mercy); (2) the *Gloria* (Glory to God in the highest); (3) the *Credo* (I believe in one God, Maker of heaven and earth); (4) the *Sanctus* (Holy, Holy, Holy, Lord God of Hosts); *Benedictus* (Blessed is He Who cometh in the Name of the Lord), and *Osanna* (Hosanna in the highest); (5) the *Agnus Dei* (Lamb of God). This section of the Mass is called the "ordinary" and is unchangeable. The other part is called the "proper" of the Mass, with definite assignments following the church year. Originally the music of the entire Mass consisted of a single line of melody, unmeasured in the modern sense, based upon one of the church modes rather than upon the major and minor scale. This is known as Plain Chant or Gregorian Chant, and portions of this music as well as entire Gregorian Masses are still used in the Roman Catholic Church.

The polyphonic setting of the Mass found in compositions of the Renaissance often bases the music upon a theme derived from Plain Chant or from a secular song. The title of the Mass is an indication of the source of the principal theme.

PALESTRINA—*Sanctus* (with *Benedictus* and *Osanna*) from the Mass *Assumpta est Maria*

This Mass, for six-part chorus, is based upon a theme from the Antiphonal for the first Sunday in October. The theme, an ascending figure, is heard at the beginning of the Sanctus in the second soprano part (Example 1). It is immediately imitated by the first soprano in augmentation. The other voices enter separately, either with an imitation of the theme or in free counterpoint. Notice that the sopranos and altos are boys' voices, more penetrating in the lower registers and lacking the warmth of women's voices. The voices overlap, making it difficult to follow each independent melodic line but giving the music a changing harmonic texture which, although almost entirely lacking in dissonance in the modern sense, keeps the music moving along. This music is somewhat austere, lacking in tunefulness and surface emotional appeal, but full of the exalted spirit that we associate with Gothic architecture.

EXAMPLE 1.

The six-voice counterpoint gives an added effect of splendor.

The Benedictus is a four-part setting, more expressive as befitting the text. The voices enter in pairs, the second soprano and tenor imitating the first soprano and alto.

The Osanna, also based upon the Gregorian fragment, is in six parts, each voice entering separately with either the theme or a countertheme of reverse motion.

THE MOTET

The Renaissance motet is a polyphonic song on a Latin Biblical or sacred text. It frequently employs the canonic entrances of the separate voices which are found in the Mass. In its strictest design, each phrase of the text is associated with a line of melody or theme, which appears in succession in every voice. These several melodies frequently overlap so that the voices are singing different text phrases and melodies at the same time. This naturally does not lead to great clarity of words, but forms a pleasing musical design for the ear. This type of treatment is varied by alternation with passages in which all voices move as a rhythmical unit and achieve an effect more harmonic than contrapuntal.

VICTORIA—*O magnum mysterium*

Victoria's style is perhaps warmer and more intense in feeling than that of his friend and colleague, Palestrina. This motet is especially tender and full of devotional spirit. The translation of the text follows: "Oh wonderful mystery and sacrament which permits animals to see the newborn God lying in his cradle. Oh blessed Virgin whose body was deemed worthy to bear the Saviour, Jesus Christ. Alleluia."

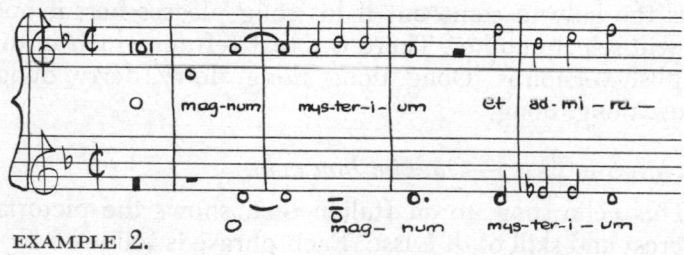

EXAMPLE 2.

The first part of this motet is in canonic style with separate themes and with the voice groupings entering singly (Example 2). The second part, beginning with "O beata Virga," employs the voices in harmonic relationship. For the final Alleluia the contrapuntal style is resumed.

THE MADRIGAL

The madrigal is a secular song, usually sung *a cappella,* which had great vogue in Italy and England during the latter half of the sixteenth century. Like the motet, which it often resembles in design, it is a polyphonic song, but is written to a secular text in the vernacular, which it attempts to interpret with utmost fidelity. It is freer and more vivacious in texture than the motet and is usually written in five voices.

1. Italian and English Secular Songs, Madrigals, etc.

ORLANDO DI LASSO—*Matona mia cara*

This is a gay love song to an Italian text by the great Renaissance master. Although there are four parts of equal interest, the voices usually move together rhythmically. It is a serenade, resembling a madrigal, in which the singer asks the lady to come out if his song pleases her; if not, he will select another. There is a text refrain which in the English version is "Dong, dong, dong, derry, derry, dong, dong, dong, dong."

ORLANDO DI LASSO—*Ola che bon echo*

This echo song, to an Italian text, shows the pictorial interest and skill of di Lasso. Each phrase is followed by a duplicate in echo chorus, and the color and rhythmical effect of this alternation is masterly.

GESUALDO (c. 1560–1614)—*Resta di darmi noia*

Gesualdo, Prince of Venosa, was a tempestuous figure of the Renaissance whose colorful life (he murdered his wife's lover) is reflected in music both daring and intense. His harmonies, chromatic and surprising even to twentieth-century ears, are said to have disturbed his more placid contemporaries.

This madrigal is a despairing love song. The translation is: "Cease to torment me, cruel delusion, that I shall never again be the one whom you love. Joy for me is dead. I dare not hope ever to be happy again."

MORLEY—*Now is the month of Maying*

This spring song with melodious top voice is an indication of the tendency in the madrigal toward the simple harmonic chorus, later to be a feature of the opera. Morley's song has been widely sung by modern glee clubs, but, since this is really vocal chamber music, the effect is better without doubling of the voices.

GIBBONS—*The silver swan*

An expressive setting of the legend of the swan whose only song is voiced in death. This madrigal, also modern in its harmonic arrangement, is frequently performed today.

2. German Part Song

ISAAC (c. 1450–1517)—*Innsbruck, ich muss dich lassen*

In Germany the madrigal was not as readily welcomed as in England, and German composers used it sparingly toward the end of the sixteenth century. Its place was taken by the simple four-part song with melody in the top voice. This type of song was upon occasion taken over into the Lutheran service to serve as a chorale melody. The above example (*Innsbruck, I must leave Thee*) was written by the Netherlandic composer Isaac, who had been in that city at the court of Maximilian and who had applied for leave to attach himself to the court of Lorenzo the Magnificent, in Florence. It is an appealing melody suggestive of the German student songs later to become so popular. It also appears as a chorale to the words *O Welt, ich muss dich lassen* (*O World, I must leave Thee*).

THE CHANSON

The chanson of the French Renaissance (not to be confused with the many medieval varieties known by the same name) was the French equivalent of the Italian madrigal. It was also a polyphonic song on a secular text and, as in the case of the madrigal, it was often performed by one voice, the others being taken by instruments. As a rule it was set for four voices to the five of the madrigal, and its texture was less complicated. Toward the end of the sixteenth century the influence of motet and madrigal resulted in a more involved polyphonic idiom in the chanson. Of paramount importance is the clear formal design of these Renaissance chansons, which often follow the modern ABA design.

JANEQUIN (c. 1485–c. 1580)—*Ce mois de Mai*

Janequin was a delightful composer of a great variety of chansons. He especially enjoyed pictorial effects in music, and wrote representations of such things as the song of birds and women's chattering, which he depicted in extended compositions which are really vocal tone poems. A spring song, this is one of his short chansons. Renaissance poetry is frequently difficult to translate because of its racy humor. Blushes are usually spared because of the difficulty of hearing the words in polyphonic passages, even when one is familiar with the language. This poem, in which a young lady looks forward to the coming of her lover, is untranslatable. The music is as spicy as the words.

ORLANDO DI LASSO—*Quand mon mari*

This is an example of late-sixteenth-century French chanson and shows the influence of the madrigal in its polyphonic complexity. Although gay and amusing, the text may be translated without censorship: "When my husband comes home it's my lot to be beaten. He takes the spoon out of the pot and throws it at my head. I am afraid he will hit me. He is false, ugly, jealous. He is ugly, riotous, grumbling. I am young and he is old."

Renaissance Instrumental Music

Although instrumental music is as old as vocal music, our knowledge of its earlier medieval phases is meager because such music—mostly improvised—was seldom written out in notation. Another reason is that much of the vocal music of the thirteenth through the fifteenth centuries was performed by both voices and instruments, and a specific instrumental style arose only when, with the advent of the true *a cappella* style in the sixteenth century, the two branches, vocal and instrumental, acquired independence. Throughout these centuries there was a growing demand for special music for instruments to perform, but for many years such compositions as were made available were usually patterned on the models of sacred and secular vocal music, and were often simple transcriptions of madrigals, chansons, and motets. These were known by such names as *canzone* and *ricercar*.

EARLY CHANSONS TRANSCRIBED FOR INSTRUMENTS

PIERRE DE LA RUE (d. 1518)—*Autant en emporte le vent*
OBRECHT—*Tsat een meskin*

These chansons, the second one of Dutch origin, are of strict polyphonic design with canonic imitations and separate entrance of voices suggesting the motet, although the melodies are secular in style. They are performed, as presented in Volume 3 of *L'Anthologie Sonore,* by an ensemble of flute, viols, lute, and harp, the individual coloring of which makes the polyphony very clear. Since the parts were found with only the first line of each verse indicated, it is assumed by the musicologist Curt Sachs that they were intended to be played rather than to be sung.

CHANSONS WITH VOICE AND INSTRUMENTS

GARNIER (first half of sixteenth century)—*Resveillez-moi*
GENTIAN—*La loy d'honneur*
CLAUDIN DE SERMISY (c. 1490–1562)—*En entrant en ung jardin*

These chansons, from Volume 2 of *L'Anthologie Sonore,* are simple, tuneful melodies sung by a single voice and accompanied by an ensemble of guitar, flute, and piccolo. The choice of accompanying instruments was left to the performers and usually depended upon whatever instruments were available.

INDEPENDENT INSTRUMENTAL MUSIC

1. French Dances of the Sixteenth Century

Dance music of the period has a more modern sound than the instrumental music derived from the chanson and the madrigal. As a matter of fact, in a much earlier period simple, recurrent patterns in duple and triple rhythm using the modern major and minor scale may be found, but, since this music was frowned upon by the church, not much of the earlier literature was preserved and examples from the thirteenth and fourteenth centuries are rare.

These simple and gay tunes were used to accompany the dances in fashion at the French aristocratic courts in the middle of the sixteenth century. The *pavane* was a stately dance in duple rhythm usually coupled with a more lively figure in triple time, known as the *gaillarde.* The grouping of these contrasting rhythms led in a later epoch to the instrumental dance suite. The *branle* was a popular round dance in duple rhythm in which each couple imitated the figures executed by the leading couple. The music was

played on various types of instruments, but in France preference was given to bowed stringed instruments. (From
L'Anthologie Sonore, Volume 2.)

2. German Dances Around 1600

Not much difference is to be noted in these somewhat
later dances by German composers since they followed
French and Italian models. The first is a pavane by Mel-
chior Franck (1573–1639). The second is a lively dance
of the round variety. (From *Album—2000 Years of Music.*)

WILLIAM BYRD—*Pavane and gaillard*

This is an example of similar dances written in England
in the time of Queen Elizabeth. It is played by viola da
gamba and harpsichord. The viola da gamba (knee viol)
corresponds approximately in range to the violoncello.

3. English Virginal Music

Very interesting independent instrumental music was
written during the second half of the sixteenth century for
the English variety of the harpsichord, known as the virginal. This instrument lent itself to various descriptive effects and to elaborations of simple tunes with rhythmic
changes of increasing motion, leading to the type of classic
theme and variations.

GILES FARNABY (c. 1560–1600)—*The new sa-hoo*
MARTIN PEERESON (c. 1580–1650)—*The fall of the leafe*
GILES FARNABY—*A toye*

The first of these three pieces from Volume 2 of *L'Anthologie Sonore* is a set of elaborations on a popular Dutch
air. The other two are of the pictorial variety, the one sad,
the other gay.

4. Spanish Lute Music

The Spanish School of the sixteenth century rivaled the great musical nations in every field. Of particular interest and originality was their lute music, songs and solo pieces. The lute, being able to render both polyphonic and chordal styles with equal ease, was the most versatile and popular instrument of the Renaissance.

LUIS MILAN (sixteenth-century Spain)—*Three pavans for lute*

These dances are played on a *vihuela de mano,* or "hand viol," as distinguished from the *vihuela de arco,* the bowed viol, an instrument shaped like a guitar with six strings. (From *L'Anthologie Sonore,* Volume 4.)

5. Renaissance Sonata

In the late Renaissance the term "sonata" is used not to indicate a form but a composition for instruments as opposed to a cantata, a composition to be sung.

G. GABRIELI (1557–1612)—*Sonata pian e forte*

This beautiful sonata is by Gabrieli, one of the great musical figures of the Venetian School and organist at St. Marks. Like the paintings and architecture of the period in Venice, the music is opulent and impressive, a foretaste of the splendors of the baroque period to come. The music is an imitation of the effect of two antiphonal choruses and resembles the transcription of a late Renaissance vocal piece with chordal rather than polyphonic interest.

3 THE BAROQUE

Introduction

THE term "baroque" was originally used by historians of art to describe certain architectural and pictorial tendencies which developed at the end of the Renaissance, a sort of theatricalism which displayed itself in elaboration of design and proportions, effects of light and shade, a sought-after impressiveness of size and of setting. The moving spirit behind this tendency, which originated in Italy, to spread later to the rest of Europe was the Catholic Counter Reformation, which sought to oppose the Protestant movement and regain the lost provinces by overwhelming the world with a grandiose, emotional, and conquering church. The spirit of this movement found adequate expression in all the arts connected with the church; thus music reflected the same tendencies apparent in the architecture and painting of this period, which extended from the latter part of the sixteenth century to the middle of the eighteenth century. In music it is characterized by a sudden break with polyphony (which, however, was later reintroduced) and by the coming to the fore of new dynamic and dramatic types, such as opera, oratorio, cantata, and various categories of instrumental music.

In its first stages opera was an expression of the classic dreams of certain late Renaissance men of letters. As first presented, it was an attempt to unite the arts of music and drama as they were supposed to have existed in the Age of Pericles. The somewhat artificial and anemic result was soon enlivened by fusing it with the rich resources of the madrigal and the festival and religious plays, and opera—this time a true product of the baroque—sprang into great popularity, not only as a feature of court life but also as a feature in the life of the rank and file of the Italian people, whose enthusiasm was later shared by much of the rest of Europe. Opera influenced the whole future course of music, exploiting the dramatic elements inherent in the madrigal, the poignant choruses of the Venetian composers, the natural aptitude of the Italians for expressive singing, and all the resources of opulent theatrical art and fondness for display of the baroque. It provided in the symmetrical aria, the so-called *da capo* aria, the design which was to serve as a basis for practically all subsequent music, both vocal and instrumental; and in the overture and other purely instrumental sections it created independent instrumental types and forms which were to become important ancestors of the classic symphony.

Unfortunately for us, baroque opera is still more important historically than as a part of our own musical life. The operas, once so popular, seldom appear on the stage today and were practically unknown in the nineteenth century. This is not because the music is in any way inferior to the instrumental music of the period, which we hear so often, but because classic and romantic opera coming afterward established new standards of taste which made the old operatic conventions appear stilted and ridiculous. The books of the period were based upon mythological or historical subjects and were treated in the most perfunctory fashion without any element of naturalism, a succession of formalized stage episodes with the chief objective of maneuvering the singers into situations where they could best display their elaborate vocal art. Italian operas, which set the fashion, always featured the male soprano and alto, the vocal skill of these performers apparently compensating for their strange appearance. Even as late as the time of Handel, the vogue of the *castrati* continued, and it was only in the latter half of the eighteenth century that they gradually disappeared.

But if the splendor of the baroque opera cannot be re-created on the contemporary stage no such difficulty attaches itself to the choral music of the period. The oratorio, the Passion, and the Mass, under the influence of the opera, were infused with a dramatic spirit and a splendor of effect that have lost none of their power to impress with the passing of the years. No one can listen to such a work as Bach's *B minor Mass* or Handel's *Messiah* without sensing the magnificent breadth of baroque style. There is nothing in the literature of music, not even the great symphonies of Beethoven or the epic music dramas of Wagner, which excels it in grandeur of conception or richness of sound.

Simultaneously with the spread of opera, instrumental music was greatly extended and expanded in a literature now definitely emancipated from choral transcriptions. A purely instrumental style suitable to the artistic capabilities of the various instruments was evolved. Instrument making reached a new level of perfection with the violins of such craftsmen as Stradivari and Guarneri, and the violin family with an enhanced emotional quality of tone displaced the pallid sonorities of the viols. The harpsichord and clavichord, now at the height of their perfection, the one with a wide variety of color effects, the other with sensitive and expressive dynamics, achieved the popularity formerly accorded to the lute. The organ became more flexible, adopted modern notation, and was the inspiration of a succession of Italian and German composers culminating in the masterpieces of J. S. Bach. The orchestra, which was, of course, indispensable to the opera, was for a time a miscellaneous collection of instruments varying with the fancy of the individual composer, but in later baroque operas it was permanently established as a group of winds in combination with the standard string ensemble of violins, violas, cellos, and basses.

Although the music of this first great instrumental age was somewhat overshadowed by the subsequent coming of the symphony and the development of the modern orchestra, baroque instrumental music plays an increasingly large part in our musical life today. In the field of organ music the compositions of the Italian and German masters of the seventeenth and early eighteenth centuries are the backbone of the literature. The great fugues of Bach, his exquisite choral preludes, the organ concertos of Handel, the various short compositions of the Italian and French organists are the chief reliance of the recitalist today, who has discovered that the organ music of later periods is bleak and trivial by comparison.

The recent revival of interest in the harpsichord has revealed the true importance of the keyboard music of the period. Now that we can hear this music on the instrument for which it was intended rather than on the piano, so unsuited to its style, the clavier music of Couperin, Scarlatti, Bach, and Handel is emerging from the "historical" group, dutifully prefacing piano recital programs, and is finding an enthusiastic public in its own right.

Violin music of such baroque composers as Corelli, Vivaldi, and other Italians has always been admired by string players, who consider the music of this period unexcelled in its feeling for the nature of the instrument. The baroque ensemble music, which was lost sight of in the great popularity of the symphony orchestra and which is admittedly still a small voice when placed beside it, is now more frequently heard, and, although often distorted by the coarsening effect of too large a body of players, the concerto grosso and the solo concerto, typically baroque in their spirit and style, are today an important part of the orchestral repertory.

In its own time baroque music was naturally greatly admired and was handsomely subventioned by the nobility, which had now definitely supplanted the church as chief patron of the art. Not that the church was at all unappreciative, but secular music was more and more coming to the fore in social and artistic importance. All the various European courts employed bodies of musicians, whose performances were important features of the social life of the time. In Italy and France opera became a brilliant spectacle, staged with the most lavish display. Singers were greatly in vogue and circulated from opera house to opera house exercising a bland sovereignty over their publics and over the music which they graciously consented to sing. Although in Germany the larger courts, such as Dresden, Berlin, Stuttgart, etc., all had their well-endowed opera houses, the many smaller princely, grand ducal, and episcopal courts, not able to maintain such costly musical organizations, contented themselves with small orchestras. This accounts for the extensive cultivation of instrumental music in Germany. Even small principalities often boasted of instrumental bands for civic occasions.

Church music reflected the popular trend of the times. Even modest churches had good choirs and orchestras for elaborate musical services often lasting several hours. In the Roman Catholic Church the influence of the admired operatic style made itself felt in the increasingly dramatic quality of the music and the newly important instrumental accompaniment to the Mass. Operatic elements, such as aria, arioso, and recitative, also found their way into Protestant church music. In the meantime the Lutheran Reformation developed a new popular style of church music based upon the chorale, a simple hymn with text in the vernacular, well adapted to congregational singing. The fusion of the popular and contrapuntal elements in German music with the dramatic-operatic coming from the Italian Catholic baroque reached its final synthesis in the works of J. S. Bach.

The principal vocal forms of the baroque were the opera; the oratorio, similar to the opera in plan but more contemplative in nature, set to a religious text and generally presented without scenery or costumes; the cantata, a shorter choral work, religious or secular; the Passion, a choral work resembling the oratorio but based upon the story of the New Testament; and the Mass.

The instrumental forms were the fugue, an outgrowth of the transcribed motet or ricercar; the *sonata da chiesa* (church sonata), a composition for two or three instruments in several movements; the *sonata da camera* (chamber sonata) and the instrumental suite, which consisted of several dance movements; the *concerto grosso,* an ensemble piece of several movements; and the *solo concerto,* an outgrowth of the latter. The so-called *opera sinfonia,* or overture, belongs likewise to this group, for the curtain raisers soon became detached from the opera and were often performed as independent pieces. Short pieces in free style, such as preludes, fantasias, and toccatas, were sometimes associated with fugues, but often appeared separately. The *passacaglia,* a composition constructed upon a fixed bass pattern, was a popular type, especially for the organ.

The music lover of limited experience is sometimes puzzled by preliminary encounters with baroque style, for it is really very different in effect from the more familiar designs of the classic and Romantic periods. To begin with there is the matter of harmony. We are accustomed to striking modulations and key contrasts and the lush harmonic backgrounds of the Romantic composers. The baroque composer was interested in modulation chiefly because of the direction which it gave to the music. Almost all the forms are based upon a succession of planned tonalities, proceeding generally from the starting key to that of its nearest neighbor and then returning to the original. (In the case of major, tonic to dominant; in minor, tonic to the relative major.) Other modulations are made in the same purposeful manner, not to surprise, but to extend the length of the composition. All of these key relationships are very clear and are hardly ever beclouded by incidental modulations.

Harmony, then, is a feature of the design; harmonic color, highly seasoned chords for their own sake, is sparingly used. The texture of a great deal of the music is polyphonic. That means the momentum of the music is increased by the simultaneous flow of several melodies. Baroque music seldom is concerned with contrasting themes, but with a singleness of purpose, and generally only one idea goes ahead with irresistible forward motion. It is this insistent progress which provides its interest and excitement, for the crescendo, the device of gradual increase from piano to forte, upon which the classic and Romantic composers depend so much for their dramatic climaxes, was never used as a principle. Forte and piano passages appear in alternation for purposes of contrast, but are used in abrupt succession without gradation between them.

Baroque melodies also have a style of their own. We seldom find the simple phrase construction or the tunefulness of, let us say, Mozart or Schubert. The melodies tend toward longer periods and more elaborate organization. They are often ornamented and embellished with trills and shakes, especially in melodies intended for the harpsichord, where they serve to emphasize the accents of the rhythm. Sometimes there appears to be no melody at all, but merely a pattern of rhythmic figuration which will continue throughout an entire piece with little contrasting motion. Except in the fugue, the concentrated motive so characteristic of the later symphony is seldom employed. The treatment of the central subject of the fugue is quite different from that of the motive in the symphony. There is no development except the occasional modification of the subject by the devices of augmentation, diminution, and inversion, or the piling up of the subject upon itself in stretto. The essence of the fugue is its repetition of a short pattern in the various melodic strands as they are woven together. Its unity comes from the subject, its forward motion and flow of thought come not from development but from its logic of key succession.

Baroque music is only incidentally chromatic and seldom employs keys of many flats or sharps. The tempered scale of equal semitones as opposed to the old "natural scale" had been accepted, but although Bach affirmed its more extensive use in the forty-eight preludes and fugues in every key, major and minor, his example was not widely followed by others, and for many years *The Well-Tempered Clavier* was regarded as a theoretical work.

When the listener has become adjusted to the values of baroque music so that he is no longer disappointed in not finding the familiar characteristics of later compositions, he will derive much pleasure from this music, so solid in its architecture and so rich in its texture.

Some Important Composers of the Baroque

Italy

Monteverdi, 1567–1643	Composer of madrigals, church music, and operas
Frescobaldi, 1583–1644	Organ and church composer at Rome
Corelli, 1653–1713	Violin composer at Rome
Alessandro Scarlatti, 1659–1725	Opera and church composer at Naples
Vivaldi, c. 1680–1743	Violin and opera composer
Domenico Scarlatti, 1685–1757	Harpsichord composer

France

Lully, 1633–1687	Opera composer at court of Louis XIV
Couperin, 1668–1733	Harpsichord composer
Rameau, 1683–1764	Theorist, opera, and harpsichord composer

England

| Purcell, 1658–1695 | Composer of opera, church, and instrumental music |

Germany

Schütz, 1585–1672	Church composer
Pachelbel, 1653–1706	Composer of church and instrumental music
Buxtehude, 1637–1707	Composer of church and instrumental music (notably keyboard)
J. S. Bach, 1685–1750	Composer active in all fields of music, with the bulk of his work for the church
Handel, 1685–1759	Opera and oratorio composer, also active in many other fields

The Fugue

The fugue is an outgrowth of the transcribed motet of the Renaissance via the ricercar. The pattern of the beginning remains the same, that is, there is a melodic fragment which each voice, entering separately, states. But while in the motet the various text phrases invite new melodic fragments for separate statement, the fugue, except in the case of the occasional double and triple fugues which are designed to include two or three subjects, is limited to a single central idea. The earlier transcribed motet, with a succession of subjects, proved somewhat unsatisfactory because, without the various text phrases to justify the parade of unrelated subjects, the composition lacked coherence. When the ricercar, the title of which suggests "research," i. e., to seek out the possibilities of a given subject, eliminated all but the first subject and confined itself to this as a central feature of design, the instrumental fugue was established.

The subject of the fugue contains the essence of the music. It establishes not only a rhythmic and tonal pattern but also sets the mood of the entire composition. The invention of a good subject is two thirds of the composer's problem. It must have a definite personality so that it is readily recognizable, must contain rhythmic elements which can be isolated and repeated as the basis for episodes, and if it lends itself to combination upon itself, or *stretto,* so much the better. In Bach's fugue subjects we have an encyclopedia of musical imagination. Magnificent as was his ability to manipulate his ideas, it is in the ideas themselves that his genius shows its compelling force. Few other composers could endow a brief melodic pattern with so much significance. When the subject itself is lacking in all the elements necessary to the piece, it is supplemented by a countersubject which is usually stated in combination with the *answer,* (the subject transposed to the dominant). In cases where the subject is all sufficient, the countersubject is replaced by free counterpoint.

The fugue subject is spun out rather than developed as in the case of the symphonic theme. It is transposed to the dominant and often to neighboring keys. It may be augmented, diminished, or inverted. It may be combined in stretto, but it remains essentially the same, and its frequent repetition in one voice or another established a pattern of great unity altogether different from the dramatic progressive flow of the symphony. The dynamic values of the fugue, as in the case of all baroque music, are an alternation of piano and forte without gradation between them. The successive entrances of voices, or the manipulation of the rhythm, may sometimes give the effect of a crescendo, but this is a building up of texture, not the increase of dynamics. In listening to one of the great fugues of Bach there is often a feeling of growing excitement, caused by the persistent repetition of rhythms which beat upon our emotions with similar effect to the ostinato figures of primitive music. When one has become accustomed to the polyphonic style, so that its ever-changing patterns cease to be a confusion and present a clear picture to the mind, the fugue is a source of intense musical enjoyment.

J. S. BACH—*Prelude and Fugue in B flat major (The Well-Tempered Clavier, Volume I)*

The first volume of *The Well-Tempered Clavier* was written by Bach in 1722. It is a series of preludes and fugues in the twelve keys of the "standardized" chromatic scale,

EXAMPLE 3.

major and minor. The preludes are free in design, sometimes polyphonic in the nature of two- or three-part inventions, sometimes homophonic with a constant rhythmic figuration. The mood of the preludes parallels that of the fugue, but there is no obvious thematic relationship between them. This prelude is distinctly a virtuoso piece, a repeated homophonic arpeggio pattern, punctuated occasionally by scales. The mood is bright and joyful. In the second part there are several series of massed chords.

The fugue is in three voices, which enter in descending order. The subject, in a triple rhythm, with somewhat the effect of a scherzo, is composed of staccato eighth notes featuring the downward skip of a sixth, contrasted with legato sixteenth notes moving in stepwise fashion (Example 3). The countersubject contains a repeated note figure which reappears several times in one voice or another (Example

EXAMPLE 4.

4). Bach gave no phrasing indications in his manuscripts, leaving these matters, according to the custom of the times, to the musical understanding of the performer. Almost all modern editions supply phrasing and expression marks, and these are therefore the editors' prescription and not Bach's and the performer has the right to disagree. Since the effect of the whole fugue may depend upon the phrasing of the subject, such matters are of great importance.

This fugue consists almost entirely of repetition of the subject, which is relatively long. There are few episodes.

J. S. BACH—*Prelude and Fugue in C sharp minor* (*The Well-Tempered Clavier*, Volume I)

The mood of these pieces is serious, with an expressive melancholy in the prelude which is succeeded in the fugue by a more impersonal note of tragic grandeur. The prelude is a polyphonic invention based upon a melody heard in the top voice in the first bar. This melody is imitated by the other voices but never loses its independent interest as it expressively unfolds throughout the movement.

The fugue is in five voices. The subject is a four-note figure of even rhythm with a tonal pattern not unlike the principal motive of Liszt's *Les Préludes* and the Franck *Symphony* (Example 5). The voices enter in ascending order from the bass. Since the rhythm of the subject is regular, Bach introduces not one but three countersubjects.

The first one almost immediately disappears, but the second, a pattern of stepwise eighth notes, is thereafter a constant feature of the design (Example 6). The third subject,

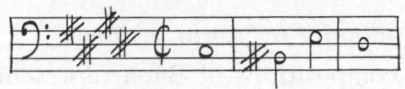

EXAMPLE 5.

somewhat like a trumpet figure with a very definite personality, does not appear until the forty-ninth bar, but from this time on it vies in importance with the central

EXAMPLE 6.

subject, which it ideally complements (Example 7). This fugue, in its cumulative grandeur, is perhaps the most impressive of the entire forty-eight.

EXAMPLE 7.

D. SCARLATTI—*Fugue in G minor (The Cat's Fugue)*

The entertaining possibilities of the fugue are shown in this odd little piece by the Italian harpsichordist Domenico Scarlatti. The subject, unexpectedly defiant of the regular conventions of harmony, is somewhat like a modern atonal theme. It suggests that the cat in walking over the keys was the unconscious author of the musical idea. Though the piece is in no way descriptive and follows the strict conventions of the fugue, its subject provides an insight into the whimsy and fantasy of Scarlatti's musical imagination, one of the boldest in the baroque era.

J. S. BACH—*Fugue for organ in A minor*

The organ compositions of Bach represent his most extended and serious instrumental works. The baroque instrumental ensemble used in the suite and concerto was pale in comparison to the tonal splendor of the contemporary

EXAMPLE 8.

organ, and it was to this instrument, the perfect vehicle for baroque dynamic contrasts and sustained linear polyphony, that he turned for his greatest inspiration. The fugue was likewise the instrumental form which offered to him the greatest opportunity for extended musical thought. His great compositions for organ are analogous to the symphonies of Beethoven in their importance to instrumental literature. In this age of preoccupation with the symphony orchestra, Bach's organ works have frequently been transcribed and performed at symphony concerts, so that the concert public has been afforded a glimpse of their magnificent architecture, and as a result Bach has become a box-office attraction. We must not forget, however, that they were designed for the organ and appear to greatest advantage in this medium.

The *Fugue in A minor,* like many other organ fugues, has a much more extended subject than the fugues of *The Well-Tempered Clavier.* The melodiousness of the subject is probably responsible for the popularity of this great tonal edifice, which has the element of charm blended with aus-

EXAMPLE 9.

terity (Example 8). The entrances of the subject and answer are in descending sequence and the countersubject is a repeated rhythmic figure used throughout the work (Example 9). Entrances of the subject are spaced between long episodes based upon its melodic design. There is a free fantasia with pedal cadenza to conclude.

The Suite

A succession of dances of contrasting rhythm, but all in the same key and in the same simple binary design, formed the basis of the baroque instrumental suite. When these were written for a solo instrument and continuo they were called sonatas (*da camera*); for an ensemble of strings or winds, suites; and, when written for harpsichord, various names were applied, among them suites, partitas, and lessons. The different dances used were derivations of old dances, but by the eighteenth century most of them had lost their dancelike qualities and were standard instrumental forms, consisting of rhythmic patterns often of considerable complexity.

The first three movements of the suite usually are the

allemande, a serious allegro in duple rhythm; the *courante,* a rapid movement in triple rhythm; and the *sarabande,* a slow expressive melody in triple rhythm. The last movement is almost always a *gigue,* a rollicking dance pattern generally in six-eight time. In between sarabande and gigue there are inserted two or three pieces of a less sophisticated character, such as *minuet, gavotte, bourrée, rigaudon, loure, polonaise, air,* etc.

This type of composition was especially popular in France. Couperin wrote a number of pieces in suite form with programmatic titles, charming but not necessarily influencing the music. Rameau, another French composer, wrote a number of harpsichord suites. The most familiar compositions of this style, however, are the French suites, English suites, and partitas of J. S. Bach. Usually heard today on the piano, they were conceived for the harpsichord and are more effective when played upon that instrument.

J. S. BACH—*French Suite in E major*

Each movement of this suite is in E major and is divided into two sections with indicated repeats. The purpose of the first section is to bring about modulation with cadence on the dominant. The second half, which is usually the longer, is concerned with the problem of finding its way back to the tonic. When this is achieved the piece comes to an end. This music makes its appeal as abstract design. It is undramatic, there being no contrast within the movement, no identifiable theme or even melody which returns, no dynamic shading. It is simply a rhythmic figuration, a pattern constantly repeating itself as in a textile design, except that in the case of the music this pattern has a kaleidoscopic quality, with constant transposition of its melodic outline, and, unlike the aimlessness of wallpaper or textile designs, it is given logic and ordered progress by the underlying scheme of the tonality.

Allemande
Courante
These two movements are polyphonic, consisting each of only two voices.

Sarabande
An expressive melody with rhythmic features often repeated, supported by harmonies which have a certain melodic independence but are subordinate to the top voice.

Gavotte
A dance in duple rhythm, each phrase of which begins on the third beat. It is harmonized in three voices.

Polonaise
A dance in triple rhythm in two voices.

Bourrée
The bourrée is the peasant counterpart of the gavotte. This dance is written for two independent voices.

Minuet
In triple rhythm. Two voices rhythmically punctuated by the entrances of a third.

Gigue
Two independent voices with the rhythmic features of one imitated by the other.

J. S. BACH—*Orchestral Suite in D major, no. 3*

Bach wrote four suites of varying instrumentation for orchestra. The third one is scored for two oboes, three trumpets, tympani, and string quintet. In the collected Bach works these suites are called *overtures* because each one begins with a lengthy piece in the form of the French opera overture, a slow introduction and allegro in fugal style. This is followed by short pieces in the binary form of the suite.

Grave—vivace

The introduction is an impressive polyphonic piece of broad outline and sharply defined rhythm, for full orchestra. The vivace commences with a rhythmic subject

EXAMPLE 10.

(first oboe and first violin) (Example 10). The answer to this is stated by the second oboe and second violin, followed by subject on violas and answer on the cello, in the manner of the fugue. The trumpets and tympani are then added to enforce the accents of the rhythm. The trumpets are also used melodically as the movement proceeds. The plan of the movement is somewhat like the concerto style, with the subject serving as refrain for full orchestra and episodic material connecting the tuttis. At the conclusion the introduction returns in shortened form.

Air

The second movement will be recognized as the familiar *Air for the G string* so often played by violinists. It was thus transcribed by a famous violinist, Wilhelmj, in 1871. In this suite the effect is different, and, while the melody lies higher and therefore does not employ the rich, low violin register, the accompaniment is vastly more beautiful on the sustained tones of the strings than as customarily heard on the piano. The melody is of the decorative sort in which Bach excels. Its sustained notes against the complementary rhythm of the second violins and violas and ostinato figure of the bass give it an especial poignance. In this movement strings alone are used.

Gavotte

The gavotte has a hearty rhythm and obvious melodic

appeal. If proof were needed that Bach was not an academic composer this would be Exhibit A. As in the symphony minuet, the gavotte has a contrasting trio followed by repetitions of the first part.

Bourrée
This dance moves at a somewhat faster tempo than the gavotte. In the second part amusing cross-accents develop in the rhythm.

Gigue
The gigue is lilting and popular in style, although there are unexpected effects in the phrasing of the rhythm which give it a certain sophisticated quality.

The Baroque Sonata

The sonata of the baroque period should not be regarded as a primitive ancestor of the classic sonata but as a highly perfected type of composition of entirely different design, with an extensive literature by the best composers of the period. One reason for the great success of this type of composition was the popularity of the violin and the skill of the composers in dealing with its technical possibilities. But sonatas were also written for flute, oboe, viola da gamba, and other instruments. There was a variable element in the sonata of this period, the accompaniment usually provided by an instrument of the harpsichord type. The accompanying harpsichord, however, had no part of its own; only the bass voice was written out by the composer, and the performer, guided by figures written over the notes, was expected to fill in suitable harmonies. This accompaniment was known as the *basso continuo,* or figured bass, and it will be easily understood that skill in the realization of this part varied with different performers.

So-called solo sonatas for violin or other instrument and continuo are played today with the continuo part written out for piano by a modern editor with varying results, according to the individual's taste and feeling for style. The violin sonatas by such men as Corelli, Vivaldi, Tartini, Geminiani, Locatelli, Veracini, Porpora, Vitali, and Handel, which figure so largely upon recitalists' programs, are of this type. Bach, in addition to sonatas for violin and continuo, wrote six for harpsichord and violin, three for harpsichord and cello, and three for harpsichord and flute, in which the keyboard part was written out. They give somewhat the effect of trios, since the right-hand keyboard part is treated as an individual instrument, often in polyphonic combination with the solo instrument.

Corelli established the form of the baroque sonata as a four-movement work. It begins with a slow movement, is followed by an allegro in fugal style and a melodious andante in homophonic style, and is concluded by a rapid movement, usually in triple rhythm. This type of sonata was known as the church sonata (*sonata da chiesa*), because of its serious nature and because it was frequently performed during church services. In contrast to this were the chamber sonata (*sonata da camera*) and the instrumental suite, which were groups of dances of various contrasting rhythms. Bach also wrote several sonatas and suites (called *partitas*) for unaccompanied stringed instruments, violin or cello.

A characteristic type of baroque sonata, unfortunately not played in concert so often today, is the trio sonata. This was written for three instruments, usually two violins and cello or gamba. The number of players performing such a composition, however, was at least four; the ubiquitous harpsichordist played the continuo from the figured bass part and other players could join the ensemble by doubling any of the parts.

In general the sonatas of the Italian composers are more tuneful and less polyphonic than those of the Germans, although Handel's style in instrumental music greatly resembles that of the Italian masters. It is interesting to note that this remarkable activity of the Italian instrumental composers in the baroque period was not followed by significant contributions to the literature of the classic sonata. Italian genius, which appears so brilliant in the baroque violin compositions, later devoted itself almost exclusively to the opera, while German and Austrian instrumental composers, developing the models of their southern contemporaries, combined the dramatic quality of the opera with instrumental design and dominated the field of symphonic music.

HANDEL—*Sonata for violin and continuo in E major*
Adagio in E major

This singing diatonic melody for the violin (Example 11), with complementary rhythmical accompaniment in

EXAMPLE 11.

the bass, is in four phrases, the fourth resembling the first but extended for several bars to end on a deceptive cadence. The purpose of this is to lead without pause to the following movement, which is in the same key.

Allegro in E major
A tuneful rhythmic melody is heard in the violin (Example 12). Two parallel five-bar phrases are succeeded by a greatly extended third phrase, in which the rhythmic features of the melody are developed, and a fourth phrase,

EXAMPLE 12.

similar to the first two but lengthened to seven bars, with cadences in the key of the dominant. This section is then repeated. The second section, likewise repeated, is in similar design but in five phrases with a final cadence in the tonic.

Largo in C sharp minor
A broad, dignified melody of a simple expressiveness which is characteristic of Handel (Example 13) leads from

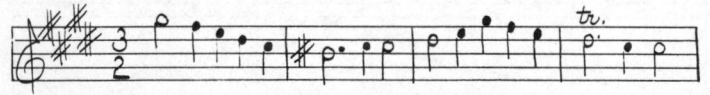

EXAMPLE 13.

C sharp minor to E major and then returns to the tonic. The ending is extended with a pause on the chord of G sharp minor so that the following movement will proceed without interruption.

Allegro in C sharp minor
The finale is a dancelike movement with a figuration in

EXAMPLE 14.

triple rhythm in two sections with repetitions, similar in design to the second movement (Example 14).

HANDEL—*Sonata for flute and continuo in G major*

The plan of this sonata is very much like the preceding violin sonata but the character of the music is influenced by the sound of the flute.

Adagio in G major
The lyric design is in unequal phrase lengths and there are more rhythmical features about this melody than in the

EXAMPLE 15.

first movement of the violin sonata to compensate for the lack of intensity of the instrument (Example 15). A deceptive cadence leads to the second movement.

Allegro in G major
The bass part of the continuo is much more important here than in any movement of the violin sonata (Example

EXAMPLE 16.

16). The plan is a polyphonic dialogue between the two voices with bass part entering in imitation as in the fugue and continuing in a free fugal style.

Adagio in E minor
The sustained tones of the flute are used to advantage in a lyric melody against a scale pattern of the bass part (Ex-

ample 17). The ending, as in the case of the second movement, is a deceptive cadence.

Bourrée in G major

The bourrée, which, as we have said, is the peasant counterpart of the gavotte, is a duple dance rhythm of

EXAMPLE 17.

hearty vigor. This melody is one of the most familiar Handel tunes and has been frequently transcribed for other instruments (Example 18).

EXAMPLE 18.

VIVALDI—*Sonata for violin and continuo in A major*

The sonatas of Vivaldi are of great brilliance but are lacking somewhat in the profundity and simple melodic appeal so characteristic of Corelli.

Prelude a capriccio in A major

The prelude is an alternation of presto and adagio, consisting entirely of broken-chord violin figures, first on A

EXAMPLE 19.

major and then on E major (Example 19). The continuo simply sustains the chords.

Presto agitato in A major

This is a brilliant rhythmical melody in a single section over a constant figure of the accompaniment (Example 20).

EXAMPLE 20.

Corrente in A major

The courante is a rapid dance movement in triple rhythm divided into two sections, each of which is repeated. The

EXAMPLE 21.

melody is very effectively written for the violin, alternating staccato and legato passages, with trills and wide leaps a feature of its design (Example 21).

Adagio in F sharp minor

The adagio, *quasi recitativo,* is little more than a rhapsodic phrase serving as transition to the finale (Example 22).

EXAMPLE 22.

Giga in A major
The gigue is the characteristic last movement of the suite and the *sonata da camera*. It has the rollicking triple rhythm of the English jig. This movement has the traditional binary

EXAMPLE 23.

form with pause on the dominant and return to the tonic (Example 23).

The sonatas for harpsichord of Domenico Scarlatti constitute a unique category among the various forms of the baroque sonata. Since the majority of these sonatas are complete in one organic movement, sometimes even prophetic of the design later to be found in the classic sonata, it is evident that Scarlatti, already emerging from baroque style, was using the term "sonata" (Italian *suonare,* to sound) in its earliest connotation, to distinguish pieces of instrumental music from cantatas (Italian *cantare,* to sing), pieces composed for vocal performance. The free usage of musical terminology of the time is demonstrated in the title of the only book of music which Scarlatti published on his own account. The pieces of this collection, *Esercizii per gravicembalo* (Studies for Harpsichord), are separately entitled "sonata." Though each composition is complete in itself, it was not unusual for later publishers and editors to arrange these sonatas into suites and to add descriptive titles; thus "Pastoral," "Cortège," and "The lover-passionate and sentimental" were associated with some of the sonatas and have persisted to the present day.

The importance of these pieces in the evolution of keyboard music, and, in fact, in all instrumental music, can hardly be exaggerated. Departing from the traditional polyphonic style of the period, they forecast the new homophonic style which found fuller expression in a later epoch. From a purely technical point of view the sonatas are equally significant. Scarlatti's long and brilliant career as a harpsichordist provided him with an intimate understanding of the technical resources of the instrument and its virtuoso potentialities. Among the technical devices associated with Scarlatti, all of which have been used by later composers, are rapid repetition of tone, crossing of hands, double notes, wide skips, and arpeggios. The sonatas are short, and usually follow a basic pattern of binary form. Several musical ideas, concise and epigrammatic, are stated in the first section, which ends in the key of the dominant. The second section of the piece consists of repetitions of this material with variation in a sequence of tonalities re-

EXAMPLE 24.

turning to the home key. There is little development of thematic material in the true sense of the word, and repetition of short rhythmic and melodic motives is frequent, but there are occasional glimpses of a tendency in this direction.

SCARLATTI—*Sonata in D major, Longo 107*

Three musical ideas are presented successively with the utmost clarity (Examples 24, 25, and 26). In the second

EXAMPLE 25.

EXAMPLE 26.

section they are repeated in contrasting keys. One notes here the use of a favorite technique of Scarlatti's, the crossing of the hands.

SCARLATTI—*Sonata in D minor, Longo 108 (The lover-passionate and sentimental)*

The affixed title of this sonata is suggested by the alternation of themes, the first demure and simple (Example

EXAMPLE 27.

27), the second intense and impatient in its insistent repetition (Example 28). It is the second theme which assumes greater importance by virtue of its strong rhythmic nature.

EXAMPLE 28.

SCARLATTI—*Sonata in C major, Longo 205* (Neapolitan folk dance)

Again Scarlatti shows his predilection for triple rhythm (Example 29). The whole movement is dominated by a strong rhythmic figure which is ever present.

EXAMPLE 29.

SCARLATTI—*Sonata in B flat major, Longo 327*

An ascending staccato arpeggio opens this ebullient sonata, so replete with technical fireworks (Example 30).

EXAMPLE 30.

The crossing of hands and the extremely wide skips give an ample sonority to the music while dazzling the listener with virtuosity.

The Concerto Grosso

During the last years of the seventeenth century and the first half of the eighteenth the most popular form of instrumental ensemble was the concerto grosso. This is a composition in several movements in which two tone masses are set off, one against the other. The one, called the *tutti* or *concerto,* is generally a four-part string choir of violins, violas, cellos, and basses. The violins are divided into two groups: the violas take the part beneath the second violin, while cellos and basses, playing together, furnish the fourth part. The bass part is reinforced by a keyboard instrument, usually the harpsichord, which also provides suitable harmonies. These are not written out in the part but are supposed to be improvised by the performer, who is guided by numerical symbols over each note indicating the proper chord. The bass part is usually referred to as the *continuo* or *figured bass*. All baroque instrumental music written for ensemble, whether concerto, sonata, suite, or accompaniment to choral music, contains this feature. Often, in the case of choral music, the organ is substituted for the harpsichord. It is only in the time of Haydn that it ceases to be a necessary part of ensemble music. Generally the keyboard performer also served as conductor of the ensemble.

The second tone mass is a group of solo instruments, usually three, called the *solo* or *concertino*. This may consist of solo strings, winds, or a combination of both. The essence of the concerto is the antiphonal relationship, a veritable rivalry, between these two groups. Although the concertino instruments are given more elaborate parts as a rule, the purpose of the music is not so much virtuoso display, as developed in the classic concerto, as it is contrast of single voices of individual color with the more impersonal and full-bodied tone of the tutti.

The concerto grosso, as frequently performed today by our large orchestras, overemphasizes this contrast with tuttis of grotesquely disproportionate size. Audiences have come to expect massive string tone from the modern orchestra, and no doubt the concerto grosso as properly played by a small ensemble would sound rather thin, but, if it is to be played at all, it should be remembered that the concerto grosso was chamber music and its delicate beauty should not be distorted by a full-throated tone entirely foreign to its conception. In modern performances also the continuo part is sometimes left out, leaving certain passages bleak and denuded where the intended chords should support them. One reason for this is that the harpsichord tone is too small for the large concert hall, and the piano, the tone of which does not, like the harpsichord, blend tactfully with the strings, is an unsatisfactory substitute.

The number of movements of the concerto grosso varies as do their design and tonality. Polyphonic movements of a rapid tempo generally alternate with expressive homophonic melodies. The most characteristic form is that in which the tutti states a refrain in a succession of keys, and the concertino elaborates features of its melodic design or occupies itself with solo subjects in the transitional passages. In all its forms, orderly progression from one key to one or several others and return is the guiding principle of the music.

The Italian masters, Corelli and Vivaldi, and the Germans, Handel and Bach, are the composers of the concerto grosso most frequently heard today. Archangelo Corelli is credited with the standardization of the forms of both concerto grosso and baroque sonata. He was a constant experimenter in musical design and anticipated many later discoveries of the German School. A great violinist himself, he was the first composer to realize fully the genius of the instrument. His music is of sturdy organization and profound thought, but it is all irradiated by the melodic beauty which is characteristic of Italian music.

CORELLI—*Concerto Grosso in G minor, no.* 8 (first published in 1714)

This concerto bears the subheading "Made for Christmas Eve" (*Fatto per la notte di natale*), and is known as the *Christmas Concerto.* It is exceptional in that there is an added last movement, a pastorale, evidently related in program to the shepherds' song at the nativity. The concertino consists of two violins and cello with the customary tutti.

Introduction—Vivace-grave in G minor

A few bars of rapid music establish the key. There is a pause and then both concertino and tutti are heard in an expressive, somewhat chromatic music in which the voices enter singly, each time bringing about a gentle dissonance which is resolved as the music proceeds. All parts are of equal melodic importance and the feeling is one of harmonic tension and relief.

Allegro in G minor

In this movement the relationship between concertino and tutti is simply one of tonal reinforcement by the latter. The concertino is a vigorous polyphonic duet between the solo violins in which the parts overlap and serve as a rhythmic foil, one to the other. The solo cello adds an even rhythmic figure of arpeggio and scale design as counterpoint. The music of the concertino continues uninterruptedly but is punctuated by frequent doublings of the voices by the tutti, affording vivid dynamic contrasts.

Adagio in E flat major

The concertino is now an expressive trio based upon a decorative chordal melody that is heard first in one voice and then in another against a background accompaniment by the tutti. The effect is one of serenity and joy. A rapid middle section with regular rhythm dealing with a succession of harmonies is an exuberant contrast. The third section is a continuation of the mood and style of the first.

Vivace in G minor

A short, gay movement in triple rhythm, with the effect of the minuet, is enforced in accent by entrances of the tutti.

Allegro in G minor

This is a robust polyphonic trio with the three voices entering separately in imitation, rhythmically supported and underlined by entrances of the tutti. There is a middle section in which effects of piano and forte alternate rapidly, followed by a parallel third section and coda with further contrasts of dynamics.

Pastorale in G minor

This movement, which is an addition to the usual plan of the concerto grosso, is a flowing melody harmonized in thirds on the concertino with support from the tutti, sometimes sustaining, sometimes reinforcing the voices of the solo instruments. Its gentle *berceuse* movement suggests the music of the shepherds at the nativity. According to Forkel, the historian, Corelli had in mind a picture of the angels hovering over the town of Bethlehem.

J. S. BACH—*Brandenburg concerto no. 2 in F major* (Composed in 1721)

The six Brandenburg Concertos of Bach are scored for a variety of instruments. The one in F major has a concertino consisting of trumpet, flute, oboe, and violin, and the tutti comprises the customary strings and continuo. It is profitable to compare the respective recordings of Adolf Busch and Leopold Stokowski. All six concertos are recorded with a small ensemble directed by Busch which, with the exception of an unfortunate substitution of piano for harpsichord, faithfully re-creates the type of performance intended by Bach. Stokowski, with the magnificent trappings of the Philadelphia Orchestra, gives a performance which is both thick and lush. Perhaps it serves to bring Bach closer to our own age, but one wonders if the Leipzig master would recognize his own handiwork. Tempo indications are seldom supplied in the Bach manuscripts. The performer is expected to use his own judgment, based upon the character of the music.

First movement in F major

A fine vigorous melody given out by all the instruments serves as refrain for the first movement, which is a good example of typical concerto grosso design (Example 31). Appearances of this refrain on the tutti in various related

EXAMPLE 31.

keys are alternated with solo passages by the instruments of the concertino. This movement is characteristically baroque in spirit in its richness, in alternation of dynamics, and in the uninterrupted flow of its stalwart rhythm.

Second movement—Andante in D minor

This expressive slow movement is a remarkable example of thematic unity. A single brief motive (Example 32) is the source of all the melody of the piece. It is woven into a

EXAMPLE 32.

series of lovely designs played by three solo instruments, violin, oboe, and flute. To accompany this the indicated tutti is merely an ostinato figure on cello and continuo, to which supporting chords on the harpsichord should be supplied. The pattern of the music is so beautiful in itself that nothing in the way of "expression" should be added. The notes speak for themselves.

Finale—Allegro assai

A jovial tune for solo trumpet (Example 33) with cello and continuo accompaniment introduces the refrain of this piece, which is also in standard concerto design. The other

EXAMPLE 33.

instruments of the tutti do not make their entrance until all the other soloists have had a turn at the refrain, joining in the proceedings one at a time. When they do arrive they are restricted to simple accompaniment. The main interest of the music remains in the four solo instruments and supporting bass.

The Solo Concerto

The solo concerto as found in the works of Vivaldi, Bach, and Handel retains the principle of competing sonorities which is the hallmark of the concerto grosso, but, because the concertino is here confined to a single solo instrument, admits a greater degree of virtuosity. The baroque violin concertos represent such a highly developed technique in the treatment of the instrument that they are a regular part of the solo violinist's repertory today, and are played more frequently than other solo concertos of the period. This is due to the fact that the modern violin is the same instrument that served the baroque player, and is played with approximately the same technique, whereas the trumpet or oboe player of our day finds great difficulty in coping with the virtuoso demands required of his eighteenth-century predecessors, whose instruments were quite different. If you refer back to the *Brandenburg Concerto in F* you will note the extreme difficulty of the trumpet part which lies very high and demands much rapid passage work. In general plan of architecture the solo concerto greatly resembles the concerto grosso from which it developed.

J. S. BACH—*Concerto for violin in E major*

Bach is supposed to have written a number of solo violin concertos during his service as musician to Prince Leopold of Anhalt-Cöthen, but only the two in E major and A minor have been found. Like Corelli, Bach was also a fine violinist, and the influence of the instrument is felt in all his instrumental music, even in that for harpsichord and organ. This concerto is in three movements, an extended allegro in typical concerto style, an adagio, undoubtedly one of his most beautiful compositions, and a lively rondo. The violin appears to great advantage throughout, and the solo part, while of considerable difficulty, is always an integral part of the musical idea, not an ornamental accessory calculated to dazzle the audience into an admiration of the performer's technical accomplishments.

Allegro in E major

The opening refrain played by the tutti is forthright and melodious, complete in itself in the fashion of a rondo theme (Example 34). It contains several independent rhythmic ideas, notably the first three notes, which are used somewhat as the motive of a symphony, appearing separately by transposition as a basis for the unfolding of passages of figuration on the solo instrument. These passages alternate with the refrain, either in part or in entirety, as the music passes through various keys. After a cadence in E major there is a middle section in the relative minor, with passages of increasing difficulty over fragments of the refrain, and then the music surprisingly comes to a halt in G sharp minor, featured by a short adagio passage on the

EXAMPLE 34.

solo violin. Now the entire first section is repeated without change. The design is therefore like the aria, ABA, with the middle section more in the nature of development than contrast.

Adagio in C sharp minor

The plan of this movement is unusual in the concerto although we find a similar scheme in two other pieces of Bach, the slow movements of the *A minor violin concerto* and of the *Italian concerto for harpsichord*. The principal idea does not appear at all on the solo instrument, but serves rather as a point of departure or setting for a rhapsodical and ornate melody on the violin. It is stated immediately on the cello, bass, and continuo, is harmonized by chords on the strings above, which join the melody in octaves each time that it cadences. This theme (Example 35), if performed in proper baroque style, should not be played with any crescendo, but its expressive melodic organization has an implicit feeling of crescendo which is sensed even though quite properly unrealized. It is a theme of haunting sadness, of a grief intense but controlled. The violin enters against this with a long, sustained note which is followed by melodic flights of touching beauty of a sort which Bach alone could conceive. There is a middle section which passes into E major, where the violin is supported by the simplest chord accompaniment on violins and viola. Against this design the bass again appears with

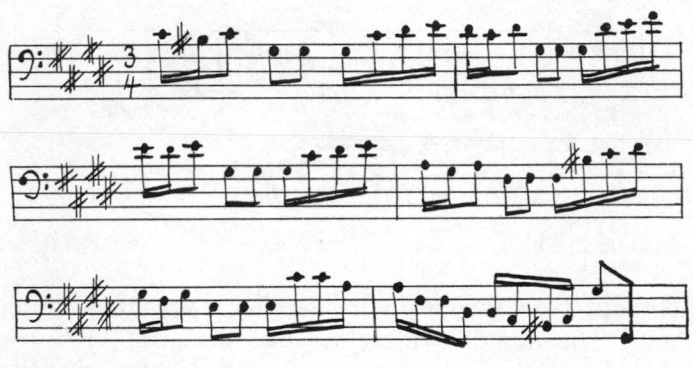

EXAMPLE 35.

the background theme leading back through related keys to a cadence in C sharp minor. The movement concludes as it begins, with the cello theme and supporting harmony. The solo violin again is silent.

Allegro assai in E major

The form of this piece is extremely easy to follow. There is a dancelike refrain of sixteen bars played by the tutti five times, each time in E major (Example 36). In between

EXAMPLE 36.

the appearances of the refrain the solo violin plays a virtuoso interlude supported by a simple accompaniment, each interlude increasing in difficulty; thus the last interlude is the most brilliant and is twice the length of the others. This music is Bach in his most jovial vein, high spirited, melodious, and imposing no intellectual problems upon his listeners.

The Chorale and the Chorale Prelude

The chorale is the German equivalent of the familiar English Protestant hymn. It was incorporated into the church service by Martin Luther (1483–1546) with the deliberate purpose of establishing a music suitable for the congregation to sing. The Lutheran Reformation stressed democratic principles of worship: the worshiper himself was to participate in the service as much as possible. Instead of merely listening to the priest and the choir, who spoke and sang in Latin, he was able to take a more active part because the service was conducted in German and the music was of a sort to be sung by the layman rather than by the expert.

The words of the chorales were adaptations of old hymns or were written by contemporary poets. The music was composed by church composers or rearranged from familiar Gregorian hymns. Sacred and secular popular songs were also pressed into service. In the chorale, therefore, German music was subjected to a genuine popular strain, characterized by simple melody of tuneful quality, organized in regular phrases. This music, unlike many later Protestant hymns, never wallows in sentimentality. It is strong and masculine, and even when most expressive it never loses its devout, somewhat austere, religious feeling. Bach was a man of great piety and for him the chorale was a source of rich inspiration. Almost all the chorales which were used in the service were arranged by him in four-part harmonization for congregational singing. He also used them freely in his cantatas and Passions, and arranged them as short organ pieces which are known as *chorale preludes.*

The chorale prelude originated as an improvisation by

the organist upon the hymn which the congregation was to sing. Later it developed into several distinct types of composition. One of these, under the influence of the motet, is a polyphonic piece with characteristic fugal entrances based on each phrase of the chorale. Another is an ornamental elaboration of the chorale melody in the sumptuous baroque style. Still another is a fantasia, developing freely some of the elements of the melody. Perhaps the most appealing type is the one found most often in Bach, in which the chorale appears without alteration in the top voice and the accompaniment is a poetic interpretation of the mood of the poem.

Chorale preludes were written exclusively for the organ, but, along with recent symphony concert trends, many of them have been transcribed for orchestra, frequently with very good effect, although there is a danger that incidentally they may be oversentimentalized or generally overblown. Piano recital programs sometimes also include arrangements of the chorale preludes.

1. SIMPLE CHORALES

Vater unser im Himmelreich (*Our Father Which art in heaven*)

The words are an adaptation by Martin Luther of the Lord's Prayer and the melody is by a sixteenth-century church composer. This chorale is used by Bach in his *St. John Passion* and in several cantatas. It is also used by Mendelssohn in a sonata for organ.

Herzlich thut mich verlangen (*My inmost heart doth grieve*)

This chorale is one of the most widely known and loved melodies of the church. It was originally a secular love song by Hassler, one of the early baroque composers, who adapted it as a hymn. It is also used as a setting for the words *O Haupt voll Blut und Wunden* (*O Sacred Head once wounded*), and is often referred to as the Passion Chorale. It is used by Bach in *St. Matthew Passion,* the *Christmas Oratorio,* and in several cantatas.

2. CHORALE PRELUDES BY J. S. BACH

Wachet auf ruft uns die Stimme (*Sleepers Wake*)

This chorale prelude is a transcription of one of the parts of his chorale cantata of the same name. It is a three-voiced composition with the chorale appearing without alteration in the middle voice. The top voice consists of a lovely pastoral melody, entirely independent of the chorale.

Jesu, meine Freude (*Jesus, My Joy*)

The chorale melody is by one of the best-known composers of the Reformation, Johann Crüger. The chorale prelude is a polyphonic arrangement with the melody unaltered in the top voice. The mood is one of quiet happiness.

Christum wir sollen loben schon (*Christ, we shall praise*)

The chorale melody comes from an old Catholic hymn. The treatment in the prelude is poetical, a representation of the mystical adoration. The melody is in the second voice. Above it lies an expressive melody of perpetually descending line.

O Mensch bewein (*O Mankind bewail Thy grievous sin*)

This is a most moving treatment of an Easter hymn, which is a lament for Christ's death on the Cross. The chorale melody is amplified in each phrase so that it is practically unrecognizable, but is replaced by a melodic line of the most inspired beauty. This is an example of the baroque decorative melody, which in spite of its elaborate organization is highly expressive.

In dir ist Freude (*In Thee is gladness*)

This is a joyful New Year's piece, based upon a chorale

adapted from a secular melody of spirited rhythm. The prelude is a free fantasia where phrases from the chorale melody appear as motives in the various voices. There is a cadence refrain appearing frequently in the pedals. The effect is somewhat like the pealing of festival bells.

3. CHORALE PRELUDES ARRANGED FOR ORCHESTRA

Ich ruf zu dir (I cry to Thee)

There is a quality of supplication in the melody of this chorale by a sixteenth-century German church composer. This is greatly enhanced by Bach's treatment in the prelude. The melody stands simply in the top voice, and is accompanied by a flowing expressive melody in the middle voice, and a bass part which consists of repeated notes, giving an effect of the accents of grief. In the setting for orchestra, Stokowski uses every opportunity to stress the emotional feeling of the piece.

Wir glauben all in einen Gott (We believe in one God)

This is a brilliant fantasia based upon a long and rather complicated chorale by Johann Walter, a German composer of the sixteenth century. Bach uses little more than the introductory melodic phrase for this triumphant musical affirmation of faith. The three upper voices are in polyphonic imitation with separate fugal entrances. The pedal part consists of a vigorous ascending refrain which, like a fanfare, salutes the arrival of each new key.

The Mass

The Lutheran service did not abandon the Catholic Mass but shortened it, including only the first two divisions, the Kyrie and the Gloria. Bach wrote four of these short Masses for inclusion in the regular service. The great *Mass in B minor,* however, is a complete Catholic Mass, and because of its great length (it takes at least three hours to perform) as well as its non-Lutheran character, it is unsuitable for liturgic purposes and is usually performed today as a "concert Mass." Bach presented a section of it to the Catholic sovereign Augustus III, Elector of Saxony, in the hope that he might be named court composer. The title was eventually granted, but there is no record of the Mass having been performed, or for that matter even examined, at the court.

J. S. BACH—*Mass in B minor* (composed 1733–1737)

For accompaniment to the Mass, Bach uses an orchestra of three trumpets, two flutes, two oboes, two bassoons, strings and continuo with organ. The text follows the prescribed liturgic sections of the Mass, each with many subdivisions. There are choruses ranging from four to eight parts, solos, and duets. A surprising feature of the work, from the historical point of view, is that no less than eight choruses are adaptations of music written by Bach for other works, generally cantatas. One of these is the familiar *Crucifixus* from the *Credo,* which is so perfectly an expression of its text that one can hardly believe it was originally composed to other words.

The music of the Mass ranges in mood from splendid austerity to touching simplicity. The grandeur of the first *Kyrie* and the *Sanctus* has probably never been surpassed in choral music, but there are moments when the music is filled with the most intimate human expression, either appealingly tuneful or picturesquely dramatic. Many of the choruses are fugal; others, with text fragments set to motives, resemble the motet. The *Sanctus* and *Osanna* are antiphonal with one part of the chorus set against the other. The solos and duets have a special form unlike the symmetrical pattern of the aria. There is usually a refrain, played by one or two solo instruments, which begins and ends the piece. This is woven in and out of the texture of the music in polyphonic combination with the solo voices, with the effect of continuous development.

No. 1—Kyrie (first part)

The *Kyrie* is divided into three parts: the first a great five-part chorus to the words *Kyrie eleison;* the second a melodious duet between two soprano soloists to the words *Christe eleison;* and the third a four-part chorus, quieter in mood than the first, repeating the words *Kyrie eleison.* It has been suggested that Bach intended to represent in these three pieces a musical interpretation of the Father, Son, and Holy Ghost of the Trinity.

The first part begins with full chorus in a short phrase which is like an agonized cry for mercy. This is followed by an instrumental introduction in which the subject of

EXAMPLE 37.

the movement is heard in two of the inner voices and finally in the bass. This subject, which appears more clearly when the singers enter in the order of tenor, alto, soprano 1, soprano 2, and bass, begins with a repeated note for the word *Kyrie* and a chromatic, melismatic figure based upon chord intervals for the word *eleison* (Example 37). The underlying harmony proceeds from dissonance to resolution and gives this subject an effect of inevitable and relentless forward motion. The entire movement is occupied with statements of this subject by the various voices. There are short related episodes and a brief instrumental interlude, after which there is another fugal exposition with the voices entering in ascending order, leading to a tremendous climax shortly before the end.

No. 15—Et Incarnatus from the Credo

This is a five-part chorus to the words "And was incarnate by the Holy Ghost of the Virgin Mary, And was made man." The form is a free adaptation of the motet with a

EXAMPLE 38.

descending arpeggio figure for the words *et incarnatus* which enters separately in the voices (Example 38). The accompaniment is a repeated melodic figure on the violins, expressive in character, with a constant bass rhythm of repeated notes. At the end, with the words *et homo factus est*, there is a feeling of suspense which adds to the note of mystery maintained throughout the composition.

No. 16—Crucifixus from the Credo

This is the most dramatic part of the Mass, a four-part chorus setting of the text "was crucified also for us under Pontius Pilate, He suffered and was buried." There is an accompaniment of chords over a fixed bass fashioned on a descending chromatic scale and resembling a passacaglia (Example 39). Over this moving accompaniment the voices enter fragmentarily in accents of deep grief with the word *crucifixus*. With the words *etiam pro nobis sub Pontio Pilato passus et sepultus est*, the choral texture is richer and there is an effect of climax. The voices again

EXAMPLE 39.

enter separately with the word *crucifixus* and the conclusion upon the words *et sepultus est* leads the voices into the extreme low register with a feeling of profound dejection.

No. 17—Et resurrexit from the *Credo*

The tragic feeling of the *Crucifixus* is dispelled by the jubilant chorus which follows immediately upon the words "And the third day He rose again according to the Scriptures, and ascended into heaven, and sitteth on the right

EXAMPLE 40.

hand of the Father. And He shall come again with glory to judge the quick and the dead. Whose kingdom shall have no end." This piece is in three main divisions dealing with the Resurrection, the Ascension, and the Second Advent. It is built upon the refrain which is heard at the beginning in the voices and the orchestra (Example 40).

No. 23—Aria—Agnus Dei

The concluding portions of the Mass are quiet and unspectacular. For the words "O Lamb of God, that takest away the sins of the world, Have mercy upon us," Bach has written a solo for alto of great beauty, with an expressive chromatic melody on the violins in imitative relationship with the solo voice. This melody contains an unusual

EXAMPLE 41.

motive continually moving to a dissonant tone which is resolved by the next chord of the accompaniment (Example 41). The frequent appearance of this motive which appears at the beginning on the violins gives a feeling of great poignance to the music.

No. 20—Sanctus

To the words "Holy, holy, holy, Lord God of hosts, Heaven and Earth are full of Thy glory," Bach has written the most inspired music of the Mass. It is a six-part chorus in two sections. The first part is an antiphonal chorus in which the heavenly choirs seem to be vying in ecstasy.

San-ctus Do-mi-nus De-us Sa-ba-oth

EXAMPLE 42.

There is a descending theme in the bass of rugged power over which the upper voices sometimes move in whirling figures, sometimes are stationary (Example 42). The second half is a fugue based upon a brilliant subject first announced by the tenors (Example 43).

Pleni sunt coeli et terra glo— — — ri-a e-jus

EXAMPLE 43.

The Oratorio

The term "oratorio" has a number of meanings, but the most familiar interpretation is that of a choral composition on a religious subject for soloists, chorus, and orchestra, generally performed without costumes or scenery. The opera and oratorio originated at about the same time and at the same place—in Italy in the early seventeenth century. Many of the composers of the period wrote both operas and oratorios, and indeed for a while the difference between them was slight except in subject matter. Both used the recitative for plot passages, and included solo arias, duets, and choruses of formal design for purely musical purposes. Toward the middle of the seventeenth century, however, the opera and oratorio began to part company, each to fulfill its separate destiny.

While in Italy the oratorio continued along the Catholic pattern of the seventeenth century, in Germany, as a result of the Protestant environment, a special form of the oratorio, of a devotional nature suitable for church service, developed and reached its climax in the choral works of J. S. Bach. This was known as the Passion Oratorio, or Passion Music.

The most spectacular flourishing of the concert oratorio developed in England in the career of the German-born composer George Frederick Handel. Handel, a composer of opera in the Italian style, became not only the dominating influence in opera in the first half of the eighteenth century but an impresario as well. He undertook the composition of oratorios as a device to keep his opera singers and opera house in London busy during the Lenten doldrums, when the public was inclined to forego the worldly joys which opera represented. It was discovered that religious subjects, presented without scenery and costumes, constituted no violation of the public conscience, and the oratorios were enormously successful.

Ironically, although the oratorio was therefore chiefly a by-product of Handel, the great opera composer, his oratorios have eclipsed his operas in survival value. This is not really the fault of the operatic music, which has perhaps even more of the tunefulness and vigor that have delighted singers and public in his oratorios, but because many of the operatic conventions of Handel's time, so happily ridiculed by Addison and Steele in the *Spectator Papers,* perished with the age and are not acceptable to modern audiences. At this time singer worship was at its height and operas were vehicles for the popular stars. Each star required a variety of arias, pathetic, flowing, declamatory, bravura, etc., no two alike in succession and, if possible, with the stars rotating. It will be imagined that the unfortunate plot, generally historical in character, crowded into the recitatives so as to make room for the vocal display of the arias, could have little theatrical interest. Furthermore, the male soprano and alto were much in vogue and complicated matters by assuming the leading male parts such as Julius Caesar, Nero, or Orestes. Choruses were infrequent and rather perfunctory. In the oratorio, however, although the various types of arias are found, the choruses are more important, and the subject matter, not designed for theatrical representation, is less perishable.

HANDEL—*The Messiah* (composed in 1741)

The Messiah, Handel's most familiar work, was composed in 1741—in twenty-three days—and was first produced in Dublin in 1742. Unlike most of the other oratorios, it is devotional and lyrical rather than militant and dramatic. The text consists of Biblical excerpts, divided into three parts which relate to the coming of the Saviour, His death and resurrection, and prophecies of the last judgment and the life to come.

PART ONE

Chorus—And the glory of the Lord
The text relates to the prophecy of the coming of the Messiah:

> "And the glory of the Lord shall be revealed
> And all flesh shall see it together for the
> Mouth of the Lord hath spoken it."

The chorus is constructed in motet style with a musical phrase corresponding to each phrase of the text. The orchestra furnishes harmonic support and frequently doubles the voices. The mood is jubilant.

Aria and Chorus—O Thou that tellest good tidings to
Zion
This is preceded by a recitative dealing with the prophecy "Behold, a virgin shall conceive and bear a son, and shall call his name Emmanuel, God with us." It is a melody of quiet happiness sung by contralto with accompaniment of violins, bassoon, and continuo, divided into several verses, each beginning with the same refrain.

Aria—The people that walked in darkness
This bass aria is preceded by a recitative "For behold, darkness shall cover the earth and gross darkness the people; but the Lord shall arise upon thee, and His glory shall be seen upon thee, and the Gentiles shall come to thy light, and kings to the brightness of thy rising."
This is a dramatic example of the unison aria in which the accompaniment of bassoon, strings, and continuo doubles the melody of the voice throughout.

Duet—He shall feed His flock

Two versions of this famous melody exist: one is for alto followed by the soprano in transposed key; the other remains in the same key and is sung throughout by the soprano. The mood is a representation of the words "He shall feed His flock like a shepherd, and He shall gather the lambs with His arm and carry them in His bosom, and gently lead those that are with young. Come unto Him all ye that labor and are heavy laden and He will give you rest. Take His yoke upon you, and learn of Him, for He is meek and lowly of heart, and ye shall find rest unto your souls."

PART TWO

Chorus—And with His stripes we are healed

This is a fine example of choral fugue modeled after the instrumental fugue. The four voices enter in descending

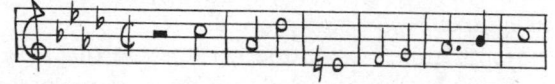

EXAMPLE 44.

order, doubled by the orchestra. The fugue subject is a reflection of the mood of the text (Example 44). There is a contrasting countersubject (Example 45). There are no

EXAMPLE 45.

episodes, the subject constantly reappearing in one voice or another.

Chorus—Hallelujah

This chorus, the conclusion to Part Two, is probably

Handel's most famous composition. The triumphant refrain, "Hallelujah," constantly recurs to punctuate the phrases of the text with inspiring effect. The style alternates between mass chords of great sonority and fugal passages on the words "and He shall reign forever."

Aria—I know that my Redeemer liveth

The appealing simplicity of this air is a perfect expression of the words "I know that my Redeemer liveth, and that He shall stand at the latter day upon the earth; and though worms destroy this body, yet in my flesh shall I see God. For now is Christ risen from the dead, the first fruits of them that sleep."

The Passion

The origin of the Passion Music dates back to the fourth century, when during Easter week the story of the Passion and death of Jesus, according to the New Testament, was recited in church.

As the art of music developed, the style of presentation changed. In the Renaissance period composers set the Passion *a cappella*. In the seventeenth century, Heinrich Schütz, the most important German composer of the early baroque, established a pattern of Motet Passion which was influenced by the Italian opera. The Bible text was used throughout. The narrative was sung by a solo voice, the Evangelist, in recitative style, and the various characters of the drama appear also in recitative passages. Four-part choruses are used to represent groups such as the disciples, the high priests, and the crowd on the street. Many of the effects are extremely dramatic. After Schütz, there appeared a new type called Passion Oratorio, in which the Bible text was supplemented and later even supplanted by rhymed verses of contemporary poets.

Although the bulk of Bach's choral works is made up of

cantatas, ranging from short solo compositions to extended choral works approximating the oratorio in scope and design, he is supposed to have written four Passion Oratorios. But only two have been discovered: the *Passion according to St. John,* written in 1723, and the *Passion according to St. Matthew,* written in 1729. Bach used a verse text, selecting portions of poems by Brockes and Picander, but collaborated on both libretti, and restored the Biblical text for the narrative parts. In these Passion Oratorios Bach's choral style as exemplified in the cantatas is enhanced by the dramatic implications of the Biblical narrative.

J. S. BACH—*The Passion according to St. Matthew*

St. Matthew Passion was first heard at St. Thomas Church in Leipzig on Good Friday, 1729. One hundred years later the work was reintroduced at a public performance under the direction of Mendelssohn, and from this time on appreciation of the greatness of Bach, who had been little known in the intervening years, has steadily grown. Today performances of the work are heard frequently in church or in concert hall. Because of its great length, it is seldom given in its entirety but is sometimes performed in two successive evenings without cuts.

St. Matthew Passion is really a tremendous drama in twenty-four scenes dealing with the last days of the Saviour. Each scene consists of a musical and dramatic unit. The story is told by the Evangelist, a tenor part written in recitative. When the various characters are introduced in the course of his narrative, they also sing in recitative. The crowd is represented by dramatic choruses, often with remarkably realistic effect. The more important scenes also include solos or duets, which do not form a part of the story but are an expressive commentary upon the action. The lesser scenes are set off from the others by devotional chorales which are supposed to be sung by the congregation. The music is scored for soloists, double chorus, and two orchestras, each consisting of two flutes, two oboes, first and second violins, violas, organ, and continuo (cellos and basses). During the recitatives the accompaniment is provided by organ or harpsichord alone, except for the part of Jesus, which is always accompanied by strings.

Opening Chorus—Come, ye daughters

This magnificent introduction to the work is a double chorus which, although of great polyphonic complexity, is extremely dramatic. It suggests the procession to the Cross,

EXAMPLE 46.

with the choruses, one composed of the lamenting disciples and the other of the crowd of bystanders, filled with curiosity. Above these two choruses a separate group sings a devotional chorale, "Oh Lamb of God Most Holy." The style is fugal, rather freely developed. In the instrumental introduction the principal subject in E minor appears in the top voice with supporting harmonies (Example 46). There is a persistent rhythmic figure in the bass which runs through the entire piece. When the voices enter, the principal subject appears first in the bass, followed shortly by the tenor. It is presented simultaneously with a countersubject in the soprano part, answered by the alto (Example 47). There is a modulation to the major mode, and the first two phrases of the chorale appear and are repeated. The second half returns to E minor and the last three phrases of the chorale appear over the other voice. In this section the second chorus, which up to this time

EXAMPLE 47.

has been confined to short interjections, now doubles the first and adds to the mass sonority.

Two Chorales—O Lord who dares to smite Thee. No. 44
(After the scourging)
O Thou with hate surrounded. No. 63
(The crowning with thorns)

These two chorales, simple four-voice harmonizations of Lutheran hymn tunes, appear as devotional interludes following two of the short scenes.

Duet and Chorus—No. 33—Alas my Jesus now is taken
This follows immediately the scene in which Judas betrays Jesus by a kiss and the guards of the high priests arrest Him. It is a lament, sung by two women's voices, interrupted by furious cries of protests from the disciples. The

contrast between the wailing voices of the women and the angry shouts is extraordinarily dramatic. This is followed by a stormy chorus of the disciples, who call upon the lightning and thunder to blast their tormentors.

Aria No. 47—O pardon me, my God

This contralto aria is perhaps the most famous solo from the Passion. Coming after the scene of Peter's denial of Jesus, it is a plea for forgiveness:

> "O pardon me, my God
> And on my tears have pity.
> Look at me,
> Heart and eyes do weep to Thee
> To Thee, bitterly."

Formal, of operatic design, this aria is in three parts, with a beautiful instrumental introduction in which an appealing melody, the chief element, is played on a solo violin. With the entrance of the singer, the violin continues, sharing the melody in imitation with the voice part.

Closing Chorus—No. 78—In deepest grief

The final chorus, representing the disciples watching at the tomb of Jesus, is much simpler in texture than the elaborate first chorus, but deeply moving in accents of grief. It is arranged from an earlier instrumental sarabande, which it resembles in design and rhythm, with modulation from C minor to E flat major; but, unlike the usual form, there is a full repetition of the first part to conclude.

The Opera

Although the opera was the most popular and perhaps the most characteristic form of music of the baroque period, performances today of the operatic literature are rarely undertaken and we shall include no example of baroque opera for study. Works of Monteverdi, Purcell, Handel, Rameau, and others are sometimes presented in concert version, and operatic excerpts frequently appear on singers' programs, but the operas themselves are not regarded as a part of the standard repertory. This is not because of any shortcomings of the music, but may be attributed to the fact that modern conventions of the theater are different from those which were in vogue in the seventeenth and early eighteenth centuries, and modern audiences find the operas difficult to comprehend.

The oldest operas which are included in the regular repertory are those of Gluck, who was not a baroque but a classic composer, a connecting link between the ideals of Scarlatti and Handel and the classic opera as represented by Mozart. As a matter of fact, Gluck's earlier operas, now practically never performed, included examples of post-baroque *opera seria* (serious opera) as well as Italian and French comic operas of a pleasing and witty nature. He is best known, however, for his last operas composed for performances at the Paris Opéra under the patronage of Marie Antoinette. These brought about certain reforms which marked the transition from the ornate and artificial baroque style to the relatively simple and naturalistic vein of the classic composers.

Gluck is often cited as the great operatic reformer who paved the way for the music drama of the nineteenth century. In the preface to *Alceste* he calls attention to the abuses of certain operatic practices and evidences his desire to bring about a greater unity between text and music. With this in view, he abolishes virtuoso passages for singers and attempts to bridge the gap between recitative and aria, increasing the musical importance of the former and lessening the formal rigidity of the latter. Modern operagoers will not be overly impressed by the naturalism of the Gluck operas, which are based upon mythological subjects and have an impersonal quality in their exalted treatment of the great human emotions. They are completely lacking in suspense, and there is little characterization when compared, for example, with the operas of Mozart. Their great appeal, however, lies in the noble simplicity of the melody and in their absolute sincerity. Compared to the serene divinity of Gluck's creations, Wagner's gods and goddesses seem restless and earthy indeed.

GLUCK—*Orpheus and Eurydice* (composed in 1762; Paris version, 1774)

The story follows the familiar myth beginning after the death of Eurydice, with Orpheus mourning at the tomb. He is persuaded by Amor to attempt her rescue from the kingdom of Hades, and the condition is imposed that if successful he must not look back as she follows him out of the underworld. After winning his way past the Furies to the Elysian Fields, where he finds Eurydice, he loses her again when she betrays him into violating the terms of the agreement. The intervention of Amor prevents the tragic conclusion which usually prevails in the story, and the lovers are happily reunited in the end.

In the original production staged in Vienna the part of Orpheus was written for male alto in accordance with the custom of Italian opera. For the Paris version the part was revised and sung by a tenor. During the nineteenth century the unfortunate tradition was established of having the part sung by a contralto. This prevails today except upon rare occasions.

Act I—*Opening chorus—Ah, dans ce bois tranquille*
Orpheus is mourning at the tomb of Eurydice. His companions call upon Eurydice to witness the suffering of her husband, who is dying of grief. The melancholy song of the chorus is occasionally interrupted by the voice of Orpheus, who despairingly cries the name of his beloved.

Act II—*Dance of the Furies and Chorus—Quel est l'audace*
Orpheus has penetrated the kingdom of the dead and is

surrounded by the Furies, who dance about him and impede his further passage. The introduction suggests the challenging authority of the spirits and the timidity of Orpheus. As the notes of his lyre are heard the spirits cry out in rage against this mortal who dares to direct his steps into their dread country. They dance about him and call upon Cerberus to frighten him away. There is an amusing realistic effect in the orchestra of the barking of Cerberus.

Act II—Appeal to the Furies—Laissez-vous toucher
Orpheus, accompanying himself upon the lyre, sings to the Furies asking that they have pity upon his distress. They are not at all mollified by the song and interrupt him with angry cries of "No."

Act II—Dance of the Furies
After considerable effort Orpheus has persuaded the Furies to let him pass and enters the underworld. Left by themselves, the Furies now engage in a wild dance, at the conclusion of which they disappear. This music is effective pictorially and dramatically and is the ancestor of many diabolic orchestra effects which appear in later compositions.

Act II—Dance of the Blessed Spirits
The scene now changes to the Elysian Fields, where the spirits of the blessed have their happy dwelling place. This music is a remarkable expression of beatific joys. It consists of three parts, a serene melody for two flutes and strings with a contrasting middle section of great intensity in which the feeling of joy approaches ecstasy. The first part is then repeated. In the records of the complete opera the first section is omitted.

Act II—Aria of the Happy Shade—Cet aisle aimable
The indication is that this song may be sung either by Eurydice or by a Happy Shade who is also a soprano. Since there are so few principal characters in the opera, the lat-

ter solution is generally adopted. Here again Gluck has been remarkably successful in depicting heavenly joy. The refrain of the melody is little more than an ascending and descending scale, but with this simple means a melody of the sheerest loveliness is achieved. A chorus of blessed spirits accompanies sections of the air.

Act II—Orpheus's Aria—Quel nouveau ciel

Enchanted by the vision of the blessed spirits, among whom he hopes to find Eurydice, Orpheus sings of his happiness but cannot restrain his impatience to find her. The spirits gather about him and reassure him that Eurydice will soon appear.

Act III—Orpheus's Aria—J'ai perdu mon Euridice

This famous air is a moving expression of the grief of Orpheus when, after he has broken his promise at the urging of Eurydice and has looked behind as she follows him out of Hades, he sees her die once again. There is a recurrent refrain of the most touching sadness—not a hysterical outpouring of grief, but a deeply felt sorrow which is all the more expressive because of its restraint. It is as if Gluck, with the exalted power of his inspiration, had raised the somewhat academic misfortune of Orpheus to the expression of a universal sorrow.

4 THE CLASSIC ERA

Introduction

THE so-called "classic period" extends roughly from the death of the last great masters of the baroque to the end of the Beethovenian era. Both its beginning and its end are inextricably connected with other currents. At its beginning the rococo, the dainty and playful tapering off of the baroque, and at its end the early Romantic movement both left unmistakable marks upon Classicism—and both these influences are felt in the music of the period. Owing to the great number of Austrian composers who occupied the leading positions in the classic era, and to the prominent role that Vienna, the capital, played in musical life, the classic period is also called the Viennese Period or School, although the style was not restricted to Austria.

The term "classic" is rather vague, but since it has become a household word, and since this period is usually known and designated by this term, we shall use it to denote a style characterized by fine sense of roundness of form, equilibrium of means of expression and content, discipline of mind, and an absence of any vulgar or sensational effects, especially the overemphasis of emotional content which made its appearance in a later age. The classic composer builds and constructs with highly developed skill, but that does not mean that form is stressed at the expense of emotional values. On the contrary, Haydn, Mozart, and Beethoven and many of their colleagues were deeply interested in human problems, and their compositions glow with warm human feeling. Even in the somewhat stereotyped entertainment music of the age, to which they all contributed, their character and personality endow the music with a spirit far above the level of perfunctory Kapellmeister music.

From the economic point of view, the position of the musician during this period was bettered and progress was made toward the more democratic nineteenth century. The music publisher, profiting by the spread of printed music and the public demand for certain types of composition, became an increasingly important factor in the support of music. The institution of public concerts and the rise of the instrumental virtuoso also affected the situation. The chief patron of music, however, was still the nobility. Retinues of musicians, often including composers, were to be found in many noble households. Haydn, Mozart, and Beethoven, all were supported during portions of their careers by noble patrons and received many commissions for compositions from wealthy amateurs. To the proud spirit of Mozart and Beethoven this dependence upon the rich and eminent was somewhat of a trial, but the impoverishment of Mozart after his resignation from the intolerable service of the Archbishop of Salzburg is an indication that the time had not yet arrived when the composer could hope to be economically independent.

All the music of the period was influenced by the growth of the sonata form, the large architectural order of classicism. An instrumental design capable of great expansion, especially as expressed in string quartet and symphony, it was the characteristic contribution to the musical style of this period and a feature of practically all types of instrumental music. Although chamber music and orchestral music were now separated, each with its own artistic purpose and sphere, the forms and devices which eighteenth-century composers employed were quite similar. In the mature works of Haydn and Mozart they tended to draw apart, a process even more marked in the music of Beethoven.

The significant change from the harpsichord to the modern hammer piano was another important factor in shaping the musical style of classicism, bringing with it enhanced rhythmic and dynamic possibilities for musical expression. This is shown in the piano sonatas of Haydn and Mozart but is especially striking in the thirty-two piano sonatas of Beethoven which comprise one of the most valuable aspects of his art. However, the full effect of piano style, calling on the rich dynamic and coloristic resources of the instrument, was not felt until the Romantic era, at which time this instrument virtually took the place of the orchestra.

As regards form and content, we find the classic sonata greatly changed from its baroque prototype. It still consists of several movements, but these are seldom all in the same key and a greater variety of forms is to be noted. The chief difference is that the linear interest, the spinning out of motive figuration, is replaced by dramatic opposition of moods, themes, and tonalities, and by many-sided development of concentrated thematic materials. The texture is rarely polyphonic in the sense of uninterrupted contrapuntal progression, but excellent use is made by all the great classical masters of a free and pliable contrapuntal technique in the manipulation of their thematic material, especially in the development sections of their sonata constructions.

The classic period brought with it a standard of organization hitherto lacking in ensemble music for instruments. Before the time of Haydn the line of division between chamber and orchestral music was not clearly marked.

Players often doubled the parts of trio sonatas so that the effect might resemble a small string orchestra, and such orchestral compositions as the concerto grosso were frequently played by small groups with the effect of chamber music. The keyboard instrument, adding a continuo part, was a feature of all ensemble music. But the improvised continuo part disappeared along with the harpsichord, and chamber music, with careful part writing for each single instrument, was established in the form of trios, quartets, quintets, etc. Various instruments were used in these groups—strings, wood winds, occasionally the piano—but the standard chamber music organization was the string quartet, with two violins, viola, and cello.

The orchestral principle of duplicated parts resulted in the symphony orchestra, an organization of strings, wood winds, brasses, and percussion which has served subsequently as the standard large instrumental ensemble. For this larger grouping (it was by no means the mammoth affair of the late nineteenth century) the classic composers wrote symphonies and concertos. The symphony resembled the sonata in formal organization, and the classic concerto merged this design with the concerto principle of the baroque solo concerto, with added emphasis upon the virtuoso possibilities of the solo instrument. The instrumental suite of the baroque was replaced by a form of entertainment music known as the divertimento, serenade, or cassation. In orchestral works such as the symphony and the concerto there was a growth of tone color for dramatic contrasts, although orchestral color still did not exist for its own sake. The period showed a tendency toward enlargement and expansion of the proportions as well as the subjectivity and expressiveness of all instrumental music.

Perhaps the greatest glory of the classic period was the symphony of Haydn, Mozart, and Beethoven. As a general rule musical forms develop and mature slowly. The Renaissance motet and the instrumental fugue of the baroque were the result of long periods of experimentation. But within little more than half a century the classic symphony not only was established and perfected, but reached a level of artistic achievement unsurpassed in the literature of music.

Opera and church music of the period reflect the same stylistic and social changes. The solemn but static splendor of the baroque opera disappeared under the irresistible vivacity of the lifelike human theater that was the opera buffa and the opéra comique. Gluck's musical tragedies attempted to endow the old baroque *opera seria,* or "serious opera," with a somber and eloquent tone, devoid of the senseless frills of the outmoded bravura style. Adhering uncompromisingly to his lofty aims and curbing the singer's extravagances, Gluck reformed opera, but even his truly noble music dramas, which in fact effected a transition from the baroque to the new opera, could not stave off the impending merger of "comic opera" with "serious opera" which gave us the classical opera and the imperishable masterpieces of Mozart.

Oratorio and Passion, typical creations of the baroque, declined markedly after the death of Bach, but the Mass knew a new era of glory by assimilating much of the operatic and symphonic technique of the period. This course of affairs is explained by the fact that whereas the great baroque masters came from the Protestant north of Germany, the focal point of the classic style was the Catholic south.

Principal Composers of the Preclassic and Classic Periods

C. P. E. Bach, 1714–1788	Second son of J. S. Bach. Versatile composer contributing to the evolution of the classic idiom
Johann Stamitz, 1717–1757	Composer at the Mannheim court. Early composer of symphonies

Gluck, 1714–1787
Haydn, 1732–1809
Mozart, 1756–1791
Beethoven, 1770–1827

The Classic Sonata

It was in the classic period that the piano sonata came into its own. Haydn, Mozart, and Beethoven composed extensively in this medium and also wrote sonatas for violin and piano. Originally intended for music making in the homes of the many excellent amateurs of the time, the classic piano sonata became in the Beethovenian era, when concert life began, an entertainment piece devised for public performance. Although tending occasionally toward virtuoso display, it subordinates its keyboard effects to the general symphonic design, and is always compact and clear in thought. In the Romantic period the sonata was replaced in general esteem by the single-movement piece, generally of song form pattern. But in the late eighteenth and early nineteenth centuries the sonata was regarded as a natural form of expression, widely understood and enjoyed because of its logic of design and its melodic and dramatic features.

The sonata's great contribution to musical design was the pattern known as first movement or sonata form. At this point musical nomenclature is a bit confusing. The term "sonata" indicates a type of composition in several movements. The term "sonata form" is a principle of construction which is embodied in one or more movements of the sonata, almost invariably appearing as the basis for the design of the first movement. It is a musical plan in three sections. The first, known as the *exposition*, is in two related keys with modulation from the first to the second serving as a *bridge*. The thematic material of the movement is presented in this section, and it is a convention of the design that the most important musical ideas are included in the part before modulation, subsidiary and contrasting themes usually being stated in the bridge and thereafter. The second section, known as the *development* or *working-out* section, includes such thematic material as the composer may select, varied in repetition by change of key, of rhythm, melody, accompaniment, or of any of its essential features. At the conclusion of the development the principal key of the work is reintroduced. The third section, known as the *recapitulation*, restates the material of the exposition, but does not modulate, making such musical adjustments as may be necessary. A *coda*, appearing as a second, shorter development section, may be added as a conclusion. The movement may also be preceded by an *introduction* with or without thematic relationship to the main body of the movement. It is traditionally slower in tempo than the movement proper, which when serving as first movement is almost always some form of an allegro. This design, perfected in the classic period, is susceptible of considerable expansion, and forms the basis of a majority of large instrumental compositions.

The standard design of the sonata is in four movements, like that of the symphony: the first is a sonata-form allegro; the second a lyric andante in either song form, modified sonata form, or theme and variations; the third a minuet or scherzo; and the fourth an allegro in rondo or sonata form, occasionally theme and variations. However, the sonata varies this procedure much more than does the symphony. Many sonatas have only three movements, choosing between either minuet or rondo, and some are written in only two movements. Very occasionally the first movement is found to consist of a theme and variations (Mozart—*A major;* Beethoven—*A flat major*). The so-called *Moonlight Sonata* of Beethoven begins with a slow movement. In his later sonatas great freedom of form and originality of content are to be observed, but freedom from rigid formal pattern is a characteristic of the works of Haydn and Mozart as well.

HAYDN—*Sonata for piano in C minor, opus 17, no. 6* (composed in 1780)

First movement—Allegro moderato in C minor

The first movement, in sonata form, reverses the customary treatment of themes; the principal theme, in minor (Example 48), is of an expressive character and is con-

EXAMPLE 48.

trasted with subsidiary major themes which are chiefly of rhythmic interest. They are connected by modulatory material of some length which alternates rhythmic and expressive features. The development section begins with the expressive subject, first in major, and continues with

EXAMPLE 49.

an extended treatment of the second subsidiary theme (Example 49) leading to a fine dramatic climax. The recapitulation lays greater emphasis on the expressive theme, and shortens both the transition and subsidiary sections. There is no coda. Notice the harpsichord figure which accompanies the second subsidiary theme.

Second movement—Andante con moto in A flat major
The second movement has somewhat the feeling of the sarabande, a lyric dance movement in triple rhythm used in the earlier instrumental suite. The principal features of the melody are the repeated note accompanied by a descending scale in the left hand and the offbeat melody accompanied by left-hand thirds which is introduced in the

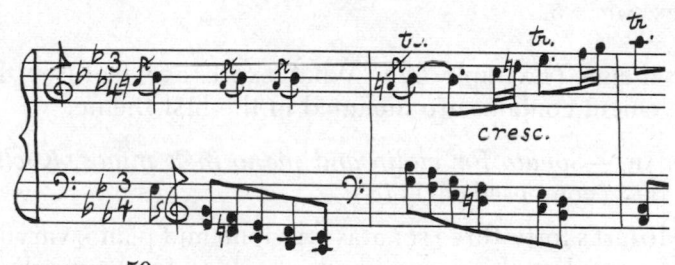

EXAMPLE 50.

third phrase (Example 50). As in the old suite, the movement is divided into two sections, for each of which a repeat is indicated. The melody is continually developing as it unfolds with contrast of dynamics and several climaxes.

Finale—Allegro in C minor
The third movement, rhythmically vigorous, uses a number of keyboard effects, among them crossing of the hands. It is in sonata form with a suggestion of the rondo, in that

EXAMPLE 51.

the first theme also serves as a coda (Example 51). The development especially emphasizes the dynamic subsidi-

EXAMPLE 52.

ary theme (Example 52). What expressive features the movement contains are included in the first theme.

MOZART—*Sonata for violin and piano in E minor, Köchel no. 304* (composed in 1778)

Mozart's forty-three sonatas for violin and piano, varying in the number of movements from one to four, furnish an excellent example of entertainment music of the classic period—music designed to be enjoyed informally in the home, not too difficult to be played by amateurs, graceful, melodious, and gay. The imitative possibilities of the two differing timbres of the instruments are stimulating to the composer, who had a natural gift for polyphonic combination, and beneath the unpretentious exterior of the music there is deft and scintillating craftsmanship. The *Sonata in E minor* consists of two movements, a sonata form allegro and a minuet.

First movement—Allegro in E minor
The principal theme (Example 53) is stated at once in octaves between the violin and piano, followed by a subsidiary theme (Example 54) also in octaves. The first theme is then repeated on the violin with harmonized accompaniment on the piano. A second, subsidiary theme (Example

EXAMPLE 53.

55) on the piano induces the violin to amplify a melodic feature of the main theme, which is to be further expanded

EXAMPLE 54.

in development. The bridge introduces a new rhythm (Example 56) and prepares for the rhythmic personality of the chief subsidiary theme in G major (Example 57), in-

EXAMPLE 55.

troduced by the piano alone. The rest of the exposition re-echoes this material, concluding with a canonic imitation between the instruments of the principal theme.

EXAMPLE 56.

The development is short and consists mainly of the principal theme set against an expressive descending figure which has its origin in the theme itself. These elements appear variously in the violin and the two principal voices

EXAMPLE 57.

of the piano. The recapitulation, starting with the main theme accompanied by new harmonic features, proceeds with the material of the exposition occasionally varied. There is a short coda to conclude.

Second movement—Tempo di menuetto in E minor
One thinks of the minuet as a rather worldly affair, genteel and graceful, but somewhat on the stuffy side. This piece is quite different, an intimate little melody, rather sad and appealing, as if one were remembering a dance rather than actually engaging in it. The melody is introduced by the piano, the violin joins in, and the music goes

EXAMPLE 58.

on with expansion of the melodic elements thus pronounced. After a pause and a short, spectacular run on the piano, the first part comes to an end with some charming imitation between the violin and the top voice of the piano. The trio in E major, despite its change from the minor, is still rather tender and ruminative. Again the piano introduces the melody and is later joined by the violin. The complementary third section is written out because it chooses not to be symmetrical but is shorter, has a new accompaniment figure, and introduces a new melodic fragment (Example 58) which makes the music more wistful than ever.

BEETHOVEN—*Piano Sonata in C major* (*Waldstein*), *opus 53* (composed in 1804)

Beethoven's thirty-two piano sonatas are rather like a library of classic piano music, ranging as they do from simple, unpretentious pieces for the amateur to magnificent works suitable only for the virtuoso. One has to be careful about superlatives in dealing with Beethoven because they are so soon exhausted, but these piano sonatas are so perfect an expression of the composer's genius, of his profound mind and noble character, of his rich and very human personality that it is no exaggeration to say that music, even life itself, would be immeasurably the poorer without them.

The sonata dedicated to Count Waldstein is from the middle period of the composer's life, the time of the *Fifth Symphony, Fidelio,* and the *Rasoumowsky Quartets,* when he was at the height of his strength and productivity. It is a work of large proportions, so brilliant in its treatment of the piano, so original and eloquent in material and design that it seems hardly recognizable as a descendant of the modest sonatas of Haydn and Mozart.

First movement—Allegro con brio in C major
The principal theme is a pianissimo series of repeated C major chords modulating abruptly at the end into G major (Example 59). A scale fragment descends in the

EXAMPLE 59.

form of an added motive (Example 60). The theme is repeated in the key of B flat; the scale fragment is extended
and descends in a five-note arpeggio (Example 61) to a
pause on G. A tremolo version of the theme leads to a whirl-

EXAMPLE 60.

wind bridge, a moment of expectancy, and the key of E
major in which a choralelike theme (Example 62) appears. This theme does not succeed in getting into C major
until the coda. In the recapitulation section it arrives un-

EXAMPLE 61.

expectedly in A major and A minor, with only its variation
appearing in C. A second subsidiary theme based upon
arpeggio figures used prominently in the development
(Example 63) follows the chorale. It is in the tempestuous

EXAMPLE 62.

spirit of the first theme, but the mood is differently expressed. The closing material is calmer and induces a moment of comparative relaxation. The development is divided into two parts: the first is an exploitation of the descending fragment of the first theme with dynamic contrasts and a variety of keys; the other engages the second subsidiary theme in similar pursuits and leads to a rum-

EXAMPLE 63.

bling in the bass, from which flying bits of scale arise in a great crescendo to lead to the recapitulation. For the most part, this is a repetition of the exposition, but there is an expansion of the descending arpeggio fragment interjected between the two versions of the principal theme. The coda continues the process of development of the fragments of the main theme, precipitates a climax, and pauses. Then, with grateful contrast, the chorale theme arrives in the proper key. The ending is a final dramatic statement of the principal theme.

Second movement—Adagio molto in F major
The original second movement of the sonata was discovered to be too long for inclusion in the work and was later published separately as *Andante in F*. To replace it,

EXAMPLE 64.

Beethoven wrote a short adagio in the reflective, highly subjective style that came to be more and more a characteristic of his music. It is built upon a single rhythmic fragment with frequent modulation (Example 64). There is a brief lyric middle section suggesting a dialogue between cello and violin. The third section resembles the first, but the material is extended and varied.

Third movement—Rondo—Allegretto moderato in C major
When some people express the sentiment "God's in His heaven, all's right with the world," they are open to suspicion on various counts. When the turbulent, defiant, and suffering Beethoven surrenders to a mood of sunny optimism it is somehow the triumph of all humanity over the dark forces that beset us. The finale to this sonata is the reflection of such a mood. The theme of the rondo is a joyful melody of great simplicity, made exultant and glowing

by the rushing arpeggios which accompany it (Example 65). There are five appearances of the refrain interspersed with contrasting couplets, two of which are of similar ma-

EXAMPLE 65.

terial. A development in the central portion occurs before the third refrain. The movement, while long, is not difficult to follow, but this music is so completely beguiling that one is tempted to say do not try to follow it, simply let yourself bask in its warmth and loveliness.

Chamber Music—The String Quartet

In the time of Haydn a distinction was first made between music designed for the large group, orchestral, and music for small ensemble, chamber music. The orchestra lent itself naturally to the creation of large mass effects, dramatic crescendi, and varying tone colors. The small group, although unsuited to these, had certain advantages in presenting clearly independent melodies in combination, and in directing the attention to subtlety of design and delicacy of subject matter. The tradition has come down to us that chamber music represents musical composition in its most refined expression, calculated to appeal to our sense of design rather than to overwhelm us with emotional and sonorous power.

Various chamber music combinations have been employed by composers since the time of Haydn, but the most typical and the one endowed with the richest literature is undoubtedly the string quartet. This consists of two violins, a viola, and a violoncello. There are many famous organizations which devote themselves entirely to this literature, and, as in the case of the symphony, the contribution of the classic masters is the most important and most frequently played.

The quartet bears the same relationship in plan to the sonata as does the symphony, in that it generally consists of the four characteristic movements. Beethoven modified this plan somewhat in his last six quartets, which are notable for greatly increased subjectivity and originality of design.

HAYDN—*Quartet in C major (Emperor), opus 76, no. 3* (composed in 1797)

This quartet is one of six great works composed by Haydn toward the end of his long career, six years after the death of Mozart. That the older man profited greatly by the example of Mozart's magnificent works in this category cannot be doubted if one compares these later quartets with those written before Mozart's. There is a compactness of design, free interplay of parts, and saliency of thematic material which Haydn, whose music had been the chief inspiration of Mozart, learned in turn from the younger man. Together the two men fully realized the possibilities of the medium and set a standard for chamber music never to be eclipsed, not even by Beethoven, whose quartets, larger in proportion and frequently more dramatic, are among his greatest compositions. The subtitle *Emperor* is given to this quartet because the second movement is based on Haydn's famous hymn to the Austrian emperor.

First movement—Allegro in C major
The principal motive, which appears at the outset as a part of the first theme played on the first violin (Example 66), has a certain affinity with a motive from the first theme of the D major *London Symphony*. It is used chiefly as a rhythmic design to dominate the entire first movement,

serving sometimes as the foundation of a developed melody in combination with other rhythms, or again in a stretto-like formation of the four string voices. There is a dotted-

EXAMPLE 66.

note accompaniment rhythm, frequently used as a counter-melody (Example 67), and a closing theme (Example 68) which reappears at the end of the coda, but the main

EXAMPLE 67.

interest lies in manipulations of the central motive. The most vivid of its appearances is as a fully developed melody in E major at the climax of the development section. Here

EXAMPLE 68.

it is accompanied by open fifths with heavy accents on the cello and viola, giving the effect of a peasant dance with drone bass.

Second movement—Poco adagio; Cantabile in G major
This movement is a set of four formal variations on the
Austrian Hymn. The Hymn itself, without modification
and with simple four-part harmony, is first stated as a
theme. The first variation is confined to first and second
violins. The second violin plays the theme, above which
the first violin weaves a contrapuntal elaboration, a mixture of staccato and legato patterns. The second variation
has the theme in the cello, again without change, accompanied by supporting harmonies above on the other three
instruments. The viola has its turn at the theme in the third
variation, with a somewhat more independent rhythmic
scheme in the accompanying melodies. In the fourth variation the theme returns to the first violin, but after the first
phrase all the instruments are transposed to the higher
register with heightened and fresh color.

Third movement—Menuett—Allegro in C major
A simple melody on the first violin begins with a four-

EXAMPLE 69.

note motive (Example 69), which is elaborated into the
design throughout the minuet proper. A similar motive in
the trio, in A minor, is enlarged in the same fashion (Ex-

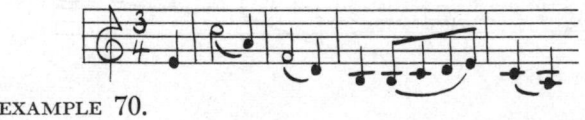

EXAMPLE 70.

ample 70). In the second part of the trio, after a pause, this
becomes an enchanting melody in A major played pianis-

simo on the first violin. A return to A minor brings the trio to a close.

Finale—Presto in C minor—C major

Classic ensemble pieces with first movements in minor are frequently terminated by a finale in major, but the reverse is seldom found. Haydn follows the latter plan in the *Emperor Quartet,* and the last movement has an un-

EXAMPLE 71.

accustomed gravity of mood. The thematic material, too, is of an unexpected seriousness. The first theme has two elements, rhythmic and expressive. The first is contained in three introductory chords with double and triple stopping on the instruments (Example 71). The second imme-

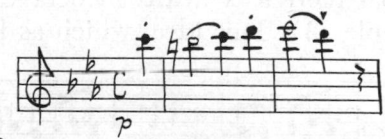

EXAMPLE 72.

diately follows, a short lyric idea on the first violin, the rhythm of which is imitated by the other instruments (Example 72). To this material is added a triplet accompaniment figure on the cello, and the lyric motive is elaborated into this design. These three elements furnish the thought of the movement which follows the plan of first-movement sonata. At the end of the recapitulation the lyric motive appears in C major and brings about a conclusion in that key.

BEETHOVEN—*Quartet in F major, opus 18, no. 1* (composed in 1800)

Beethoven's first quartet is one of six written during the same year. It belongs to his first period of composition, but the style is characteristically his own and makes scant acknowledgment to the works of his predecessors. The design is polyphonic and concentrated as to subject matter, but the strong rhythmic and dynamic contrasts give it a dramatic quality which adds to the freshness and vigor of the music. Beethoven's approach to the quartet is never orchestral, although at times the sonorous capacities of the four instruments are taxed to the limit. He is able to include a large measure of dramatic power in quartet writing without losing sight of the limitations of his medium. The music at all times is conceived in terms of the strings, and in the transparent quality of the small ensemble rather than in the massed tone of the orchestra.

First movement—Allegro con brio in F major

The principal motive is heard in octaves on the four strings (Example 73). This idea, which as first presented

EXAMPLE 73.

is strongly rhythmical, is also endowed with expressive melodic possibilities which are explored immediately thereafter. It penetrates all divisions of the movement, serving as the basis for melody, countermelody, or accompaniment figure. All other thematic material of the movement is of relative unimportance, merely episodic contrast or for purposes of combination with the central motive, which dominates the movement much as does the subject of a fugue. In the development section the motive is heard in four-part stretto.

Second movement—Adagio affettuoso ed appassionato in D minor

There is little passionate love music to be found in Beethoven's work. He often writes tenderly of love, but his passion is generally of a defiant sort, not the kind to be directed toward one's beloved. But this slow movement, which he is quoted as having identified with the story of

EXAMPLE 74.

Romeo and Juliet at the tomb of the Capulets, is a romance of great emotional intensity. Against a rhythmic pattern of repeated notes a broad melody is heard on the first violin which is later taken up by the cello (Example 74). This melody, occasionally interrupted with dramatic pauses, progresses in long phrases which are accompanied by rhythmic figures of increasing intensity suggestive of despair. The design employed is tonally that of the sonata form, and there are passages in which features of the melody are developed, but the general effect of the movement is one of sustained lyricism.

Scherzo—Allegro molto in F major

The mood of the scherzo is one of reckless gaiety. The symphonic subject matter is contained in the music of the first two bars, one motive stated by the first violin, the other

EXAMPLE 75.

simultaneously by the cello (Example 75). The trio contrasts two new ideas, one of staccato octave skips and the other a sustained, scalewise theme heard on the first violin (Example 76).

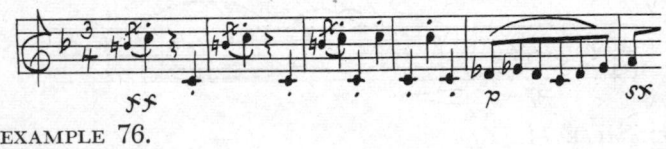

EXAMPLE 76.

Finale—Allegro in F major

The last movement is a rondo with a rhythmic refrain suggestive of the dance. This rhythm is a pattern of four

EXAMPLE 77.

triplets followed by three staccato eighth notes (Example 77). The contrasting material emphasizes duple rhythm of melody and accompaniment (Examples 78, 79, 80). These two rhythmic schemes alternate throughout the movement.

EXAMPLE 78.

EXAMPLE 79.

EXAMPLE 80.

The Divertimento

The divertimento, a type of composition known also as serenade, nocturne, or cassation, is a form of instrumental ensemble which was especially popular in Austria in the eighteenth century. It is essentially outdoor music of an entertaining quality, occupying a middle ground somewhere between chamber music and the symphony. The ensemble may consist of strings alone or other instruments may be added. The number of movements varies to include assorted dances, marches, and the like, with occasional pieces of symphonic architecture. Haydn wrote some seventy divertimenti, and Mozart twenty-two, many of which are indistinguishable from their early symphonies.

MOZART—Serenade *Eine kleine Nachtmusik, K.* 525 (composed in 1787)

This charming composition of the mature Mozart is the most familiar example of the divertimento to present-day audiences. It is written for small string orchestra, and although the design resembles his quartets and symphonies, with only the traditional minuet for a dance movement, it differs from the quartets in that each part is to be played by several performers, and from the symphonies in that only strings are indicated and the proportions of each movement are smaller.

First movement—Allegro in G major
A rhythmic arpeggio (Example 81), the principal theme of the Allegro, is stated by the instruments in octaves. This

EXAMPLE 81.

goes on to a festive music, which after a short time induces modulation, and a second theme, graceful as opposed to the boisterousness of the first, is introduced on the violins in

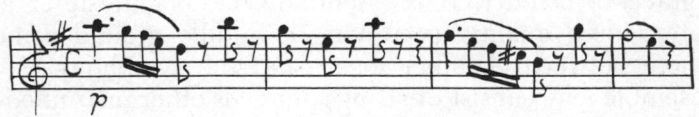

EXAMPLE 82.

D major (Example 82). A sprightly theme which also appears in the development brings the exposition to a close (Example 83). The development section, after a recollection of the first theme, occupies itself briefly with a few

EXAMPLE 83.

transpositions and extensions of the closing theme and moves on to the recapitulation, where only the necessary transpositions and a short ending are used to modify the exposition material.

Second movement—Romanze—Andante in C major
The term "romance" is an indication that this movement is unsymphonic and a simple melodic design, with a suggestion of the informality and intimacy of a song. In the slow movements of his symphonies Mozart often employs a somewhat sophisticated lyricism, but in this composition we have an example of that same naive loveliness which appears so often in the melodies from his operas. The contrasting middle section in C minor is a dialogue between the first violin and cello, supported by a fixed design of repeating harmonies on the second violin and viola. The third section resembles the first, with the omission of some melodic episodes.

Third movement—Menuetto-Allegro in G major
The minuet is forthright and rhythmical, with the violins for the most part in octaves. The trio in D major is feminine by contrast, as if the gentlemen had stepped aside and permitted the ladies to grace the boards alone.

Finale—Rondo—Allegro in G major
This is a bustling, gay little piece, high spirited through-

EXAMPLE 84.

out. The short introductory refrain (Example 84) is repeated a number of times with only slight variation, usually in the key of G major, but wanders occasionally into such

EXAMPLE 85.

neighboring countries as D and E flat major. There is a little contrasting figure for rhythmic diversion (Example 85) and a second theme (Example 86).

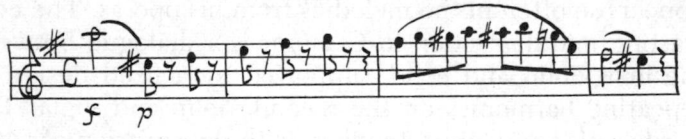

EXAMPLE 86.

The Classical Symphony

The greatest achievement of the classic period was undoubtedly the symphony. In the works of the Viennese masters this form of composition reached heights of artistic organization unexcelled in the history of music. Emerging from a music often of dry formalism, it progressed toward the more subjective and democratic music of the Romantic era, anticipating much of the popular appeal of the latter but never yielding to the structural weakness which was destined to accompany it. The classic symphony represents the ideal balance between logic of form and expressiveness of content. As such, its appeal is almost as great to audiences of today as it was to its contemporaries. In this respect alone, were there no additional evidence to be presented, the classic period is truly a golden age of music.

The essence of the symphony, as in the case of all music based on the sonata principle, is dramatic, and at its best it is a pattern of irresistible momentum, once the elements of conflict have been presented in the themes. Often these appear fused in a single initial idea. Subsidiary themes, when not necessary to complement the symphonic contribution of the principal theme, are included for purposes of melodic relief and are strictly controlled, so that they do not arrest the sense of forward motion. Even in the greatly expanded symphony movements of Beethoven this channeling of thought is strikingly evident. The listener who is able to grasp the musical substance of the thematic ideas will never find these great compositions tedious.

The enormous advantage in popular appeal of the symphony over the sonata lies in the expressive possibilities of the orchestra. Simultaneously with perfection of form, the classic masters achieved an orchestral style which, although far less colorful and dramatic than that of the late nineteenth century, was admirably adapted to the crispness and compactness of the material. While the principal role is played by the strings, and the wood winds and brass are usually given the task of building up sonority in climax or sustaining the harmonic background, there emerges during this period a lively sense of the melodic possibilities and tone character of the flute, the oboe, the clarinet, the bassoon, the horn, and other brass instruments. Trombones are used occasionally by Haydn and Beethoven; trumpets and horns are restricted to the overtone series and are therefore generally unsuited for melodic statement. The classic orchestra also was a relatively small body of players designed for a concert hall of moderate size, and best results in these symphonies, even those of Beethoven, which seem to transcend their anticipated medium in breadth of conception, are usually obtained in performances which bear these facts in mind.

The four movements of the symphony correspond to the plan of the sonata described in earlier pages. Beethoven's symphonies differ from those of Haydn and Mozart in the enlarged proportions of each movement, in the substitution of the scherzo for the minuet (except in the *First* and *Eighth Symphonies*), and in the change in spirit of the finale from an entertainment piece to a composition of greater seriousness and breadth.

HAYDN—*Symphony in D major (London), no. 104* (composed in 1795)

The *London Symphony*, written four years after the death of Mozart, is one of the crowning achievements of the mature Haydn. In this work perfection of form and instrumental technique are combined with the geniality and wit which are an essential part of Haydn's musical personality. It is a mistake to regard the symphonies of Haydn as merely amiable entertainment. Because they do not abound in the shattering climaxes and full-throated emotionalism which are typical of the nineteenth-century symphony, they often appear to the inexperienced listener as rather tame. After one has become accustomed to the less rhetorical style of Haydn, beneath the surface charm is discovered an unsuspected vigor and depth of feeling.

First movement—Adagio-Allegro, in D minor, D major
As a general rule, the first movement of the Haydn symphonies begins with a short introduction unrelated in the-

matic material to the subsequent allegro, but serving to establish a mood. This introduction is in minor, in contrast to the major of the allegro. It is based on a rhythmic motive (Example 87) heard on the full orchestra which is then de-

EXAMPLE 87.

veloped melodically against an expressive figure (Example 88) on the first violin, and later the oboe. The mood is one of great sadness.

The allegro which follows is forthright and untroubled by melancholy. The first theme (Example 89) contains two motives which are the principal source of the movement.

EXAMPLE 88.

The one appearing in the first two bars is developed incidentally in the course of the exposition and recapitulation. The second motive, in bars three and four, is a series of four repeated quarter notes followed by two half notes, the step above and return; it is the sole thematic basis of the development section, there being no contrasting lyric theme. The second half of the exposition consists of repetition and development of the first theme with the addition

EXAMPLE 89.

of a new rhythmic idea to conclude. The recapitulation is not an approximate duplication of the exposition, as is customary, but consists of further developments of the two principal motives.

Second movement—Andante in G major

The slow movements of Haydn are extremely varied in design, are less ornate melodically than those of Mozart,

EXAMPLE 90.

and are characterized by a simple lyricism both touching and profound. This andante is in three sections. The first part is an expressive melody (Example 90) of four irregular phrases on the strings, with an added figure of repeated descending notes against moving inner voices to conclude (Example 91). The middle section is a lyric development

EXAMPLE 91.

of features of this melody in various keys, using the full resources of the orchestra. The third section is an enlarged repetition of the first with new accompaniment figures, melodic embellishments and expansions, and varied orchestration. Notice particularly the added expressiveness of the

EXAMPLE 92.

chromatic inner voices in the concluding phrase (Example 92).

Third movement—Menuetto in D major

The minuet is based upon the rhythmic idea which is stated in the beginning (Example 93). The accented weak beat with syncopated effect is the main feature of the movement. Notice that there is little of the suavity of the tradi-

EXAMPLE 93.

tional minuet about this music. It is very close to the scherzo mood of the Beethoven symphony. The trio, by contrast, is sedately charming and less rhythmic. The beginning

EXAMPLE 94.

melodic figure (Example 94), the skip of a third on oboe and violin, is ingeniously developed throughout.

Finale—Allegro spiritoso in D major

This movement has the flavor of the rondo, but the design is that of the first movement sonata form with development. Two themes are of equal importance: the first is a rollicking

EXAMPLE 95.

tune of folk-song quality (Example 95), and the second, which serves as lyric contrast, is a slow-moving melody of even rhythm heard on the strings and delightfully imitated by the bassoon (Example 96). A modification of the first theme concludes the section. The development is concerned with both these themes in alternation. The second theme is especially lovely as its imitative possibilities are

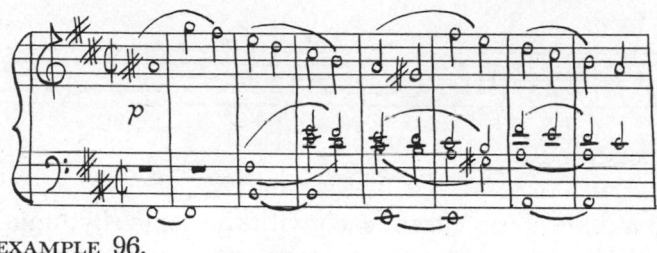

EXAMPLE 96.

exploited in a strettolike pattern on winds and strings. There is a short coda based upon the first theme.

MOZART—*Symphony in G minor, Köchel no. 550* (composed in 1788)

One has the impression that Haydn thought and felt in terms of instruments. His music is an almost perfect expression of the personalities of wood winds and strings. Mozart, on the other hand, while a great master of instrumental writing, seems much more influenced by the sound of the human voice, and particularly by that dramatic and ornamental type of singing which is characteristic of the opera. Mozart's melodies, spontaneous and ever fresh, are found in purest essence in his operas. His symphonies and chamber music reflect this musical style and are invariably dramatic. The *Symphony in G minor,* the most frequently heard, is an unusual combination of vivacity with underlying sadness. This feeling of sadness is not to be explained merely because three of the movements are in the minor mode. Despite the almost headlong rush of the allegro movements and the bustle of the finale, all the melodic essence of the work is somehow melancholy, at times extremely poignant.

First movement—Allegro molto in G minor

The principal theme is stated immediately in octaves by the violins (Example 97). This theme has an ascending

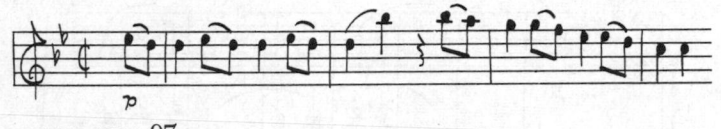

EXAMPLE 97.

and a descending curve, each with the same rhythmic design. The first three notes constitute a motive which is separately treated in the latter part of the development

EXAMPLE 98.

section and elsewhere. Notice that the theme itself as repeated hastens toward a modulation wherein a staccato theme of four notes appears, to be used as additional material for development (Example 98). This theme is much extended in the parallel section of the recapitulation. The lyric subsidiary theme (Example 99), an expressive chromatic melody, leads deftly into a closing passage based on the motive from the first theme.

EXAMPLE 99.

The development section employs the principal theme, first in its entirety and then by its motive alone. The recapitulation differs from the exposition in the extended bridge and the changed effect of the subsidiary themes in minor. There is a short, expressive coda based upon the principal theme.

Second movement—Andante in E flat major
The second movement follows the tonal design of sonata form but the effect is that of a long developing melody with

EXAMPLE 100.

two distinct features, one a broad lyric statement (Example 100) and the other a crisp motive of two ascending thirty-second notes which appears toward the end of the first

EXAMPLE 101

phrase (Example 101). These two elements, either in dialogue or in combination, are the source of the entire movement.

Third movement—Menuetto in G minor

The minuet is vigorous and unusually polyphonic in style. The two rhythmic ideas of the first three bars serve

EXAMPLE 102.

as motives for continuous development (Example 102). By contrast, the trio is in major and is engagingly tuneful, with a passage for the horns which is as much feared by the players as it is enjoyed by the listeners.

Finale—Allegro assai in G minor

This is a rapid and compact sonata allegro with two motives stated at once in the principal theme, the first an ascending arpeggio in quarter notes and the second an

EXAMPLE 103.

emphatic melodic cadence of eighth notes (Example 103). The bridge and concluding theme are based on the second motive. The subsidiary lyric theme is a simple melody of much charm which is heard first on the strings and then is varied slightly on the oboe (Example 104). In the recapitulation there is a brief passage where both the melody and its accompaniment appear in the winds, a rather unusual color. The development section is based entirely upon

EXAMPLE 104.

the first motive and moves in breathless fashion through various keys and devices. There is a short coda relating to the second motive from the principal theme.

THE SYMPHONIES OF BEETHOVEN

Practically every Beethoven symphony is a law unto itself. Each is unmistakably imbued with his dynamic and forceful personality—even the *First,* which outwardly resembles the symphonies of Haydn—but if one were compelled to select one as a basis for generalization the task would be difficult. All nine of them are four-movement works based upon the general plan of Haydn and Mozart, except that in all but two the scherzo is substituted for the minuet. He uses the familiar forms of Haydn and Mozart, first-movement allegro, symphonic song, theme and variations, etc., but the whole canvas is greatly expanded. Proportions everywhere are larger. There is an anticipation of the spirit of Romanticism to be noted in heightened orchestral climaxes, less restrained emotionalism, dynamic and rhythmical effects of violent contrast, and a subjectivity that is a marked departure from classical feeling. In spite of the change in content and style which Beethoven brought to the symphony, he remains firmly entrenched in the tradition of well-knit and logical musical thought, which is the main strength of the classic symphony. In the process of expansion the symphony did not lose its architectural solidity. Beethoven may be said to have increased its human content, and his example may have led the way to forces which were eventually to weaken it, but in his hands the classic symphony reached its fullest expression.

BEETHOVEN—*Symphony in C minor, opus 67, no. 5* (composed in 1805)

This is the most famous of Beethoven's symphonies, a favorite of musicians and audiences alike, which has withstood the ravages of the years and cannot be battered into commonplaceness by either overperformance or overfamiliarity. Even the appellation of *Fate Symphony*, of fictitious origin, and the literal explanation of the first movement as Fate knocking at the door, which usually is fed the culture-hungry individual to prevent him from thinking and feeling about it for himself, cannot dim the savage splendor of the music.

First movement—Allegro con brio in C minor

This is one of the most compact and swiftly moving pieces in the literature of music. Its power and strength are

EXAMPLE 105.

summed up in the four-note motive on strings and clarinets which appears immediately (Example 105), a motive which is the source of the entire movement. Its rhythm is heard continuously in one melodic guise or another, even punctuating the brief interlude of lyricism which appears on the violins after the bridge (Example 106). The development is a remarkable example of theme disintegration, a device especially characteristic of Beethoven. The short figure of the bridge, twice repeated here in expanded design, is then gradually reduced to a whispered single note and is finally interrupted with devastating effect by the

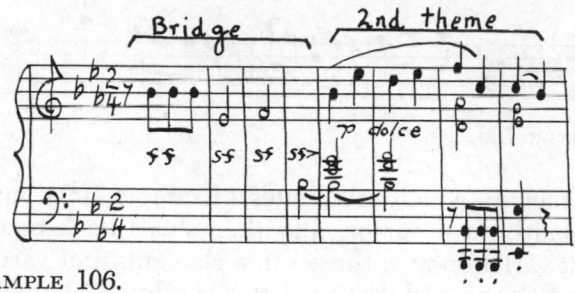

EXAMPLE 106.

principal motive on the full orchestra. Another characteristic Beethovenian feature is the interpolated oboe lament which comes after the first phrase of the recapitulation (Example 107). This is an expressive comment on the way things are going musically, and shows that the thought of the movement goes forward and is enriched by its musical

EXAMPLE 107.

experiences. There is a coda of militant spirit in which, toward the end, an added expressive figure on the oboe is added to the original melody of the first theme.

Second movement—Andante con moto in A flat major
This very familiar melody is the basis for a theme and variations of modified pattern. The theme itself is twofold, a broad lyric melody in A flat major (Example 108) and a

EXAMPLE 108.

second melody which modulates (Example 109), appears triumphantly in C major, and then steals back to A flat. The first variation uses these same elements, but varies the accompaniment and changes the rhythmic character of

EXAMPLE 109.

the first melody by eliminating its inequalities and elaborating the tonal design. The second variation is similarly treated with further elaboration of increasing rhythmic motion, but here the second melody is omitted. The third variation is more properly a development of features of both melodies. The fourth variation is a repetition of the

EXAMPLE 110.

first melody, now brilliantly scored for full orchestra. There is a coda based upon the first melody, the last phrase of which is made more eloquent for its final appearance by transposition of a part of the melodic line (Example 110).

Third movement—Allegro in C minor

This scherzo has an uneasy, foreboding quality which is anything but playful. It is unconventional in design as well,

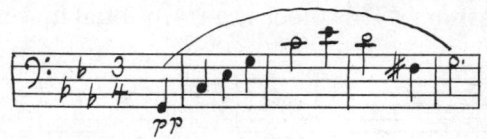

EXAMPLE 111.

except for the trio, which is regular but for its failure to cadence at the end, thereby permitting the return of the scherzo proper without a break. The principal theme of the scherzo is built upon an ascending arpeggio (Example 111)

EXAMPLE 112.

followed by an expressive melody (Example 112). There is an aggressive second theme stated by horns and echoed by wood winds and strings (Example 113), which recalls the mood of the first movement motive. These two themes in alternation and combination constitute the first section.

EXAMPLE 113.

The third section, instead of repeating the first part literally, as is customary, varies the effect of the material by different orchestration and by repeating the themes staccato and pianissimo. At the close there is a deceptive cadence and a long preparation for the last movement based on the arpeggio figure.

Finale—Allegro maestoso in C major
Without pause the finale arrives with considerable pomp and circumstance. This piece is a traditional first-movement

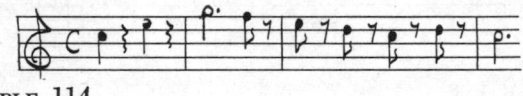

EXAMPLE 114.

sonata design with a first theme built on an arpeggio (Example 114) and several contrasting themes (Examples 115,

EXAMPLE 115.

116, 117, 118), all of them managing, however, to sustain the festival mood of the first. There is a development with a rousing climax apparently preparing for the return of the

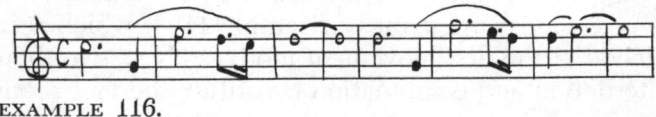

EXAMPLE 116.

principal theme in C major. Instead, there arrives the second theme of the scherzo in C minor, which suggests again the mood of uneasiness. This is soon dispelled by the ar-

EXAMPLE 117.

rival of the legitimate recapitulation, and after a triumphant coda, which does not escape entirely a touch or two of bombast, the piece comes to an end in a virtual orgy of C major chords.

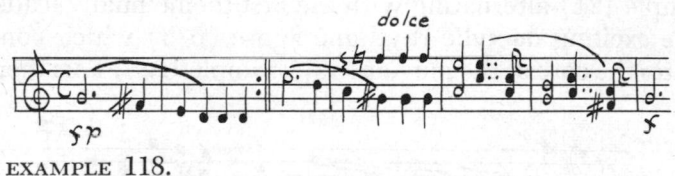

EXAMPLE 118.

BEETHOVEN—*Symphony in A major, no. 7, opus 92* (composed in 1812)

The *Seventh Symphony*, one of the most popular and frequently performed, has somewhat the feeling of the dance. Its unique feature is that unity of each movement rather than contrast is stressed. With the exception of the scherzo and trio, there is in each movement a principal rhythmic idea which dominates the entire composition.

First movement—Poco sostenuto leading to *Vivace in A major*

The slow introduction which prefaces the appearance of the exposition opens with a chordal theme played successively by the oboe, clarinets, and horns, punctuated with staccato chords by the full orchestra (Example 119). An ascending scale passage, heard first in the strings, serves as a counterpoint to this theme and becomes a motive for further development (Example 120). A second theme (Ex-

EXAMPLE 119.

ample 121) alternating with the first theme finally leads to the exciting dactylic rhythmic figure (6/8) which constitutes the core of the movement (Example 122). This theme,

EXAMPLE 120.

with its nervous rhythmic energy, dominates the movement in a manner not unlike that found in the first movement of the composer's *Fifth Symphony*. The second theme,

EXAMPLE 121.

echoing the rhythmic figure of the principal theme in the key of the dominant, brings little contrast to the movement (Example 123). The development is derived from variants

EXAMPLE 122.

of the principal theme, ingeniously treated in canonic imitation by three instruments. The insistent repetition of the rhythmic motive by the full orchestra provides a fitting preparation for a joyful and climactic return of the princi-

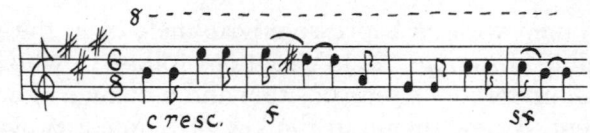

EXAMPLE 123.

pal theme in the recapitulation. An extended coda brings the movement to a brilliant close.

Second movement—Allegretto in A minor

This movement, in the form of theme and variations, has enjoyed great popularity with the public. At its first performance it was encored and later it was played between the movements of less popular symphonies to make them more palatable to an unmusical public. The principal

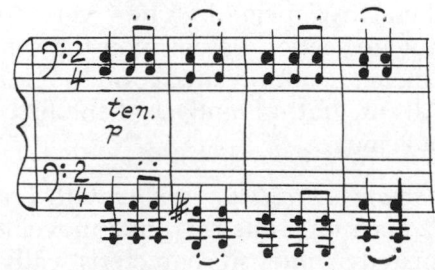

EXAMPLE 124.

theme, in the minor key, first heard in the lower strings, violas, cellos, and basses, is composed of a short rhythmic figure which repeats itself throughout the movement with *ostinato* persistence (Example 124). In the first variation the theme, transposed an octave higher to the first violins,

EXAMPLE 125.

is combined with an expressive lyric melody in the violas and cellos (Example 125). Variations follow in which this material undergoes a redisposition and a change of accompaniment. A new theme in the key of A major provides a welcome contrast to the preceding sections (Example 126).

EXAMPLE 126.

From this point on a triplet figure is frequently present, sometimes finding its way from the accompaniment into the theme itself. The principal theme, with its accompanying countertheme, reappears in a new variation to be followed by a fugato section based upon the same theme. A coda reintroducing in abbreviated form the A major theme, followed by disintegrating motives of the first theme, concludes the movement.

Third movement—Presto in F major with *Trio in D major*
The scherzo is a vigorous rhythmic movement abounding in Olympian dynamics so characteristically Beethovenian. A trio section in a quieter mood alternates with the

main section. In basing the scherzo form on the old minuet and trio of the classic symphony, Beethoven has extended the original design by a restatement of the trio section followed by the principal section. This gives a simple ABABA pattern.

Fourth movement—Allegro con brio in A major

A spirit almost bacchanalian in its wild fury pervades the brilliant finale of this symphony. The principal theme con-

EXAMPLE 127.

sists of two motives (Examples 127 and 128): the first is a rapid rhythmic figure repeated three times and ending with an upward leap of a sixth; the second, a descending scale figure harmonized in sixths. A secondary theme in con-

EXAMPLE 128.

trasting minor key employs a dotted-note rhythm derived from the end of the first motive of the principal theme (Example 129). Bold and colorful modulations contribute to the expressive quality of this material as it is worked out motive by motive in the development. The coda, presenting

EXAMPLE 129.

the principal theme in canonic imitation, builds to a powerful conclusion.

The Overture

In the classic period the overture had no independent existence as a concert piece. The great overtures of Mozart and Beethoven which so frequently appear on symphony programs were designed with one minor exception for the theater, either for opera or as incidental music to a play. It is only later, in the Romantic period, that concert overtures independent of stage performance become a regular feature of symphonic literature.

There is no standard form in the opera overtures of Mozart. Each has its own design, calculated to serve as preparation for the opera. A tendency toward sonata form is to be noted, however, especially in the overtures to *Figaro, Don Giovanni,* and *The Magic Flute.* It is Beethoven who established the classic form of the overture which was later to be imitated by Weber, Mendelssohn, Brahms, and others. This form is clearly that of the first movement of the symphony, either with or without the slow introduction, the chief difference being that the overture often contains a dramatic episode unrelated to the strict design. The themes are usually melodies taken from the opera or incidental music and, as such, are related to the story. The overture of Beethoven shows the composer in his most genial and effective vein, and there are several of his overtures which may be said to equal in greatness and eloquence any of his instrumental compositions.

BEETHOVEN—*Leonore Overture no. 3, opus 72a* (composed in 1807)

Beethoven's single opera, *Fidelio,* was produced several times from 1805 to 1813. Each time the composer, never completely satisfied, experimented with a new overture.

There are four existing overtures to the opera, the last alone bearing the name of *Fidelio*. The rejected compositions were called *Overtures to Leonore, numbers 1, 2, and 3*. At performances of the opera today it is customary to include the *Leonore Overture, no. 3* as an entr'acte. As a concert overture it is the most frequently played of the four.

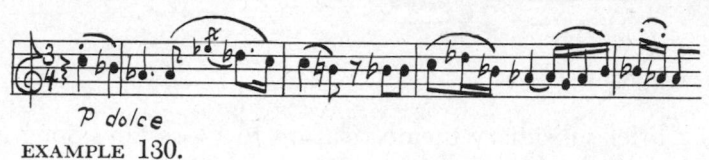

p dolce

EXAMPLE 130.

The story of *Fidelio* made a strong appeal to Beethoven, who was shocked at the immoral point of view of some of Mozart's libretti. It tells the story of Leonore, faithful wife of Don Florestan, a Spanish nobleman imprisoned on political charges. Leonore, disguised as a boy, follows her husband into the prison and obtains service as assistant jailer. She is therefore in a position to assist in his rescue by the party of a friendly nobleman, Don Fernando.

The overture begins with a slow introduction which is descriptive of Florestan waiting despairingly in his dun-

EXAMPLE 131.

geon. After a descending figure on strings and winds, the theme of Florestan, a lovely melody used also as a song in the opera, is heard in octaves on the clarinet and the bassoon (Example 130). This is followed by a mysterious triplet figure leading to a violent outburst on the full orchestra and a theme of lament on flutes and oboes. The principal theme appears at the start of the allegro section.

148 From Madrigal to Modern Music

It is a syncopated arpeggio design with upward and downward inflection (Example 131). Each half represents a symphonic motive for development. This theme is the principal basis of the composition. For lyric contrast, there

EXAMPLE 132.

is a brief subsidiary theme relating to Florestan's Song as heard in the introduction (Example 132). The development section is interrupted by a dramatic episode with off-stage trumpet call suggesting the arrival of the rescue party. There is the usual recapitulation, and a coda based on the main theme and ending with a tremendously dramatic climax.

BEETHOVEN—*Egmont Overture, opus 84* (composed in 1810)

Beethoven composed this overture for a performance of Goethe's tragedy, which also included some incidental music. The story of the play, most eloquently reflected in this overture, deals with the Spanish oppression of the Netherlandic people in the sixteenth century and with the martyr hero, Count Egmont, who led their revolt. In the play he is represented as having a romantic attachment for a young, adoring girl, Klärchen.

The slow introduction presents two thematic elements, the first a theme of somber color, suggestive of brutal strength, the other a most appealing melody of compassion (Example 133). A new melody, with the idea perhaps of suffering, now appears pianissimo on the violins, accompanied by the dark chords of the first theme. This leads dramatically to the allegro section. The principal theme is now stated on the cello. It contains the first three notes of the preceding violin theme but continues in descending arpeggio design, which gives it a feeling of resolution and strength (Example 134). This theme leads to a climax and modulation and the subsidiary material appears. This material is related to the conflicting themes which begin the

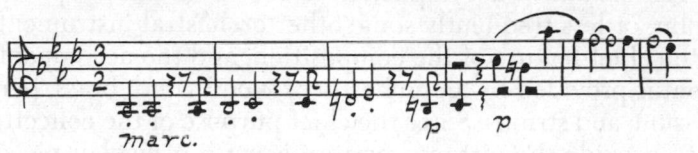

EXAMPLE 133.

introduction. A vehement closing passage prepares for the development section. This section is short but dramatically effective, consisting of the principal theme in expressive fragments punctuated by sudden fortes on the orchestra. The recapitulation parallels the exposition and concludes with violent statements of the first brutal introduction theme alternating with outcries from the violins. There is a

EXAMPLE 134.

pause, several somber chords on the wood winds, and the coda is introduced by a long dramatic crescendo. This coda is evidently representative of the triumph of the people. Episodic in content, and bearing no relation to previous thematic material, it nevertheless brings the overture to a brilliant close.

The Classic Concerto

The classic concerto established by Mozart served as a model or point of departure for all succeeding composers. It is a work, generally in three movements, resembling the architecture of the first, second, and fourth movements of the sonata and symphony. A solo instrument, piano, violin, or less frequently some other orchestral instrument, is the chief feature of the composition, and the accompaniment is provided by an orchestra of wood wind, brass, percussion, and strings. Since the chief purpose of the concerto is to provide the virtuoso performer with a display piece, the thematic material is conditioned by what will set off the solo instrument to the best advantage; the function of the orchestra is primarily to furnish an attractive background to the soloist. In the case of the piano, the sustained tones of the strings and the melodic expressiveness of the wood winds complement the dynamic but less singing tone of the instrument. The single-voiced instruments, such as the violins, naturally benefit by the harmonic background which the orchestra provides. The orchestra, furthermore, with its variety of tone color, makes an excellent foil for the solo instrument in antiphonal dialogue, in introducing themes, and in repeating themes over which the solo instrument may weave elaborations. In the first movement, generally between recapitulation and coda, the orchestra pauses while the solo instrument plays a cadenza. This was originally intended as an improvisation by the soloist upon the themes of the movement, characterized by virtuoso effects. The cadenzas now in general use are not improvised, but have been provided by various composer-performers, such as Beethoven, Brahms, Paganini, Rubinstein, etc. Shorter cadenzas sometimes appear in the second movement and usually in the finale.

The first movement of the concerto is in sonata form, the solo instrument usually making its first appearance in the repetition of the exposition. The second movement is usually in simple song form with the alternative of theme and variations. The third movement may take the form of the rondo or theme and variations.

MOZART—*Concerto in D minor for piano and orchestra, Köchel no. 466* (composed in 1785)

First movement—Allegro in D minor

The first theme is a dramatic ascending figure accompanied by an offbeat, expressive melody in minor (Example 135). Subsidiary themes in major and minor are contrasted

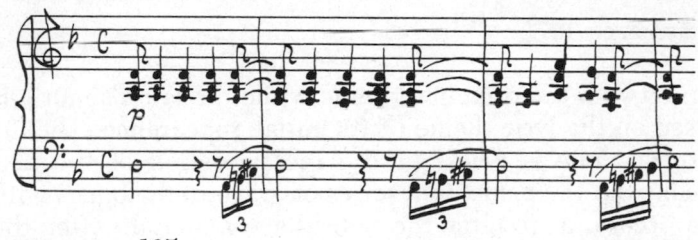

EXAMPLE 135.

with this principal theme. After an extended passage by the orchestra, the piano enters with a lyric theme (Example 136) which leads to a complete exposition in which the principal theme is repeated by the orchestra, over which the piano is heard in ornamental figurations. A new lyric

EXAMPLE 136.

theme, not stated in the introductory exposition, appears on the piano with a dotted figuration accompaniment in the violins (Example 137). The development is chiefly a dialogue between orchestra and piano. The former is con-

EXAMPLE 137.

cerned with the principal theme while the latter's music is based on the lyric theme of its initial appearance. The orchestra alone is heard in the recapitulation of the first theme, but the piano, in a series of graceful dialogues with the orchestra, restates the subsidiary material. After the cadenza there is a short coda and the movement concludes on the music of the principal theme.

Second movement—Romanze in B flat major

The piano alone introduces a melody of appealing simplicity (Example 138). Each phrase is repeated by the orchestra. The orchestra then has a short interlude leading to a related melody which the piano develops over an

EXAMPLE 138.

orchestral background. The original melody returns as before. A middle section in minor with an agitated rhythm introduced by the piano forms a dramatic contrast to this music and leads to a third section resembling the first, with a coda to conclude.

Third movement—Rondo—Allegro assai in D minor

The refrain, based upon an ascending arpeggio in D minor, is introduced by the piano alone and then is re-

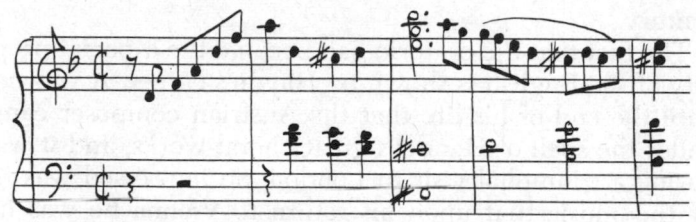

EXAMPLE 139.

peated by the orchestra (Example 139). Contrasting melodies alternate with this throughout the movement. One of these brings the rondo to a close in D major after a cadenza and a final repetition of the refrain.

The Classic Oratorio

When Handel gave the English people their own particular type of oratorio he unwittingly created a tradition which was to be the foundation stone of English musical life for many years to come. Not only was the form a constant delight to audiences and singers, but the Handel oratorios themselves have never lost their popularity and have always been regarded by the English as an integral part of their cultural heritage. This continued popularity of the works of Handel had its discouraging aspects for other composers. One would think that such a congenial expression of the musical feeling of the nation would have resulted in many fine oratorios by native-born composers. In the Renaissance, and before Handel in the baroque, English composers were forces to be reckoned with in the European scene. But, for some mysterious reason, during the latter half of the eighteenth century and for some time thereafter English music suffered an almost total eclipse. Ironically enough, the two succeeding composers who won universal esteem in this field were both foreigners, Haydn in the classic period and Mendelssohn in the nineteenth century.

The fact that the oratorio had become the especial property of the English is shown by Haydn's career. It was not until the end of his life that the Austrian composer came under the spell of Handel's great choral works, and it was during a triumphal visit to London. So impressed was he by this music that upon his return to Vienna he was inspired to undertake the composition of an oratorio. The result was one of the greatest successes of his career, *The Creation*. Its popularity was immediate, and the aging composer was prevailed upon to write another, *The Seasons*, which turned out scarcely less well.

The book of *The Creation* was an arrangement by an English author based upon Genesis and Milton's *Paradise Lost*, which had once been submitted to Handel but rejected by him, probably as being too undramatic. Haydn took it back to Vienna and, with the assistance of Baron Van Swieten, the emperor's librarian, who translated the text into German and added several arias, duets, and choruses, undertook the composition of the work. Whereas in his instrumental music Haydn wrote with great rapidity, he devoted three years, from 1796 to 1798, to this work, which he regarded as the crowning achievement of his career.

The two Haydn oratorios and Beethoven's *Christ on the Mount of Olives*, written under the inspiration of *The Creation*, represent the chief contribution of the classic composers to this type. It will be seen that little change was made in the form of the oratorio, which follows closely the model of Handel. The style of the choruses, with their vigorous polyphony and fugal passages, is also similar. The arias are generally somewhat altered in melodic design; the elaborate vocal line is replaced by a simpler, more direct type of melody, such as one would expect from the classic composers, but traces of the old ornamental style occasionally appear.

The chief difference to be noted is the greater importance of the orchestral accompaniment, which at the hands of the masters of the symphony would hardly be relegated to the perfunctory role that it formerly played. One reason that the book of *The Creation* may have appealed to Haydn where it failed to interest the earlier composer is that the many descriptive passages dealing with the world of nature —the lightnings and thunders, the fall of the snow, the boisterous seas, the great whales, and the beasts of the forest—suggest all manner of instrumental effect, which the classic orchestra was now adequately equipped to furnish. A great deal of the magic of *The Creation* can be attributed to Haydn's remarkable skill in handling the orchestra. *The Creation*, like *The Messiah* of Handel, has never lost its initial popularity. It is sung not only in concert by oratorio societies everywhere, but it is also frequently performed at church services in England and America.

JOSEPH HAYDN—*The Creation* (composed 1796–1798)

Haydn, whose work is a constant reflection of his love of mankind and the universe, gives us in this music the same mellow radiance that we find in his symphonies and chamber music. In his interpretation of the Creation there is not the elemental force and strength which Beethoven might have displayed. We may smile at the ingeniousness of some of the descriptive effects: the first picture of chaos and the rage of the accursed spirits as they sink into the abyss of darkness with the coming of the light are more quaintly than grimly expressed. But no composer could give us a more joyous, heartwarming sense of the graciousness of life and of the benevolence of God. One is also impressed by the skill which this composer, whose genius is chiefly expressed in his instrumental music, shows in handling the voices, both in the lovely arias and in the stirring choruses.

There are three main divisions of the work. The first part tells of the making of the universe, the second of the coming of life, of the birds, the fishes, the animals, and finally, man. The third part is a scene in paradise with Adam, a baritone, and Eve, a soprano, joining the angels in praise of the Creator. Three archangels—Gabriel, a soprano, Uriel, a tenor, and Raphael, a bass—are the soloists of the first and second parts.

Unfortunately as yet *The Creation* has not been recorded in its entirety, and some of the separate recordings which have been made are not available at present. But at least some of the following selections should be procurable for study.

Part One. Air for Bass—Rolling in Foaming Billows

This is a descriptive air which follows the recitative "And God said, 'Let the waters under the heavens be gathered together to one place, and let the dry land appear:' and it was so. And God called the dry land earth, and the gathering of the waters called He seas, and God saw that it was good." After an introductory passage for the orchestra suggesting the torrent of waters, the voice enters and takes up the role of courier, to describe unassumingly the various instrumental effects which accompany it. First there is "the boisterous sea," then the rivers, "flowing in serpent error" (Haydn allows the singer one pictorial serpent in the manner of Handel), and finally "the limpid brook, softly purling." The air does not employ the symmetrical plan of the aria, but follows the program. It begins in D minor and ends in D major.

Part One. Air for Soprano—With verdure clad

This air is often heard as a soprano solo apart from the oratorio. It is a lovely pastoral melody, with occasional vocal adornments, which is repeated after a short, modulatory middle section. It deals with the first fruitfulness of the earth, when the fields are green, when flowers and herbs give out their fragrance to the air, and when groves and forests appear on the hillsides.

Part One. Chorus—The Heavens are telling

Now the universe is completed and awaits the coming of man. This magnificent song of praise to the Creator is sung by chorus and soloists in alternate sections. The phrase "The heavens are telling the glory of God, the wonder of His work displays the firmament" is repeated by the chorus with the trio of archangels coming in between and fanning the flame of enthusiasm. Then the chorus in increasing measure builds up the sonorities with a succession of polyphonic entrances until all the musical forces are caught up in a tremendous chordal climax. There is a familiar hymn, "The spacious firmament on high," with words by Addison and music by Haydn, which is an arrangement of this music.

Part Two. Air for Soprano— On mighty wings

Part Two begins with a companion piece to *Rolling in Foaming Billows* which also follows the programmatic idea rather than a set musical design. This time, however, it is about the various birds that God creates. First the eagle "on mighty wings," then "the merry lark" and "the cooing dove." Finally, "the nightingale's delightful notes" are heard both in the orchestra and very elaborately in the voice, which lends itself perhaps better to bird than to water effects.

158   From Madrigal to Modern Music

Part Two. Chorus—Achieved is the glorious work

Part Two ends with another triumphant chorus, also with the co-operation of the trio of soloists. The chorus begins with the words:

> "Achieved is the glorious work
> The Lord beholds it and is pleased.
> In lofty strains let us rejoice,
> Our song let be the praise of God."

In this refrain the voices move about freely, now in imitation of each other and now joining forces in outbursts of

EXAMPLE 140.

enthusiasm. Then the trio of archangels interrupts with some polyphonic effects of its own. This is followed by a fugal chorus in which a subject to the words "Glory to His name forever" (Example 140) is combined with a counter-subject, a setting of the words "He sole on high exalted

EXAMPLE 141.

reigns" (Example 141), building into a great climax which for brilliance and excitement yields nothing to the Halle-lujah Chorus from *The Messiah.*

The Classic Opera

During the classic period Italian opera still exerted a strong influence throughout Europe, but the more lifelike and direct style of the *opera buffa* was more widely imitated than the elaborate display of the *opera seria*. In Germany the *Singspiel*, an offshoot of the English ballad opera and the Italian and French comic operas with German text, which also included spoken dialogue, became increasingly popular. Beethoven's solitary opera, *Fidelio*, is classified as a *Singspiel*, although in the high seriousness of its material and treatment it is hardly recognizable as an outgrowth of this popular form of entertainment. Mozart wrote two *Singspiele, Die Entführung aus dem Serail* (*The Abduction from the Seraglio*) and *Die Zauberflöte* (*The Magic Flute*), but the majority of his operas followed the model of the opera buffa and were written to Italian texts. Haydn wrote a number of operas, both seria and buffa, to Italian texts and *Singspiele* to German texts, but they are rarely performed today, whereas the operas of Mozart and Beethoven's *Fidelio* are a part of the standard repertory.

MOZART—*Don Giovanni* (composed in 1787)

Mozart, unlike Gluck, was no reformer of opera. He accepted the familiar Italian form of recitative, aria, and ensemble without question, but raised it to the greatest heights by his dramatic instinct, ability to characterize, and boundless melodic fertility. The dramatic ensembles in these operas have never been surpassed in ingenuity and skill by any composer.

Don Giovanni has a superb libretto by Lorenzo da Ponte, official poet to the Imperial Theater of Vienna, afterward a professor at Columbia University. Da Ponte has taken the old legend of the irresistible and heartless lover and has portrayed him in characteristic escapades leading to his downfall. From the opening scene wherein Don Giovanni has forced himself into the boudoir of a noble lady, Donna Anna, and murders her father, the Commandant, when the latter attempts to protect her, to the final scene where, confronted by supernatural terrors, the Don goes proudly to his doom, the opera moves with compelling force, now excitingly dramatic, now witty and droll. Wagner, in writing of this opera, said: "Where else has music won so infinitely rich an individuality, been able to characterize so surely, so definitely and in such exuberant plenitude as here?"

1. *Madamina*

Leporello, Don Giovanni's faithful but often despairing servant, tells Elvira, who has been promised marriage, why his master cannot reform and marry her. From a notebook he reads off the record of Don's amorous adventures, six hundred and forty in Italy, five hundred and twenty in France, only two hundred in the Rhineland, but in Spain already a thousand and three. In spite of his misgivings, Leporello occasionally likes to boast.

2. *Là ci darem la mano*

Don Giovanni has come upon some rustic wedding festivities. He charges Leporello with removing the bridegroom, Masetto, and now courts the bride, Zerlina. She is in a flutter because of the nobleman's attentions and is as arch and coy as she dares to be under the circumstances. Don Giovanni is elegant in his courtship, as befits his rank, but increasingly ardent and joyful when he supposes that he has succeeded.

3. *Batti, batti*

Zerlina later encounters Masetto and is sincerely contrite for her flirtation. She tells him to scold and then forgive her so that their days may pass in happiness together. Mozart in the simple melody characterizes the naïveté and charm of the country girl.

4. *Recitative and air—Finch' han dal vino*

Leporello tells Don Giovanni that he has invited all the peasants to the palace, including Zerlina and Masetto, but that he had some trouble with Elvira, whom he finally got rid of by locking her out. In the aria Don Giovanni exults in the plans for a carousal in the palace, surrounded by pretty girls, dancing, wine, and his accustomed paraphernalia. His reckless, gay character is perfectly expressed by the music.

5. *Minuet from Finale, Act I*

The party is in full swing. Don Giovanni orders the musicians to play. Among the guests are three masked individuals: Donna Anna, seeking revenge for the murder of her father; her faithful suitor, Don Octavio; and Elvira, the neglected fiancée. Against the background of the familiar minuet the drama goes forward. The masked trio is suspicious and watchful; Don Giovanni is pursuing Zerlina while Masetto looks on angrily. Leporello is trying to distract him. Suddenly there is a scream from behind a closed door. Zerlina and Don Giovanni have disappeared and she is appealing for help. All hasten to the door and try to force it open. In this scene both the characterizations and the dramatic continuity of the music are remarkable.

6. *Aria—Il mio tesoro*

Don Octavio, faithful friend of Donna Anna, sings of his love and desire to protect the unfortunate lady. This is an example of the beautiful melodic style in which Mozart's operas abound.

7. *Aria—Mi tradi*

Elvira, tricked and despised by Don Giovanni and Leporello, still cannot smother her love with thoughts of revenge. She is a most tragic figure, sensitive, passionate, and outrageously betrayed, and this aria brings out the force of her character.

8. *Finale—Tu m'invitasti a cena*

In a moment of braggadocio, Don Giovanni comes upon a statue erected to the late Commandant, Donna Anna's father, whom he has murdered. He mockingly invites the statue to dinner and the statue menacingly accepts. In this scene Don Giovanni is banqueting and is interrupted by the horrifying appearance of the stone guest. Now the Commandant calls upon him to repent. Leporello is terrified, but the great lover is scornful to the end. Flames arise, the spirits of the damned are heard, and Don Giovanni is engulfed in destruction. This music has an amazing dramatic power both in its vocal and orchestral writing.

5 *THE ROMANTIC ERA*

Introduction

THE Romantic period of music may be said to include the entire nineteenth century, extending beyond to the artistic revolution which manifested itself during the early years of the twentieth century and which culminated in the disillusionment of the first World War. Romanticism, however, cannot be confined to a single period of music. Since it is primarily a point of view, a youthful, experimental naïveté on the part of the artist, it is found in all ages—even, with apologetic mien, in our own. The interests of the Romantic are wide. They include literature, history, philosophy, the world of nature, and the spirit of man, all of which are brought into the vocabulary of art, which is altered and expanded in the process. The artist, conceiving himself as more than artist, sees himself as a spiritual leader of the people, a sort of interpreter of the universe. He refuses to fetter his imagination with classical doctrines. So sure is he of his role of prophet that he sometimes forgets his duty as a craftsman.

The nineteenth-century Romantic composer was an optimistic, adventurous spirit with a rapidly expanding musical language at his command, with instruments of advanced expressive and technical possibilities, and with the opportunity to address himself to a most responsive and appreciative public. He was, on the whole, more conscious of the artistic merit of his predecessors than were the composers of preceding ages; certainly he was more familiar with the music of the past. But, while he usually accepted the classic masters as his models, he was impatient with their disciplines, and therefore occasionally misunderstood their thoughts and techniques, which restrained rather than unleashed his inspiration.

Throughout the entire period we find the expressive side of music stressed at the expense of the formal, but there is a continuing classicistic strain, evident most strikingly in the works of Mendelssohn and Brahms, and often influencing the more revolutionary composers. This acted as a sort of artistic conscience, as a restraining force upon the exuberance of the times. Perhaps it is to this force that we are indebted as much as to anything else for the elements of lasting value in nineteenth-century music.

In the Romantic period music was addressed to a larger public than it had ever known before. The democratic spirit of the times made itself felt in the popularization of musical style. The growth of the large industrial cities provided enthusiastic audiences for music, performers in increasing numbers, stimulus to the publishers, and the spread of music in general education. National consciousness gave rise to a music with more national flavor. From the Near East, from Russia, Poland, Scandinavia, Spain, even from America, there came folk or popular music to blend with the established European traditions and to give music fresh color and impetus. Except for occasional instances, the aristocratic patron disappeared and the composer was compelled to make his living as performer, conductor, or teacher.

The technical possibilities of the instruments were exploited both in solo and ensemble writing, endowing music with a warmer, richer sound. The piano entered its golden age in the music of Chopin, Schumann, and Liszt; the orchestra was much enlarged in each of its constituent families; but most striking was the development of the melodic capabilities of the trumpets and horns by the adoption of the valve principle, which enabled these instruments, heretofore restricted to certain basic tones, to use the full chromatic scale. Orchestral virtuosity in dynamic and color effects became almost an end in itself, and the symphony orchestra rivaled the opera in popularity.

Symphonic style of writing was largely replaced by emphasis upon the melodic and descriptive elements of music. Although the form of the sonata was still an influence on the symphony, the concerto, and chamber music, we find less concentration of thematic material, less clarity of development, and, in general, weakened structure, especially in the large forms. The genius of the age is best displayed in the simpler song form than in the sonata. Polyphony, replaced by an interest in the dramatic and expressive possibilities of harmony, was practically a lost art. The chromatic scale was an influence not only upon melody, but also upon harmony and the tonal foundations of music. Melody itself appears less often in simple, objective pattern but usually is burdened with an underlying emotionalism resulting in periodic climaxes and oftentimes purely theatrical effect.

The Romantic period made several characteristic contributions to the literature of music, all of which exerted a profound influence upon musical style. The German *lied* (art song), which had its origin at the end of the eighteenth century, was a perfect embodiment of the Romantic point of view, and a congenial vehicle for talents which inclined to the literary and pictorial side of the art and which showed greater aptitude for melodic than symphonic invention. The more expressive style of piano writing was an admirable foil for the vocal lyricism of these songs, and the piano accompaniments to the *lied* added much to its effectiveness.

The short piano piece, resembling the song in its simple design and its emphasis upon the element of lyricism, was also an important contribution of the Romantic composers. It is easier to understand than the piano sonata, usually easier to play, and makes an impression even when played by a performer of medium skill. Such pieces as Schubert's *Moments Musicaux,* Chopin's *Nocturnes,* Schumann's *Kinderszenen,* and Mendelssohn's *Songs Without Words* were designed for the amateur pianist and show the growing importance of the nonprofessional musician in the nineteenth century.

The larger instrumental forms of orchestra and chamber music were cultivated by nearly all of the principal composers of the age under the impetus of the popularity of Beethoven's music, which continued unabated throughout the century. Symphonies, concertos, overtures, on the one hand, and sonatas, trios, quartets, and quintets, on the other, were much in demand by the large music public, which found the more colorful Romantic style greatly to its liking. The symphonic poem, a one-movement work in which the literary and descriptive fancies of the age were given free rein, and in which the program rather than any abstract design served as form determinant, made its appearance as an offshoot of the symphony. The ballet or opera suite, consisting of instrumental excerpts from a work originally designed for the stage, replaced the classic serenade as a type of entertainment music.

In the field of opera the nineteenth century was marked by the establishment of German Romantic opera and by the overwhelming success of the grand opera which made its start under French auspices only to spread all over the world. The second half of the century witnessed the triumph of the Wagnerian music drama, the culmination of Italian opera (Verdi), and of the grand opera (Gounod, Massenet). Choral music received a stimulus from the rediscovery of the great Passions and Masses of J. S. Bach.

These, with the continuing popularity of the Handel oratorios and the choral works of Haydn, Mozart, and Beethoven, rather overshadowed such contemporary compositions as were written to sacred texts. However, a certain number of Masses and oratorios were written by Romantic composers, among them Schubert, Berlioz, Mendelssohn, Liszt, Verdi, and Brahms. The music in both the Catholic and Protestant churches suffered from the invasion of operatic style, which brought with it a flood of sentimentality and sweetness grotesquely inappropriate to the tradition of church art.

Since the Romantic period extended for a century and over, it is difficult to choose among the many important composers, and in the last years of the epoch the classification of a composer as Romantic or modern is open to question.

List of Important Composers Whose Activity
Was Confined to the Nineteenth Century:

Weber, 1786–1826
Schubert, 1797–1828
Mendelssohn, 1809–1847
Chopin, 1809–1849
Schumann, 1810–1856
Berlioz, 1803–1869
Liszt, 1811–1886
Wagner, 1813–1883
Verdi, 1813–1901
Franck, 1822–1890
Bizet, 1838–1875
Brahms, 1833–1897
Tchaikovsky, 1840–1893

The German Lied

There is no satisfactory translation of the term "lied." "Song" is too inclusive and "art song" is obviously unsatisfactory. The lied is a type of composition which had its origin in the classic period but which reached its zenith as a characteristic contribution of the Romantic composers. It is the musical setting of a lyric poem for voice and piano in which an attempt is made to realize the melody inherent in the poem. To this is added an instrumental background of interpretative character, sometimes merely picturesque, often of profound psychological insight. No preconceived pattern of repetition is admitted. The design is conditioned by the content of the poem itself. The simple strophic pattern is rarely found in the lied, and only occasionally the ABA—statement, contrast, statement—design is used. Even here, however, the composer will vary the accompaniment so that little trace of the rigid formalistic aria remains.

A song of this type depends greatly for its effect upon the quality of the poem itself. The Romantic composers were fortunate in that they followed closely upon a period of great lyric poetry. Such poets as Goethe, Schiller, Heine, and Müller provided the lyrics for the songs of Schubert, Schumann, Brahms, Franz, and Wolf. The result of this collaboration is the imperishable glory of the nineteenth-century lied. These songs are popular music in the best sense. Oblivious of display, simple and melodious in design, they are more for the intimate enjoyment of the home than for the starch-bosomed concert hall, and as such they have been widely known and loved.

Schubert is undeniably the greatest master of the lied. His incomparable melodic gift was linked to a sure dramatic instinct that manifests itself in his choice of harmonies and disposition of accompaniment. His range of mood is all inclusive, from the most tender and delicate fancy to powerful and tempestuous emotion. Schumann, with lesser variety of mood, is also a composer of great melodic fertility. With perhaps a keener literary discrimination than Schubert, he sometimes surpasses him in psychological penetration of poetical thought. A master pianist, his accompaniments are often of magical beauty.

SONGS OF SCHUBERT

Who is Sylvia?

This song is a setting of Shakespeare's lyric from *Two Gentlemen of Verona*. It is a simple melody in strophic form, with three verses of exact repetition both in melody and accompaniment.

Der Tod und das Mädchen (Death and the maiden)

The poem of Claudius represents a young girl frightened at the approach of death. She begs for mercy. Death, speaking as her friend, replies kindly and says that he has not come to punish but to help her find rest in his arms. The short prelude, afterward the somber song of Death, is followed by a wild outburst from the maiden. Then the song of Death, calm and serious, yet strangely tender, is heard. Schubert later used this melody as the basis for the slow movement of a string quartet.

Der Erlkönig (The Erl-King)

This musical setting of a ballad by Goethe is a complete drama with several characters. A father is galloping on horseback through the night with a sick child in his arms. The child in terror sees the Erl-King, spirit of Death, approaching through the mist. Although the phantom speaks and is heard by the child who screams in terror, the father sees nothing. The Erl-King wheedles and coaxes, and then with sudden rage grasps the arm of the child, who utters a final despairing cry. The father rides on in deep anxiety until at last arrived at home he finds that the child in his arms is dead. Against an agitated accompaniment that suggests the galloping of the horse and the darkness of the night, the various characters speak, each with individual characterization of remarkable fidelity. This song, written by Schubert when he was only eighteen, is a tour de force of dramatic and descriptive power. Note especially the sharp, mounting dissonance which is used for each successive cry of the child.

Der Leiermann (The hurdy-gurdy man)

In vivid contrast to the last song is this little sketch from Müller's cycle *Winterreise*. Here is a picture of an old man playing the hurdy-gurdy back of the village. No one pays any attention to him; his tin cup is empty. The poet asks the old man if he may go along and sing to the music. The accompaniment pictures the monotonous drone of the hurdy-gurdy, against which the voice sings a melancholy melody, full of sorrow, plain and old.

Wohin? (Whither?)

In this song, which is from a cycle, *Die schöne Müllerin*, also by Müller, the poet pauses beside a brook and ponders upon its various adventures. He asks the brook where it is going so happily and wonders, too, if this fortunate course is to be his. The accompaniment portrays the splashing of the brook and the melody, gay and charming, suggests the simple tunefulness of a folk song.

Der Doppelgänger (The phantom double)

For profound and moving tragedy this song has never been surpassed. The poem, by Heine, tells of a man coming back to the city and to the house of someone he has loved and lost. As he stares up at the window a figure stands beside him, wringing his hands in grief. Suddenly the moon comes out and he sees the pallid face of his companion. It is his own. He begs the phantom not to mock the old sorrow that haunted him so many nights in this same place. Schubert's dramatic instinct was so true and so individual that this song might have been written yesterday. Every musical effect underlining the text is startling and eloquent. The mysterious chords of the accompaniment, the melody, now drab and monotonous, now with sudden and powerful climax, then with final touching accent, all combine to give the song a truly remarkable poignancy.

SONGS OF SCHUMANN

Die Lotosblume (*The lotus flower*)

The poem, also by Heine, is characteristically romantic in the personification of nature. It tells of the lotus flower who wilts before the fierce rays of the sun and dreams of the coming of the night. The moon is her true lover and for him she blooms and glows and exhales her perfume. The melody is full of the poetical quality of the lyric. It is supported by harmonies of subtle coloring and gentle motion.

Die beiden Grenadiere (*The two Grenadiers*)

Based on another work by Heine, this song is a narrative of two French soldiers imprisoned in Russia during Napoleon's ill-fated campaign. Now released, but still suffering from wounds, they sorrow at the news of his downfall. One speaks of wife and child at home; if he did not have them, he would like to die. The other can think only of his fallen emperor. He begs his companion that, if he dies, he may be taken to France for burial. Then when in battle the emperor rides again, he will rise from his grave to defend him. Schumann has given this song a military background by means of the rhythm of the accompaniment. The feeling of suffering and discouragement is then expressed in both melody and harmony. A final climax of patriotic fervor leads to a melodic quotation from *La Marseillaise*. At the end the voice ceases and the accompaniment again suggests exhaustion and pain.

Romantic Piano Music

The piano, the most characteristic instrument of the Romantic age, is unrivaled among solo instruments for its self-sufficiency, dynamic range, responsiveness, and brilliance. To the amateur it offers the full harmonic and tonal range of the large orchestra in return for a surprisingly small investment of talent and endeavor. The most unpretentious music can be made to sound impressive upon it. The short pieces in simple song form composed by such masters as Schubert, Schumann, Chopin, and Mendelssohn inspired a host of music lovers to set about making their own music in the home and founded a tradition of popular composition which has kept publishers' shelves heavily burdened ever since.

But the piano's advantages are not limited to performance by amateurs. In it the virtuoso finds the ideal setting for his personality and technical display. And it is at this time, in the music of Chopin, Schumann, and Liszt, that the full possibilities of this prodigious instrument are completely realized. Nothing has been added by later composers to the richness and splendor of pianistic style. In the age of these great pianist composers the virtuoso comes into his own as a demigod, strange and wonderful, a symbol of man's awe and reverence for the magic of musical sound. The crowded concert hall, fairly oozing hero worship, intoxicated and spellbound by the pianist's art—a phenomenon which has persisted even into the irreverent age which is our own—is the very essence of the spirit of musical romanticism. The virtuoso compositions are usually simple enough in plan, imposing few problems upon the listener, for they are really only the short piano pieces expanded and dressed up with technical trimmings. Although most of the pianist composers tried their hand at sonatas, they were happier and much more themselves in the informality of the single movement piece of melodic rather than symphonic design.

CHOPIN'S PIANO MUSIC

Of the several great figures of the age, Chopin must be placed first. It is hard to conceive of the piano without thinking of his music, for piano recitals are rare which do not include a Chopin group, and audiences seem never to tire of the familiar repertory of his compositions. He wrote practically nothing but piano music and succeeded most notably in the shorter forms. In spite of this limited activity, narrow in range when compared to a composer like Beethoven, he must be assigned a very high place as a creative artist for he was one of the most original composers of all time and his works are of a uniformly high level. It is hard to trace the derivation of his musical style, which comes upon the nineteenth-century scene with such freshness. The broad, sweeping melodies are influenced by Italian opera composers of the period, but his exquisite harmonies and subtle manipulation of short forms are entirely his own. His music is unsymphonic, completely lacking in polyphony. He finishes with one melody and blithely goes on to another, but for pure beauty of sound, richly inspired melody, and perfection of taste his music is unsurpassed. Even in display, with the ornamental trappings of virtuoso style, he seems able to infuse it all with musical essence. No composer has so perfectly realized the possibilities of an instrument and in Chopin's music the piano is raised to great artistic heights. His music may seem at times overly sweet or lacking in profundity, but it is always well groomed and a delight to the ear.

Polonaise in A flat major, opus 53 (first published in 1843)
The traditional polonaise was a stately court dance used for ceremonials. Chopin's A flat Polonaise is a magnificent and sumptuous piece with a martial background. There is an introduction, with a chromatic fanfare, followed by the principal melody in thirds with heavily accented first beat.

This is repeated with octave reinforcements. Two contrasting ideas lead to a second repetition and the close of the first section. The second section, in E major, introduced by sonorous rolled chords, consists first of a brassy harmonized melody over an ostinato bass figure of four descending notes, then expressive music made up chiefly of an elaborate scale pattern. This leads to a return of the first melody, now limited to one appearance, and to a short coda.

Nocturne in G major, opus 37, no. 2 (first published in 1840)

The title "nocturne" was a popular designation during the nineteenth century for short lyric pieces of reflective character. The *Nocturne in G major* consists of a melody harmonized in thirds and sixths over an arpeggio accompaniment of constant rhythm. The contrasting section somewhat resembles a barcarole. The piece continues with alternation of these two designs, shading one into the other with subtlety and charm.

Waltz in C sharp minor, opus 64, no. 2 (first published in 1847)

The waltz appears as an instrumental composition at the end of the eighteenth century, but its popularity reached its height, somewhat later, in the famous compositions of Johann Strauss, the younger. Schubert and Brahms both wrote waltzes and Chopin is the author of fourteen of them, not designed for ballroom dancing but as brilliant piano solos. The *Waltz in C sharp minor* is one of the best known, consisting of exquisite, rather capricious melodies infused with a gentle melancholy. The plan of the sections is ABCBAB.

Etude in E major, opus 10, no. 3 (first published in 1833)

Chopin's twenty-seven studies represent technical studies of remarkable variety and ingenuity. More than this, they contain some of his most imaginative writing, full of delicate sensuous effect and subtle harmonic color. The *Etude in E major* consists of a broad, songlike melody interrupted after a number of regular phrases by a series of chord clusters, increasingly chromatic, and then quietly resuming the even tenor of its way.

Mazurka in D major, opus 33. no. 2 (first published in 1838)

The mazurka, also a Polish national dance, is generally in triple rhythm with an accent on the third beat. Chopin wrote fifty-one mazurkas, using many folk melodies. His graceful style lends itself most felicitously to this type of dance, in which the feeling is closer to the actual dance than in the case of the polonaises or waltzes. The *Mazurka in D major* contains many repetitions of a simple folk-melody pattern with a contrasting middle section and a short coda.

Prelude in D flat major, opus 28, no. 15 (*Raindrop*) (first published in 1839)

The twenty-four preludes are for the most part short pieces, many of which are comparatively easy to play and hence very popular. This *Prelude in D flat major* is characterized by a reiterated eighth note, A flat (G sharp), which no doubt gives rise to its popular appellation. It is in three-part—ABA—design with a middle section in C sharp minor in which the repeated-note figure is especially emphasized against shifting harmonies. The appealing melody of the first part is considerably shortened in the last section.

Ballade in G minor, opus 23

The four ballades of Chopin are free compositions of varying design but of greater length than the majority of his compositions. These pieces are said by Schumann to have been inspired by the Polish poems of Mickiewicz and seem to suggest that they are programmatic in plan. No hint of the various programs is given by the composer. The *Ballade in G minor* shows the influence of the first-movement sonata form. There is a short, dramatic introductory passage, after which a melody of simple pathos in G minor is revealed which grows in intensity as the music proceeds. A modulation to E flat brings a second melody, which begins calmly and reassuringly but is transformed later with a passionate outburst after a return of the first melody in A minor. This is followed by an animated piano passage leading to further appearances of the two principal melodies. A tempestuous coda brings the piece to a brilliant conclusion.

Scherzo in C sharp minor, opus 39 (first published in 1840)

In his four scherzos Chopin comes closer than any other Romantic composer to the boisterous and sardonic quality of the Beethoven scherzos. This is rather curious because the two men were so different in character and personality. But while one feels that the scherzo mood of Beethoven is a natural expression of something very fundamental in his nature, in the case of Chopin this savage force is rather a surprise, a release of feeling unsuspected beneath his civilized and poetic exterior.

The *Scherzo in C sharp minor* begins hurriedly in a rough and uncompromising introduction. The main theme is an alternation between fortissimo octaves and quiet harmonies with a moving inner voice. This is the basis of the first section. The second part, corresponding to a trio, is in D flat and phrases of a vigorous chorale melody are complemented herein by delicate ornamental arpeggios. The main body of the scherzo is repeated, followed by the trio transposed to E major. A fiery coda in C sharp minor brings the piece to a conclusion.

SCHUMANN'S PIANO MUSIC

Although Schumann's music, unlike Chopin's, is not confined to the piano, the personality and spirit of the instrument dominate it at all times. His piano music was nearly all written when, as a young man, his ambition was to become a concert pianist. His zeal betrayed him into crippling his hand with a mechanical device calculated to give independence to the fourth finger; otherwise his career might have resembled that of Chopin, for there is every evidence that he was greatly gifted as a pianist. The compositions for piano are a reflection of his exquisite taste, his individuality, and his marked originality in matters of design and content. There is a suggestion of improvisation about many of the pieces, as if they were more the result of felicitous adventures at the keyboard than of sober planning. Schumann's music has a gusto and freshness about it which keeps it ever youthful. But in spite of its impetuousness it is seasoned with delicacy, and lurking beneath the surface of high spirits and bravado there is a wealth of romantic tenderness and warmth. It is also at times highly subjective. The music, rarely pictorial, is full of inner meaning, especially significant to the composer and to his circle of intimates.

Etudes symphoniques (*Studies in Form of Variations*) (composed in 1834)

This composition is an unconventional series of variations based upon a rather unpromising theme, the contribution of an amateur of Schumann's acquaintance. The theme (Example 142), in four regular phrases, is featured by a descending C sharp minor arpeggio. It contains little rhythmic or melodic interest. That Schumann could derive so much beauty and richness from such barren material is an indication of the fertility of his musical imagination. The first section, *Andante*, states the theme simply, the four melodic phrases appearing in the top voice of the piano.

Etude 1, Variation 1—Un poco piu vivo

A dotted rhythm introduced in the bass is combined with the theme in relatively unchanged state in the right hand part.

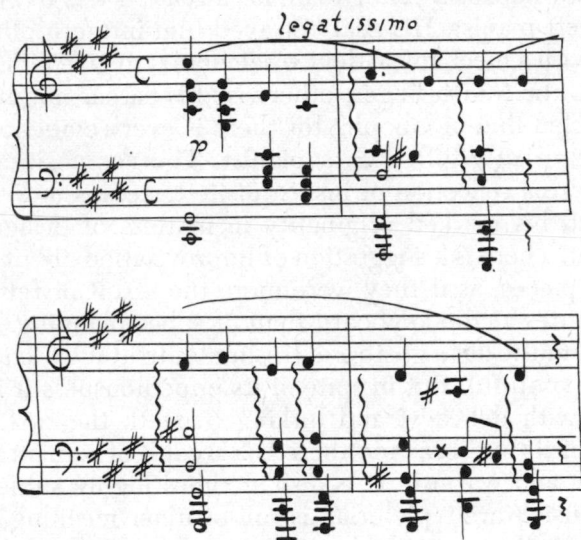

EXAMPLE 142.

Etude 2, Variation 2—Espressivo

The theme in augmentation serves as a bass over which a new expressive melody on broad lines is contrived for the upper voice. In between the two there is a chordal accompaniment consisting of a triplet figure.

Etude 3—Vivace

Schumann does not label this étude as a variation because it is one of two nonthematic interpolations added for purposes of diversion. There is a melody in the middle voice which disappears for four bars as the accompanying right-hand arpeggio figure moves to the left hand. This is followed by a third section similar to the first.

Etude 4, Variation 3—Energico

This is a canonic duet between the right hand and the left

hand, with the theme arranged in heavily accented chords, a sort of pianistic bombardment of the listener.

Etude 5, Variation 4—Scherzando

A graceful scherzo, with dotted rhythm and a suggestion of the theme in its melodic unfolding, shows the piano in contrasting delicacy of percussive effect.

Etude 6, Variation 5—Agitato

This is somewhat like a Chopin Study, a repeated pattern in both hands; the right, an even series of chords, furnishes the accompaniment, and the left, which outlines the theme, throws it into prominence by syncopated anticipations of each of the regular metrical beats. The result is dashing and brilliant.

Etude 7, Variation 6—Allegro molto

The key is now changed for the first time. This piece is in E major with a central modulation to C major. The first part is concerned with new material, against which fortissimo chords derived from the melody of the principal theme are later projected.

Etude 8, Variation 7—Grave

A return to C sharp minor brings a greatly changed derivation of the central theme, appearing in a dynamic rhythm of vigorous irregularity.

Etude 9—Presto possibile

A whirlwind Beethovenian scherzo beginning *piano* and augmenting to a *fortissimo* climax tapers off to a whispered conclusion. This étude is not indicated as a variation but suggests throughout the influence of the descending arpeggio of the theme.

Etude 10, Variation 8—Sempre con energia

A dotted rhythmic treatment of the theme in the right hand with a swiftly moving nonlegato figure accompanying in the left hand is the plan of this variation.

Etude 11, Variation 9—Con espressione

The theme, now greatly enhanced by new melodic features, appears over an agitated pianistic figure, *sotto voce,* in the bass. At the second phrase the melody is imitated canonically by an inner voice. The effect is poignantly beautiful.

Etude 12—Finale—Allegro brilliante

The finale is of considerable length and importance. Not a regular variation, it is more a fantasia upon elements of the theme in modified sonata form. The key is now changed to D flat major (the same tonic by enharmonic courtesy as C sharp minor). The first part is a joyous allegro in four regular phrases. This is followed by a singing melody in A flat major, also in four phrases, accompanied by a persistent rhythm which keeps things moving. The development section combines elements of the variation theme with the material of the last phrase of the preceding music. There follows a recapitulation, a repetition of some of the development section, and a conclusion with the beginning music repeated and varied to serve as a triumphant coda.

LISZT'S PIANO MUSIC

The adjective "Lisztian" sums up the legend that has persisted about the incredible virtuosity and dramatic personality of a showman whose heart beat warmly in tune with admiring audiences of somewhat dubious enthusiasms. A sort of Paul Bunyan of the piano, for whom no feat was too prodigious, Liszt loved life and people and savored both with relish. His career was one of fabulous success. But this picture of Liszt is a very incomplete realization of the actual man and artist. It might serve to reflect the composer of the *Hungarian Rhapsodies*, the garish delights of which, sad to relate, are the chief source of many a music lover's opinion of him. But Liszt himself would never have expected these musical confections to last beyond their own feverish day. Fortunately for the security of his fame, there is an abundance of fine, solidly constructed piano music, glowing with melodic richness, full of originality and first-rate musical invention, including the great *B minor Sonata* in one movement, possibly the finest piano sonata of the Romantic period. Unlike Schubert, Schumann, Mendelssohn, and Chopin, Liszt wrote nothing for the amateur performer; his music is difficult to play and belongs properly in the sphere of the virtuoso performer. But although the pyrotechnical effects are sometimes a trifle incongruous and forced, particularly in such lyric compositions as the famous *Liebestraum,* they are an inseparable part of Liszt's personality. Brilliant performer that he was, he simply could not conceive of music without them.

The 104th sonnet of Petrarch (first version composed in 1838–1839; version given herein composed in 1846–1858)

A number of piano compositions, most of them bearing descriptive titles, are grouped together in Liszt's published works under the heading *Années de Pèlerinage* (Years of Wandering). Among those of the second year are three sonnets of Petrarch, numbers 47, 104, and 123.

Sonnet number 104 in translation is as follows:

> Wherein He Expatiates upon Love's Paradoxes
>
> I find no peace, yet from all wars abstain me;
> I fear, I hope, I burn—and straightway wizen;
> I mount above the wind, yet stay unrisen;
> Grasp the world—thus—yet nothing does it gain me.
> Love neither lets me go, nor will detain me;
> Gives me no leave, nor yet keeps me in prison:
> I am not held, and yet the hard chain is on
> The heart; he yields no death, yet will he chain me.
> Sightless, I see; and without tongue, I sorrow;
> I cling to life, and yet would gladly perish;
> Detest myself, and yet another cherish;

Feed upon grief; from grief my laughter borrow;
Death is a spear and life a poisoned arrow,
And in delight my fears take root and flourish.

The music, restless and emotional, is a depiction of the mood of the sonnet, which doubtless elicited a sympathetic response in Liszt's own private feelings; for we learn on reliable authority that he was practically always in love, and, although his attentions seem on the whole to have been favorably received, he would be the first to understand the constant anxiety of the perennial lover. The plan of the piece is the unfolding of a songlike melody in regular phrases, involving much repetition, but enlivened by chromatic turns of the harmony and widely spaced accompaniment which is blended into a luscious unit by the use of the damper pedal. Between pauses of the melody there are showers of pianistic figurations.

Mephisto waltz (composed in 1858–1859)
This pianistic tour de force is suggested by an excerpt from Lenau's *Faust* entitled "The Dance in the Village Inn." Mephistopheles and Faust, in their wanderings, come upon a dance going on at an inn. Faust is immediately swept off his feet by one of the women dancers, a gorgeous creature with black eyes and glowing red cheeks. He is timid, however, about approaching her. Mephistopheles is scornful. Is this the man who risks his soul—this man who shrinks from a beautiful woman? Mephistopheles seizes the violin from the village fiddler, whose sleepy music, he says, is fit only for lame and sick desire, and plays it passionately. Even the walls become envious that they cannot dance. Faust approaches the woman; they dance together and disappear into the night.

This program emerges from Liszt's imagination as a piece full of crackling satanic fire and voluptuousness. The design, however, is not dependent for its logic upon the story, although it fits it very well. Only the underlying mood of the episode conditions the music. After a long introduction, which contains a suggestion of the tuning of the violin, there are two waltz melodies developed at length: the first is a vigorous affair based upon an ascending arpeggio, which serves as a motive to be developed; and the second is *espressivo amoroso,* in which the chromatically inclined melody is stated on normally unaccented beats, giving it a certain rhythmic urgency and thus adding to the erotic effect. The second waltz idea is varied in a number of appearances with new pianistic devices, each one more exciting than the last. There is an occasional interruption in the way of imitative violin passages with triple stops.

The Romantic Overture

In the Romantic period the standard form of the overture remains unchanged from the design adopted by Beethoven, and emerges as a concert piece in its own right, increasingly independent of the opera. As the overture dissociates itself from the opera, so the latter, as if in retaliation, emancipates itself from the standard form of overture. Wagner wrote several overtures of classic design—to *Rienzi, The Flying Dutchman,* and *Tannhäuser*—but for his later works—*Lohengrin, Tristan and Isolde, Die Meistersinger,* the *Nibelungen Ring,* and *Parsifal*—he calls the introductory piece a prelude, and writes more freely and often more briefly. The overtures of Verdi and other Italians are likewise generally independent and unpredictable. On the other hand, Mendelssohn, Brahms, and many later composers of the nineteenth century wrote concert overtures, as, for example, Brahms's *Tragic Overture,* with no relation whatever to stage performance. The chief change to be observed in the Romantic overture is one of color and orchestration. Weber, in his familiar overtures to *Der Freischütz, Oberon,* and *Euryanthe,* infuses the Romantic spirit into the design and his instrumental technique, so warm and glowing, is an influence upon later composers, both in the opera and in the symphony.

WEBER—*Overture to Der Freischütz* (*The free shooter*) (composed in 1820)

Der Freischütz is an example of early German opera freed from the influences of Italian style. The story concerns the attempts of a forest ranger, Max, to win a shooting contest which will lead to the position of head ranger and the hand of Agatha, the young lady of his choice. He is tempted by black forces of the forest to clinch the matter by the use of a magic bullet. This, most unwisely, he does, but dire consequences are miraculously avoided and he triumphs in spite of his weakness.

The overture is a reflection of the mood and the characters of the story. It begins rather solemnly with a theme in octaves on winds and strings answered by an expressive figure on the violins. This scheme is repeated. Then against a soft string background a lovely harmonized melody ap-

EXAMPLE 143.

pears on the horns which seems to breathe the spell of the forest (Example 143). At the conclusion of the introduction the music darkens and a poignant melody on the cello with tremolo background leads to the main body of the overture, *molto vivace*. The first section in C minor is spirited and dramatic. There is a syncopated accompaniment and various melodic figures in the section before modulation, but the thematic material is lacking in concentration and the chief motive used in the development (Example 144) appears just before the rather abrupt modulation to E flat. After a triumphant assertion of this key by full orchestra a magnificent solo passage occurs for clarinet against tremolo strings leading to the melodious second theme (Example

EXAMPLE 144.

145), which in the opera is associated with Agatha. After this a closing theme impels the music to the key of F minor and the development begins. This section is brief, and consists of appearances of the motive from the first theme noted above, followed by Agatha's melody, somewhat extended and developed. A reminiscence of the clarinet solo on the violins reintroduces the material of the exposition. The recapitulation continues in parallel fashion with the

dolce

EXAMPLE 145.

first section until just before the clarinet solo, but from this point on it is changed and enlarged to include the cello melody from the introduction, now first heard on violins and bassoon and followed by a dramatic pause. Then comes a great burst of C major harmony from the full orchestra, and Agatha's theme returns, exultantly carrying the music to a triumphant conclusion.

WAGNER—*Prelude to Die Meistersinger* (composed in 1866–1867)

Wagner's opera *Die Meistersinger von Nürnberg* centers about the guilds of artisan poets and singers in sixteenth-century Germany who were known as Mastersingers. These societies were strict in their artistic traditions and consisted of various grades of merit which could be achieved only by passing a series of exacting tests. An actual historical figure, Hans Sachs, a poet shoemaker of the sixteenth century in Nuremberg, is the chief character of the opera. With his wisdom and vision he is able to guide the progress of Walther von Stolzing, a young knight of radical artistic tendencies but great talent, to victory in a competition in which the hand of Eva, the daughter of the goldsmith Veit Pogner, with whom Walther is in love, has been offered as a prize. Sachs is able to show the hotheaded young man that tradition may be reconciled with youthful idealism. The chief comic character is a rival for the hand of Eva, one Beckmesser, a ridiculous pedant (supposed to represent Wagner's enemy, the critic Hanslick), who exemplifies the absurdity of the pompous conservative who does not even understand the true meaning of the tradition that he so fanatically reveres.

In the *Prelude,* which is an extended work often played as a concert overture apart from the opera, Wagner has really composed a one-movement symphonic poem in which the essentials of the story are fully covered. It is a striking composition, eloquent of the glory of tradition, burning with the ardor of youthful inspiration, and tinged with irony in its section devoted to Beckmesser. The general plan of the design is that of first-movement sonata form, somewhat free in its theme manipulation and disposition, but adhering to the classic succession of tonalities. By a happy contrivance, the design is made to serve the purposes of the story, for at the beginning of the recapitulation three of the themes are combined, and Wagner proves his thesis that tradition and the modern spirit can exist harmoniously even in musical counterpoint.

The *Prelude* begins with the strong masculine outline of the theme of tradition (Example 146). After a lengthy ex-

EXAMPLE 146.

tension of this idea and a contrasting lyric melody, introduced by the flute, there is a fanfare theme (Example 147) on the horns, supplemented by the wood winds, which is

EXAMPLE 147.

greeted by triumphant, sweeping scales in the strings. This is associated with the pomp and majesty of the Mastersingers. A motive from the second bar of the tradition theme is then amplified in a music of assurance and power. All this material is in the key of C major. An agitated rhythm set in an expressive melody then serves as bridge and a modulation to the key of E major is secured. Here appears the theme of Walther's *Prize Song*, a melody very different in feeling from the forthright musical thinking of the Mastersingers—impetuous, chromatic, and insistently driving forward (Example 148).

There is a sudden modulation in which the theme of the bridge reappears, and a section with somewhat the character of a development is ushered in in the key of E flat.

EXAMPLE 148.

Development or not, this section unmistakably points to Beckmesser, and is very amusing if one understands its musical implications. It consists of fussy counterpoint on staccato wood winds based upon the theme of tradition. This is interspersed with some frantic attempts with Walther's theme on the strings (in the opera Beckmesser steals some verses of the *Prize Song*). Notice the silly trills on the flutes and clarinets which are an attempt to dress up the stodgy polyphony. The strings take up the trills as Beckmesser gets more desperate, and then the strong voices of the trumpet and trombone call a halt to all this nonsense with the tradition theme in its original version, and as the clatter dies down the recapitulation arrives quietly in C major. Here is Wagner's tour de force. The first violins, first clarinet, first horn, and cellos have Walther's melody, while below, on the bassoons, tuba, and basses, appears the theme of tradition. Weaving about these voices and providing the harmonic background is the fanfare theme in the rest of the wood winds, horns, and strings (Example 149). This exciting scheme goes on for some time and is followed by an apotheosis of the fanfare theme, now practically bursting with pride. A final fortissimo blast of the full orchestra

EXAMPLE 149.

on the theme of tradition and a brassy tribute to the key of C major bring the prelude to a glowing and highly satisfactory conclusion.

The Romantic Symphony

It is difficult to generalize about the nineteenth-century symphony. Practically all the important composers tried their hand at it with varying results, but, with the exception of Brahms and possibly Schubert, none found his complete expression in this form, and most excelled in other fields. The immense shadow of Beethoven looms over the century.

He provided the model, but the genius of the Romantics seemed ill adapted to such great instrumental architecture. The extramusical interests of these composers led to a dilution of symphonic thought and their insistence upon melody, colorful orchestration, and harmony proved to be weakening rather than of benefit to the design. Audiences applauded the new symphonies as they appeared, only later to discard them as unworthy to succeed the great Beethoven. Only in the symphonies of Brahms has the spirit of the classic master found its rebirth, and Brahms was considered by many of his contemporaries pedantic and reactionary. His true importance was universally accepted only after his death.

SCHUBERT—*Symphony No. 8 in B minor* (*Unfinished*) (composed in 1822)

Schubert's first six symphonies were classical in model, following the pattern of Haydn, but rich in characteristically beautiful melodies. The *Unfinished Symphony* consists of but two movements. Sketches were also found for a scherzo, but, although Schubert was still to write his great *C major Symphony* (listed as number 7), for some reason he did not finish the one in B minor. He may possibly have felt that the work was complete in two movements. Certainly the world has come to this conclusion, for after its first performance, thirty-seven years after Schubert's death, the work achieved enormous popularity which, like that accorded his songs, seems destined to live forever.

The *Symphony in B minor,* although written five years before Beethoven's death, brings us into the very heart of Romanticism. The form, particularly of the first movement, is free, and the customary rhythmic conciseness of the classic symphony is replaced by a dramatic and colorful melodic style with an architecture of amazing strength and clarity, but very different from that of the classic masters.

First movement—Allegro moderato in B minor

The principal theme, a melody of melancholy and brooding sadness, is heard at once on cellos and basses (Example 150). This is succeeded by an accompaniment figure on the

EXAMPLE 150.

violins, suggestive of the songs, over which appears a sad, songlike melody on the oboe and clarinet (Example 151). This mounts in emotional force to a climax, and horns and bassoons effect a transition to another songlike melody, in

EXAMPLE 151.

major and of appealing sweetness, first appearing on the cellos and then transferred to the violins (Example 152). A dramatic interruption on the full orchestra is succeeded by a development of fragments of this last melody, with more dramatic interjections and a strettolike close. The

EXAMPLE 152.

development section is based entirely upon the introductory theme. This part of the movement is sheer genius in its theme manipulation, increasing in power, expressiveness, and tragic intensity. The recapitulation is an almost exact duplication of the exposition except that the initial theme, so powerfully treated in the development, is omitted here. The coda reintroduces this theme, which provides a poignantly dramatic close.

Second movement—Andante con moto in E major

Here Schubert has composed a great orchestral song, full of warmth and sweetness but occasionally rising to dramatic climaxes. The movement is in five sections, with similar material in sections one, three, and five, and con-

EXAMPLE 153.

trasting music in section two which is repeated in section four. Each section, however, is rich in varied melodies. The initial scheme is a sort of question-and-answer plan, horns and bassoons over pizzicato bass, with answering strings (Example 153). An emphatic music for full orchestra is then heard leading to return of the question and answer. The material of sections two and four is an intense melody of much dynamic variety on clarinet and oboe over a syncopated string accompaniment (Example 154). This melody is then extended and powerfully developed, first by the full orchestra and then expressively on the strings alone. The third and fourth sections practically repeat sections one and two with certain key changes, and the fifth section, serving as coda, varies the material of section one by separating and extending the question-and-answer material. Here Schubert's instrumental color and daring modulations manifest his great originality. It would be difficult to follow this movement, so long and so intense, with a scherzo and finale. Schubert evidently tried, but could not succeed to

EXAMPLE 154.

his own satisfaction. One leaves the *B minor Symphony* with no sense of incompleteness. We must regard the work as a two-movement symphony, a unique masterpiece in the literature of the orchestra.

BERLIOZ—*Symphonie fantastique* (composed in 1830–1831)

This symphony, in spite of a wide diversion of opinion as to its merits, stubbornly holds its own in the concert repertory. Conductors love it because of its brilliant orchestration, and audiences seem to enjoy its poetic flavor. Berlioz had a remarkable skill in writing for orchestra. Everything sounds well, sometimes much better than it should in terms of musical content. This music resists all efforts at transcription. Nothing drearier could be conceived than a reduction of the score for piano. Berlioz's imagination was inseparably linked to the actual orchestra sounds, and his effects which look simple on the page are fresh and brilliant in performance.

The music itself represents the paradox of the composer's mind. His great admiration was Beethoven and he believed in the formal architecture of the symphony and considered that description should play only a complementary role in design. His musical imagination, however, was almost wholly dependent upon literary inspiration: Shakespeare and Byron were responsible for two symphonies, *Romeo and Juliet* and *Harold in Italy*, and his own cyclonic love affair with a Shakespearean actress (afterward Mme. Berlioz—for a while) inspired the *Fantastic Symphony*. When not under some literary stimulus the musical results were sometimes below par, with a low blood count. He was often inconvenienced in the full realization of his poetical objectives by his reverence for classical form. His special flair was for the diabolic and macabre. In these departments of the mind he was an artist of matchless power.

The musical idiom of Berlioz shows great originality in melodic and rhythmic disposition. His use of harmony is dull and gray, and, coming in the full tide of the Romantic age, with its special richness of harmony, his music seems often rather bleak—which probably accounts for his limited popularity with music lovers. The *Fantastic Symphony* departs from the classical model in that there are five movements, each with descriptive content; it has also a central theme, called *l'idée fixe*, which appears in each of the movements.

The program upon which Berlioz built the symphony is a strange one: "A young musician of morbid sensibility and an ardent imagination poisons himself with opium. The dose of the narcotic, too weak to kill him, plunges him into a heavy sleep accompanied by strange visions, during which his sensations, sentiments, and recollections are translated in his sick mind into musical thoughts and pictures. The beloved woman has become for him a melody, and as it were, an *idée fixe*, which he finds and hears everywhere."

First movement—Reveries, Passions—Largo, Allegro agitato e appassionato assai in C major

A rhapsodical slow introduction in C minor leads to the allegro section in which the principal theme (also the *idée fixe*) is stated on violins and flute (Example 155). This

EXAMPLE 155.

theme forms the main basis of the movement, which includes the customary exposition, development, recapitulation, and coda. The following program is appended:

"He first recalls the soul distress, the wave of passion, the melancholy thoughts, the nameless joys which he has experienced before having met the loved one, then the volcanic love with which she has inspired him, the delirious agony, furious jealousy, returning tenderness, religious consolations."

Second movement—A Ball—Valse allegro non troppo in A major

This is an unconventional dance movement coming into the symphony, an introduction and waltz in the Viennese style. In the middle appears the *idée fixe* on flute and oboe. It is also heard on the clarinet shortly before the end. The program is: "He discovers the beloved one again amid the tumult of a brilliant fête."

Third movement—Scenes in the Country—Adagio in F major

This resembles the regular slow movement of the classic symphony. A dialogue between oboe and English horn is followed by a pastoral melody (Example 156) which, becoming increasingly agitated, introduces the *idée fixe* on flute and oboe. This produces a dramatic climax followed by the pastoral melody again and a recollection of the opening dialogue. The program describes the artist in the coun-

EXAMPLE 156.

try, overhearing two herdsmen piping a cattle call in dialogue. The artist relaxes amid such genial surroundings but his hopeful thoughts give way to doubts about the beloved and certain dark presentiments arise in his mind.

Fourth movement—March to the Gallows—Allegretto non troppo in G minor

This is a death march of unrelieved tension and gloom. It is built around a descending scale theme in minor, first

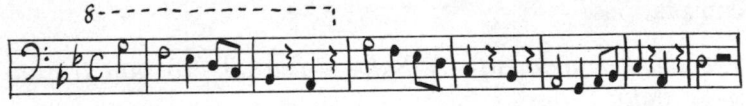

EXAMPLE 157.

stated on cellos and basses (Example 157). There is a contrasting melody in major (Example 158). At the end, after an ugly climax, the *idée fixe* appears on the clarinet followed by a brassy conclusion. The program: "He dreams that he has killed his beloved and, condemned to death, is

EXAMPLE 158.

being led to execution. The procession advances to a march, now grim and somber, now majestic and brilliant, in which the sound of muffled tread follows suddenly upon boisterous outbursts. At the end the *idée fixe* appears momentarily as a last thought of love interrupted by the fatal stroke."

Fifth movement—Dream of a Witches' Sabbath—Larghetto, Allegro in C major

High-minded Romanticists like Schumann greatly disapproved of this last movement. It is undoubtedly sacrilegious

EXAMPLE 159.

and satanic, but these very elements seem to have inspired the composer to the most original and effective part of the symphony. It consists of two introductory sections and a rondo. The introductory sections can best be explained by the program, which describes a gathering of witches and warlocks to gloat over the mock funeral of the artist. The first section is a summons to the gathering, a call upon flutes and oboes echoed by a horn in the distance, the scurrying about of dark forms suggested in strings and winds. Then first on the C clarinet and then on the high E-flat clarinet (with an acid and disagreeable tone) a travesty of the *idée fixe* appears, as the beloved now transformed into a witch rides up on a broomstick (Example 159). She is enthusiastically received by full orchestra. The second section begins with funeral bells and is followed by the *Dies Irae*, traditional hymn for the dead, heard first on the tubas and then parodied on horns and trombones (Example 160). This unholy alternation leads to the formulation of the rondo theme (Example 161) and to the rondo itself, which

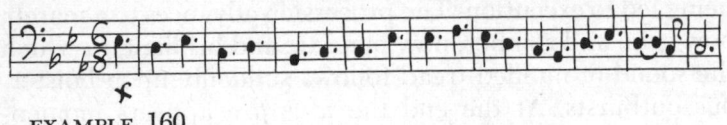

EXAMPLE 160.

is a more formal piece. The principal theme alternates with the *Dies Irae* and at the high point of the movement the two are combined in a spirit of fiendish merriment.

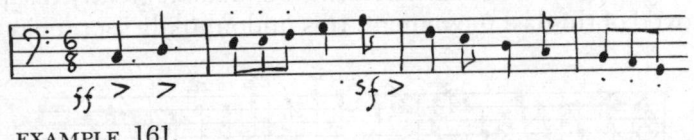

EXAMPLE 161.

BRAHMS—*Symphony in E minor, no. 4* (composed in 1884–1885)

The ever-present classic strain which lurked in the background during the Romantic period had as its chief representatives Brahms and Mendelssohn. Brahms was a composer of such importance that, practically singlehanded, he started a sizable current in the direction of revived and chastened symphonic architecture. He not only assimilated the symphonic architecture of Beethoven, but he understood and revived the lost polyphonic art of Bach. These elements, united with the rich, harmonic coloring of his contemporaries, brought new life to the symphony. Brahms discarded extramusical ideas as foreign to the nature of musical expression. If his music is inspired by poetical or dramatic subjects, that is his private affair, and he concentrates his attention upon objective design with strictly musical ideas as the substance.

Although capable of much subtlety of rhythmic organization, sometimes to the confusion of the inexperienced listener, his symphonic thought is expressed chiefly in melody. In this respect Brahms is a Romantic rather than a classic symphonist. His style is less dramatic and more sensuous than that of Beethoven; his melody is definitely less chromatic than that of Wagner and Liszt, his use of tonal relationships clearer and more disciplined. In the Brahms first-movement sonata form the themes are continually flowering and expanding. They appear even more beautiful and expressive in development than in exposition. Far from being displays of learning, the development sections are usually lyric, the themes in amplified state increasingly lovely. The recapitulations, however, unlike those of Beethoven, who tends away from symmetry of pattern, revert to the design of Haydn and Mozart and parallel the exposition with the minimum of change necessitated by the plan of tonalities. For dance movement Brahms uses neither minuet nor scherzo. The third movement is generally a piece in moderately fast tempo with a gentle reflective humor, far different from the robust comedy of Beethoven. The finale is raised to an importance scarcely less than that of the first movement.

The often-criticized orchestra of Brahms is entirely individual. There is a thickness, even occasional muddiness about it, less feeling for instrumental coloring, less brilliance than in the case of Wagner and Liszt. However, it would be difficult to imagine a different orchestral style for this music because it is so much a part of the general effect. If one is fond of Brahms he will not want the orchestration changed, whatever may be said against it.

Brahms has not the variety of mood of Beethoven. He has been said to lack the divine madness and enthusiasm of the older man. But there is a breadth and grandeur about his music. It is warm and compassionate. With all its nobility of purpose and intricacy of design it often touches the heart.

First movement—Allegro non troppo in E minor

This movement alternates its prevailing lyricism with vigorous rhythm. Reversing the Beethoven procedure, Brahms states his lyric idea first. The principal theme is

EXAMPLE 162.

heard immediately. It contains three motives: the first is an expressive chordal melody with a constant rhythm (Example 162); the second and third are differing rhythms arranged in a melodic pattern (Example 163). This ma-

EXAMPLE 163.

terial is repeated with changed accompaniment and orchestration (Example 164), with some development, and leads to modulation. Here the rhythmic contrast is afforded by an episode in B minor which dispels the mood of lyricism. This episode is rather like a march driving the music forward (Example 165). This is followed by a new lyric theme in B major (Example 166), linked by a mysterious arpeggio

EXAMPLE 164.

figure to a closing theme which is a continuation of the mood of the episode (Example 167). A quiet passage leads without repetition to the development. The principal lyric motive is now stated simply, then amplified and extended.

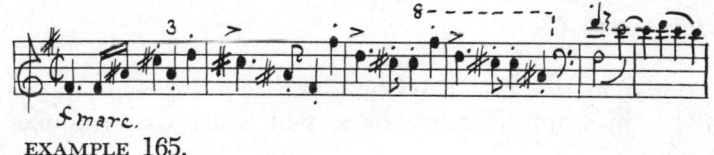

EXAMPLE 165.

The rhythmic episode and mysterious arpeggio reappear, alternate, and then are combined with the principal lyric motive. The development closes with a treatment of the second motive of the first theme. The recapitulation begins

EXAMPLE 166.

unconventionally with the first motive in augmentation, alternating with the arpeggio figure. From this point on the recapitulation is similar to the exposition. The coda commences with an extension of the material of the episode, followed by development of the motives of the first theme, the first in canonic imitation, the second merely

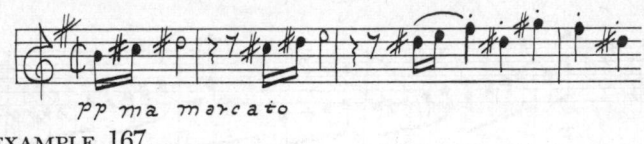

EXAMPLE 167.

stated, and the third expanded to form a vigorous and brilliant close.

Second movement—Andante moderato in E major
This movement has something of the color of the old

EXAMPLE 168.

Phrygian mode (E to E without accidentals). This appears in the three introductory bars, which are unharmonized

EXAMPLE 169.

(Example 168), and again in the last six bars, where it influences the harmony with charming ambiguous effect. The body of the movement is a symphonic song with first-movement plan of tonalities. The first theme is derived from the introductory bars (Example 169), is followed by

EXAMPLE 170.

a bridge, melodically related to it (Example 170), and a contrasting second theme (Example 171). There is no development, but only a recapitulation, with changed dispo-

EXAMPLE 171.

sition of melody, accompaniment, and orchestration. A short coda on the first theme concludes the movement.

Third movement—Allegro giocoso in C major
This movement is both brash and arch—if this is possible —with the two elements continually conflicting. Its form is

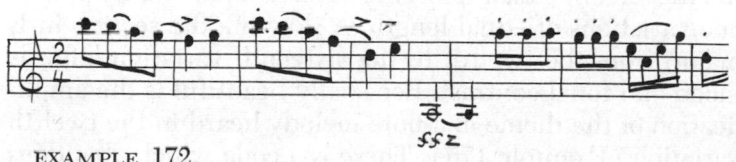

EXAMPLE 172.

first-movement sonata of brief proportions. There are a number of rhythmic motives in the first theme (Example 172) and another in the second (Example 173). These little

EXAMPLE 173.

patterns are tossed about, inverted and rhythmically altered, to sustain a mood of somewhat professorial gaiety.

Fourth movement—Allegro energico e passionato in E minor

For a finale Brahms ventures upon an old form unprecedented in the symphony, the passacaglia. The theme is stated in the first eight bars. It is an ascending scale of even

EXAMPLE 174.

rhythm with a harmonic pattern which persists throughout the movement (Example 174). This is followed by thirty-one variations of equal length. A slow middle section in E major, from the twelfth to the sixteenth variation, affords mood and tonal contrast. Especially beautiful is the amplification of the theme in a flute melody heard in the twelfth variation (Example 175). There is a coda which abandons the strict plan in favor of free symphonic development and brings the movement to a triumphant close.

In this movement Brahms has written one of the great finales of the literature. It is an amazing proof of his resourcefulness that, in spite of its arbitrary segmentation, the music flows inevitably and melodiously, with variety

EXAMPLE 175.

and absorbing interest. It is also notable for an impressive cumulative power.

TCHAIKOVSKY—*Symphony in B minor, no. 6 (Pathetic)* (composed in 1893)

As Italy dominated the opera until the time of Wagnerian music drama, so did Austria and Germany reign supreme over the symphony until the latter half of the nineteenth century. From the seventeenth century on, the operatic and orchestral field was centralized in these countries, with France the only important rival. In the late Romantic period, however, other European nations became increasingly articulate. The spread of interest in the folk song brought a new melodic freshness to both opera and symphony. This period saw the emergence of national-minded composers in Russia, Scandinavia, Bohemia, Spain, and England. Such men as Tchaikovsky, Dvořák, Smetana, Grieg, Albeniz, and others frequently based their music upon folk melodies of their native countries, and the result was an agreeable music which became very popular. The model for opera remained largely Italian, and for the symphony, German, but the net result was a gain in originality and freshness of musical style.

Tchaikovsky is characteristic of late Romanticism in that his music has a strong national flavor blended with the idiom of the German symphonists. He also inherits the symphonic style of the Romantics, with its emphasis upon melody at the expense of compact structure. His greatness lies in the appealing quality of his melody which is both emotionally intense and spontaneously lyric. He is a master of the orchestra and employs a variety of color, power of climax, and a sense of the dramatic which sometimes leads to exaggerated theatricalism. Restraint and artistic discipline, notable in the classic masters, are usually lacking in his music. The obviousness and vulgarity, which even he noticed occasionally in his own works, are defects to be admitted without invalidating his importance as a composer.

The *Pathetic Symphony* was composed a few months before his death. It is a work of compelling emotional force, now sad, now ebullient, now plunged into the depths of despair. Although subjective and possibly autobiographical, its design is clear, and the rather unusual structure supports the heavy burden of expressive feeling. Always his most popular symphony, it is also probably his best.

First movement—Adagio—Allegro non troppo in B minor

The introduction begins with a theme, stated on the bassoon, which is the principal symphonic idea of the move-

EXAMPLE 176.

ment (Example 176). Its effect is gloomy and foreboding. The allegro begins with an enlargement of this theme stated by the violas and followed by a figure of repeated sixteenth notes which usually accompanies it. Repetitions of this material lead to a suggestion of the second theme, which is to arrive shortly, and a bridge figure (Example 177). Development and combination of this material bring a di-

EXAMPLE 177.

minuendo with the sixteenth-note figure in the low strings and a pause. Now appears the lyric theme, which is the main feature of the movement (Example 178). In Beethoven the purpose of the lyric theme is merely one of relief, and it is never allowed to do more than relax momentarily the symphonic tension. Here we find that this theme overshadows everything in importance, not only in quality, but in length. It is a whole section, a complete song with

EXAMPLE 178.

statement, contrast, and restatement. It could be removed from its context and played separately, although no one appears ever to have tried it. After a cadence and pause, the development is ushered in. It consists first of contrapuntal treatment of the opening theme (Example 179), followed by a series of tremendous orchestral climaxes in which appears a brass theme possibly related to the lyric theme and interspersed with fragments of the opening theme. The recapitulation arrives with the principal theme fortissimo on the strings, imitated canonically by the wood winds and

EXAMPLE 179.

horns. In this section the material is shortened. The second theme appears in B major, omitting contrast and restatement, and leads to a quiet close.

Second movement—Allegro con grazia in D major
This movement is an alternation of two moods: grace and delicacy suggestive of a dance, and appealing pathos. It is written in a meter of five-four, combined in groups of two and three in each bar. Although more rapid in tempo than the usual second movement, the effect is that of the lyric, songlike movement in three sections and coda.

Third movement—Allegro molto vivace in G major
Instead of a scherzo, Tchaikovsky has written a brilliant symphonic march for the third movement. There is a long introduction in G major in which the outlines of the march

EXAMPLE 180.

melody gradually appear against a staccato triplet figure (Example 180). The march finally arrives in E major on the clarinets, accompanied by staccato strings and horn. It is organized with a contrasting middle section and in the midst of the movement there is a development followed by a repetition of the march in G major and a coda.

Fourth movement—Adagio lamentoso in B minor
The finale is unusual in mood and concludes the symphony with a feeling of black despair. It is a lyric movement consisting of two melodies, which are presented in the tonal plan of sonata form, but there is no development. The

EXAMPLE 181.

first melody, in B minor, is a descending figure of considerable poignancy (Example 181). The effect of this is increased, as the movement progresses, by a rapidly ascending anacrusis, which is added to it. The contrasting melody makes its first appearance in D major, and, although it, too, is sorrowful, there is a little consoling quality, probably because of the major mode (Example 182). Both melodies are intensely emotional and susceptible of climax, which

EXAMPLE 182.

Tchaikovsky does not stint. In the second half of the movement both melodies reappear in B minor. The effect upon the second one is to withdraw what little cheer there was and to make it even more depressing than the first. The movement ends on the low strings, fading away in deep dejection. This movement suggests self-pity, and an almost suicidal melancholy.

The Romantic Concerto

The growth in importance of the virtuoso performer in the nineteenth century brought about a demand for works which would provide him with the impressive setting of the symphony orchestra. The concerto with featured soloist became an indispensable part of the symphony program, along with symphonies, overtures, suites, and symphonic poems. Many of the Romantic composers were solo pianists, among them Weber, Mendelssohn, Schumann, Chopin, Liszt, Brahms, and Rubinstein. All of them contributed significantly to the literature of the concerto. Violinists such as Spohr, Paganini, Vieuxtemps, Sarasate, Wieniawski, and Joachim all wrote brilliant concertos for their instrument, although from the strictly musical point of view the violin concertos of the nonspecializing Mendelssohn, Brahms, and Bruch are more interesting.

In general, the Romantic concerto followed the design of the classic concerto as established by Mozart, a three-movement work, with the first, sonata-form allegro, overshadowing in importance the slow movement and finale. Liszt was the chief dissenter from an almost universal design; in his popular piano concertos in A minor and E flat major he experimented with the form in fusing the elements of the various movements into a single movement, but, although he achieved marked success, this innovation was not widely adopted. The four great concertos of Brahms, far from be-

ing merely display pieces, are among his most extended and serious compositions.

SCHUMANN—*Concerto for piano in A minor* (composed in 1841–1845)

This well-loved composition of Schumann is unfortunately not typical of the nineteenth-century concerto for several reasons, among them the informality of its design, its musical integrity, in which display is subordinated to quality of ideas, and its reaffirmation of the old concerto principle of equality of partnership between solo and tutti. The first movement was intended originally to stand alone as a fantasia for piano and orchestra. It was only after four years that Schumann was impelled to extend the work by the addition of a slow movement and a finale. If his single concerto is not typical of the period as an example of the form, Schumann's musical style is truly characteristic of Romanticism at its best. His sensitive approach to the instrument, which seems to respond to his confidences with the tenderness and warmth which only such devotion can inspire, results in a music of exquisite feeling and taste, fresh in originality and glowing with the warmth of his melody.

First movement—Allegro affettuoso in A minor
The piano makes its appearance immediately after an introductory chord on the full orchestra. It states an impulsive, heralding theme (Example 183) which is later used in the development. The main theme of the movement is then plaintively exposed on the oboe and bassoon, accompanied by clarinets and horns (Example 184). This theme, subject to various modifications and amplifications, is the unifying source of the entire movement. The general plan of the movement is that of a first-movement allegro with an exposition in A minor and C major. There is a development, in which the main theme is amplified and trans-

EXAMPLE 183.

formed into a tender dialogue between piano and clarinet in the key of A flat major. Transpositions of the introductory theme link this passage to another amplification of the main theme in G major, in which the piano and flute rapturously carry on the melody to a return of A minor, and the

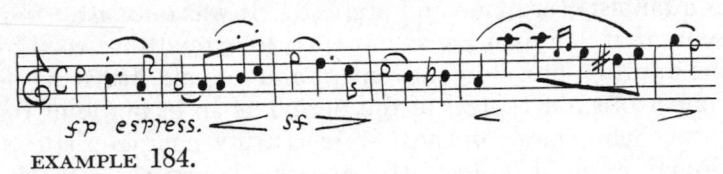

EXAMPLE 184.

recapitulation. There is a somewhat reflective cadenza and a brilliant coda, with the main theme appearing in martial rhythm.

Second movement—Intermezzo—Andante grazioso in F major

The second movement is an intimate and charming dialogue between piano and orchestra in Schumann's happiest vein. The melodic line is so divided between soloist and accompaniment that each depends upon the other. There is a second scheme in which first the cello and then the violins deal with a broad lyric melody, and the piano, gently supporting each phrase, adds a short expressive comment between them. A return to the first plan brings the movement to a close, but instead of a cadence there is a reminiscence of the first-movement theme and the music rushes on without pause to the finale.

Finale—Allegro vivace in A major

A youthful and vigorous joy dominates the last movement, which contains a number of highly entertaining themes in a design of first-movement sonata. The two most

EXAMPLE 185.

important are the first in A major, tuneful as a rondo refrain (Example 185), and the second in E major, a theme of great rhythmic subtlety because of its missing beats, more evident to the eye than to the ear (Example 186). After this theme has established itself, the piano weaves a web of arpeggios about it, until the orchestra, completely

EXAMPLE 186.

baffled, takes refuge in a development of the first theme, where it finds securer ground. A new theme (Example 187) appears in F major to give variety to the development and eventually to lead to a recapitulation, beginning uncon-

EXAMPLE 187.

ventionally not in the home key but in D major. A major reappears for the restatement of the second theme and its complexities, and, after a rousing tutti on the main theme, a coda introduced by glittering new figuration on the piano, in partnership with the main theme, keeps things moving until the end.

The Symphonic Poem

Liszt, like Berlioz, found his imagination stimulated by extramusical ideas and preferred to write to a definite program. He was careful to explain, however, that he did not believe that music should be merely representational, but that it might well yield to poetical influences and devote its power to the emotional expression of these. Granting that a composer submit to such influences—and what romantic-minded artist does not—it is only proper to share with the public the ideas which have inspired him, so that the music may be more perfectly understood.

Unlike Berlioz, Liszt did not allow his reverence for the classic masters to interfere with his originality as a musical architect. He realized that the accepted designs of the symphony might well deflect and embarrass the development of the poetic idea, and that to yield to the established disciplines at the expense of logic was a form of pedantry to which no spirited artist of an emancipated age should submit. He therefore became the leader of a left-wing tendency among the Romantics; he and his followers, including Wagner, believed that in casting loose from the shackles of classicism they were writing the music of the future.

Fortunately for the success of this school of thought, Liszt was an able champion. Among the Romantic composers before Brahms, he was master of the surest technique, a musical architect of skill, with a knowledge of instrumental resources, a flair for experimental harmonies, a fine melodic gift, and a natural instinct for effect. The symphonic poem, or, as literally translated, tone poem, was the great contribution of this movement. In inventing it

Liszt discarded the rigid form of the symphony, allowing the program itself to determine the design, and substituted for the four-movement plan an extended composition in a single movement. However, Liszt did not abandon the symphonic principle of concentrated themes, development of these, and carefully balanced succession of tonalities. His chief technical device, called theme metamorphosis, consists of kaleidoscopic transformations of a central theme. In this way he obtains variety of mood and color without sacrificing inner unity. His symphonic mastery is shown by his ingenuity in evolving from the simplest theme related patterns suitable for each change of poetical thought.

Between the years 1848 and 1861 at Weimar, to which city he retired from his concert career, he wrote ten symphonic poems and two program symphonies. From the time of Liszt the symphonic poem was recognized as the typical symphonic form of the age, and until the beginning of the twentieth century it was widely adopted and imitated. At the close of the century another gifted composer, Richard Strauss, appeared upon the scene to give fresh impetus to the form.

LISZT—*Les Préludes* (composed in 1859)

This composition has been the most frequently played of Liszt's orchestral works. Today it causes much eyebrow lifting because of its rather obvious subject matter and bombastic style. However, it has vitality beneath its surface vulgarity, is most effectively scored, and is an ingenious combination of representation and pure design, understandable when considered from either point of view. The program is based upon a prose selection from Lamartine's *Méditations Poétiques:*

What is our life but a series of preludes to that unknown song of which Death intones the first solemn note? Love forms the enchanted aurora of every existence. But where is the destiny in which the first delights of happiness are not interrupted by some storm whose mortal breath dissipates its beautiful illusions, whose fatal lightning consumes its altar? And where is the cruelly wounded soul that after one of these tempests does not seek to soothe its memories in the sweet calm of country life? But man does not easily resign himself long to the enjoyment of the beneficent serenity in the bosom of nature which at first charmed him; and when the trumpet sounds the alarm, he hastens to the post of danger, whatever the war that calls him to the ranks, that he may find again in the fight full consciousness of himself and entire possession of his powers.

It will be seen that this program is a composer's holiday of accessible moods, young love, passion's storm, pastoral joys, war, and self-mastery, in the representation of which Liszt did not stint himself. The succession of moods is easy to follow. The musical design, consisting approximately of eight sections, all of them based upon a central motive of three notes, is equally simple.

Section I

Introduction. In C major. The motive is presented in the third bar (Example 188). It is extended and repeated in crescendo leading to

EXAMPLE 188.

Section II

The motive with slightly varied rhythm and extension (Example 189) is stated with fortissimo accompaniment

EXAMPLE 189.

on trumpets and trombones. This music also serves for the concluding section, thus providing a symmetrical design. It is filled with a sort of "Captain of my soul" exultance.

Section III

Obviously dealing with young love, the motive is now transformed into a melody of romantic tenderness (Example 190). There is a key change leading to

EXAMPLE 190.

Section IV

in E major which introduces a melody of greater emotional force on the horns and violas (Example 191). The

EXAMPLE 191.

love represented is no longer idyllic. This melody is scarcely recognizable as an expansion of the central motive, and might be considered as the lyric theme of sonata form, but it is actually based upon it, as the three notes of the motive appear on the first beat of the first, third, and fourth bars, a central arch sustaining the whole. The motive in original state returns and there is a pause.

Section V

Here we have the storm in several keys and the motive in different dramatic guises. The first part is obvious and has lost whatever effectiveness it had in a deluge of banal imitations. The second scheme, however, with the theme in the brass and an agitated accompaniment also based upon the motive, is still fresh and exciting. This music leads to a quiet return of the first love music. Several keys are used.

Section VI
The pastoral section introduces a new background theme (Example 192) on the clarinet which is later combined

EXAMPLE 192.

with the love theme from section three. It increases in intensity as it modulates back to the key of C.

Section VII
The motive is now transformed into a sort of battle call on the trumpets and horns (Example 193). Both love

EXAMPLE 193.

themes return and are appropriately militarized. There is a tremendous climax.

Section VIII
The triumphant music of section two returns to serve as conclusion.

Romantic Chamber Music

The ideal of chamber music, as might be expected, persisted stubbornly throughout the Romantic period, even though it had little in common with this age of inflated musical thought. The quartets of Mozart, Haydn, and Beethoven were as active in influence as their symphonies, and even more perilous to the Romantic composer, who, with unsymphonic lyricism, increased feeling for instrumental and harmonic color, and a flair for dramatic and pictorial expression as his chief weapons, sought to emulate their delicately balanced design.

It is perhaps for this reason that quintets, quartets, and trios for strings with piano were so popular. The Romanticists were on safe ground in dealing with the rich sonorities of the keyboard, and its percussive quality lent an additional impetus to the great crescendi upon which they depended for the chief feature of their designs. It is interesting to note that in the baroque period the harpsichord was necessary to weld together the string voices in chamber music, and, after the perfected chamber music style of the classic masters had tapered off in the nineteenth century, another keyboard instrument came forward to prop up the tottering structure.

The chief composers of the early Romantic chamber music were Schubert, Mendelssohn, and Schumann. Schubert, closest in spirit to the mighty Beethoven, was most successful in preserving the essential features of the style. The classicism of Mendelssohn was artificial rather than instinctive. His works preserve the outward aspect perhaps better than Schubert, but have less to offer in the way of musical thought to compensate for weakened structure. Schumann succeeds most happily in his ingratiating piano quintet. His quartets are far below his songs and piano music in quality. Later in the century, Brahms, who revived the glory of the symphony, performed a similar service for the art of chamber music. Although apparently irreconcilable, he alone was able to fuse the elements of the Romantic idiom with the classic spirit. His trios, quartets, quintets, and sextets are a perfect expression of his genius. They may be said, perhaps, to excel in quality of design and profundity of musical thought his magnificent works for orchestra.

The end of the century brought an echo of the symphonic revival into the field of chamber music in other lands. In France, César Franck, and in Bohemia, Smetana and Dvořák among others, composed quartets and quintets which have become a part of the standard repertory.

SCHUBERT—*Quartet in D minor (Death and the maiden)* (composed between 1824–1826)

The purest essence of the spirit of classicism is to be found in the literature of chamber music. The symphony, tempted by the color and dynamic possibilities of the orchestra, might sometimes allow the drama to run away with the design, but in the string quartet strictly musical elements are almost always paramount. It is the citadel of "absolute music." But even this citadel could not withstand the spirit of Romanticism as embodied in the works of Schubert. The *Quartet in D minor* is practically a program quartet, conditioned by a mood which is revealed in the theme and variations of the second movement. Schubert chose for his theme the song of Death from his famous lied "Death and the Maiden." It is not hard to trace the reflection of this idea throughout the work. The first movement seems to be a struggle, with Death as the victor. The third movement suggests Death as the demon fiddler, and the last movement, which is an inexorable dance of Death, includes also in the second theme a quotation from the *Erl-King*, the despairing cry of the child.

This programmatic character of the music does not destroy the objective design of the movements, which follow the classic pattern, but it supplies a logic which compensates for the less concentrated character of the themes, particularly in the first movement. As in the case of the symphonies, Schubert's gift is more melodic than symphonic and his themes are lacking in the rhythmic saliency that we find in Haydn, Mozart, and Beethoven. The music drives forward not so much from the impetus of the themes themselves as from the dramatic imagination of Schubert, who can spin out his melodies to great lengths and sustain the interest with his remarkable instinct for harmony and instrumental color.

First movement—Allegro in D minor

The central motive of the first movement is a rhythmic triplet figure which is stated immediately by all four instruments (Example 194). After a short introduction of a

EXAMPLE 194.

solemn and foreboding character, the first theme is heard on the first violin with an accompaniment embodying the triplet feature on the other instruments (Example 195). The introductory pronouncement of the rhythmic motive again appears, and a melodious bridge leads on to F major and the subsidiary theme. As in the case of several symphonic movements, notably the first and last of the great *C major Symphony*, it is in the subsidiary theme that Schubert discovers his chief symphonic material. This theme,

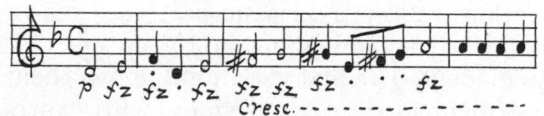

EXAMPLE 195.

in thirds on the violins against a rhythmic accompaniment, is songlike, but it has a rhythm which Schubert finds very useful in development (Example 196). The section devoted to this theme is long, and there is development as well as exposition as the music is spun out with harmonic and rhythmic devices. The interest of this theme is sufficient to continue throughout more than half of the development section. After a fortissimo climax, the triplet motive returns over a repeated A on the cello and leads to the recapitulation. In this section the first theme is omitted, and

EXAMPLE 196.

after the introductory fortissimo motive the bridge leads to D major. There the second theme again makes a lengthy appearance, with new development features. The coda brings about a dramatic reappearance of the triplet motive and of the melody of the first theme for a somber conclusion in D minor.

Second movement—Andante con moto in G minor

The song of Death now appears as the basis for a movement of five variations. It will be remembered that in the lied Death appears as friend and consoler to the frightened maiden, and it is in this mood that the music is conceived. It is dark and solemn, but in the last part, with its modulation to the major, it suggests compassion and tenderness. The variations follow the classic pattern, each one a unit of approximately equal length, and the outline of the theme is always evident. The first variation has the theme in triplet arrangement in the second violin with expressive melodic fragments above it on the first violin. The high register of the cello reveals it in the second variation, supported by fixed rhythms on the other instruments. In the third variation the theme is divided between the four instruments in a dynamic rhythmic ostinato. G major makes its appearance in the fourth variation with the melody in the second violin accompanied by a graceful triplet arabesque on the first violin. The last variation, again in minor, uses a variety of rhythmic designs and allocations of the melody among the instruments. In the second part the cello is especially emphasized. The rhythmic motion gradually disappears and the coda brings back the original sober disposition of the theme, first in the high register and then ending quietly with a cadence in G major.

Third movement—Scherzo—Allegro molto in D minor
The theme of the scherzo in octaves on the violins is vigorously rhythmic and not without sardonic implications (Example 197). Particularly in the second part, where it

EXAMPLE 197.

is played in octaves on viola and cello below heavily accented chords on the violins, does it seem to carry out the idea of demoniacal glee. The trio, by contrast, is gentle

EXAMPLE 198.

and reassuring, suggesting in its music the modulation to major of the theme of Death (Example 198).

Finale—Presto in D minor
The finale is said to have been cut down from its original length as a result of criticisms on the part of Schubert's

friends. This may account for its apparent wavering between rondo and sonata form design. There is a first (Example 199) and second theme (Example 200) with a closing melodic episode, after which an extended development section might be expected, but, instead, after a few

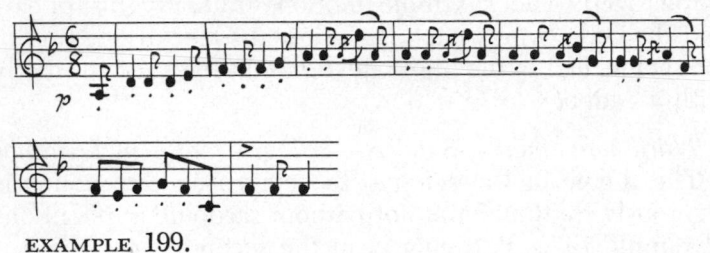

EXAMPLE 199.

rhythmic fragments of the first theme, the key of D minor returns and there is a full-fledged recapitulation. At the close of this the first theme reappears again in D minor, after the fashion of a rondo refrain. There is a rapid whirling coda on the material of the first theme. The feeling of

EXAMPLE 200.

the entire movement is that of the tarantella, with a persistent rhythm which yields only to the despairing cries of the second theme, derived from the music of the *Erl-King*.

BRAHMS—*Quintet for clarinet and strings in B minor, opus 115* (composed in 1891)

The *Clarinet Quintet* of Brahms, a work of the rarest quality, was inspired by the friendship of the composer for Richard Mühlfeld, a clarinetist of the Meiningen Orchestra, and is one of several chamber music works featuring this instrument which Brahms wrote in the last period of his career. The first impression one gains upon hearing it is the richness of its sound and the opulence of its melody. Closer examination reveals subtleties of detail and design which are of an almost alarming complexity. The fact that such an elaborate musical plan can succeed in sounding so disarmingly lovely at a first hearing is a proof of the mastery of style which Brahms achieved at the end of his career. This is truly the art which conceals art.

First movement—Allegro in B minor

The first theme, which is stated by first and second violins, contains two important motives. The first, harmonized in thirds and sixths, circling about the fifth and third degrees of the chord of B minor, serves to introduce an expressive melodic fragment which hovers about the lower D, B, and F sharp of the chord (Example 201). The clar-

EXAMPLE 201.

inet enters with a D major arpeggio and a melodic figure emerging from the first motive and descends unaccompanied to the low, dark register of the instrument. The viola and cello repeat the second motive and lead to a more fully developed exposition of this same motive in octaves on the violins, accompanied by a decorative pattern on the clarinet and viola. An abrupt change of rhythm, emphasized by silent beats, is introduced by the bridge (Example 202). This rhythm continues with the addition of triplet ornamentation to the key of D major, where the lyric subsidiary theme is introduced on the clarinet with inverted answer by the first violin (Example 203). This plan continues with subtle interweaving of the melody between clarinet and strings, the rhythm dying down in the central portion of the section, only to reassert itself in a passionate climax which tapers off to a moment of calm as the end of the exposition is reached.

The development section, introduced by a D major arpeggio on the clarinet, is in two parts, each marked by the

EXAMPLE 202.

flowering in rich lyricism of motives of the exposition. The first half is devoted to the circling motive of the introductory theme; the second is an amplification of the bridge theme. The rhythmic features persist in the lower strings as a background for an exquisite duet between the clarinet and the first violin. As the key of B minor is reached with a preparatory F sharp pianissimo in the cello, the second

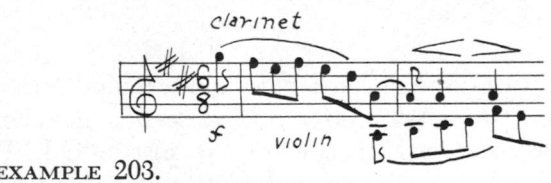

EXAMPLE 203.

motive of the first theme appears softly on the clarinet and leads to the return of the original theme and the recapitulation section. The portion before the bridge is shortened by the elimination of its rhapsodic elements. The bridge and lyric subsidiary material are essentially unchanged. The coda is a final development of the two motives of the principal theme and the movement ends on a note of pessimism.

Second movement—Adagio in B major

In this movement Brahms, inspired by the melancholy sweetness of the tone of the clarinet, has created a mood of rapture which suggests the aching loveliness of some of Schubert's music. It is in moments like this that Romanticism reaches its greatest heights of inspiration. A melody in five phrases, with clarinet and first violin alternating and

EXAMPLE 204.

then combining for the final phrase, is accompanied by muted strings with a rhythm of gentle restlessness (Example 204).

The contrasting middle section is a rhapsodic clarinet solo elaborating the first three notes of the melody of the first section. It has somewhat the passionate quality of Hungarian-gypsy violin music.

The third section is an almost exact reduplication of the first, with the addition of an expressive coda which recalls the stormy figure of the central section, now spent of its passion and imbued with the serene spirit of the introductory section.

Third movement—Andantino in D major, B minor

The form of this movement, often used to replace the traditional scherzo, is the especial property of Brahms. It begins with a simple, flowing melody of regular phrases in D major (Example 205). This is succeeded by a rapid,

EXAMPLE 205.

sparkling rondo in B minor, the refrain of which is an elaboration of the Andantino melody (Example 206). The

EXAMPLE 206.

original melody and the key of D major return for a brief third section, which concludes the movement.

Finale—Con moto in B minor

The finale is a set of five formal variations on a simple, folklike melody with a coda which brings a return of the principal theme of the first movement to serve as a cyclic conclusion to the whole work. There are other examples of this device in the *B flat Quartet* and the *First* and *Third Symphonies*.

The variations are simple and easy to follow. The first one is an elaboration of the theme on solo cello with accompanying harmonies on the other instruments. The second amplifies the melody on the first violin and clarinet with syncopated accompaniment. The third variation has the same disposition of solo and accompaniment, but induces a more elaborate melodic display. The fourth variation in B major divides the melodic line into a dialogue between the clarinet and first violin. The fifth variation is in triple rhythm with a return to B minor, and consists of a solo by the viola, later doubled by the second violin over pizzicato cello, and interrupted by ornamented melodic features on the clarinet and the first violin.

The coda, with the return of the motives from the first movement, serves to bring about a re-establishment of the note of thoughtful sadness which dominates the entire work.

The Romantic Sonata

During the Romantic period the sonata resembled a somewhat inconvenient conscience. The prestige of the classical sonata continued unabated, especially in the case of the Beethoven sonatas, which challenged the composers of the period to numerous attempts in this direction. However, as in the case of the symphony, the genius of the age was not in the line of symphonic architecture. The piano virtuoso style, the preoccupation with colorful harmony, and the songlike Italianate melodies were not elements lending themselves readily to absorption in the pattern of the sonata, even when programmatic subjects were renounced. As a result, the piano sonatas of the Romantic period contain more of the fantasy than of the sonata. Loose in construction, they depend for their interest upon their melodic charm, rich harmony, and keyboard effectiveness rather than upon their logic of design or thematic unity. An exception must be made of the remarkable one-movement *Sonata in B minor* of Liszt and the sonatas of Brahms, in which the classic order and proportion are successfully blended with Romantic idiom. In France, the Belgian-born César Franck, composer of a few highly successful symphonic and chamber works, wrote a sonata for violin and piano which exerted a wide influence and led to many imitations, especially in France.

Franck, an organist who was polyphonic minded because of long familiarity with the works of J. S. Bach, had a facility for such devices as canon and fugue which was unusual for his time. He also was devoted to the principles of form as exemplified in the works of Beethoven. He and his disciples attempted to continue Beethoven's ultimate conception of the sonata form in which emphasis was placed upon interinfluence of the movements, the cyclic sonata. His *Symphony in D minor*, his *Quartet* and *Quintet*, as well as the *Sonata for violin and piano*, all illustrate this tendency and were eventually highly successful, although not until after his death.

The carefully planned design of his works gives them solidity and clarity, but his harmonic style, influenced by Wagner and Liszt and excessively chromatic with frequent modulation, sometimes blurs the effect. His melodies are rhapsodic in late-nineteenth-century style, abounding in great climaxes and sometimes overly sweet. In the *Sonata for violin and piano*, however, he has succeeded in producing one of the truly great, post-Beethovenian compositions in symphonic style.

CÉSAR FRANCK—*Sonata for violin and piano in A major* (composed in 1886)

Three cyclic motives dominate the four movements of this work. The first motive, X, is a three-note pattern, an

EXAMPLE 207.

ascending and descending third with accent on the top note, which is stated at the beginning of the first movement (Example 207). The second, Y, an even pattern of four

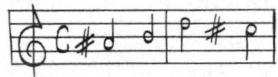

EXAMPLE 208.

tones, A sharp, B, D and C sharp, is the basis for the principal theme of the second movement (Example 208). The third, Z, first appears in the third movement. It is a melody based on the skip of the fourth and fifth degrees from F sharp (Example 209).

EXAMPLE 209.

First movement—Allegretto in A major
This is a symphonic song of two themes, more like a typical second movement than the customary opening al-

molto dolce

EXAMPLE 210.

legro. Theme X is expanded into an expressive melody on the violin against a quiet chordal accompaniment (Example 210). The second theme, also lyric, is confined to

EXAMPLE 211.

the piano (Example 211). These two themes alternate throughout the movement.

Second movement—Allegro in D minor
The second movement is a sonata allegro with an exposition, development, recapitulation, and coda based upon the classic model. The piano begins with a brilliant figuration based upon theme Y (Example 212), and leads to a first theme, similarly devised, stated on the violin. The bridge is based upon theme X from the first movement. The subsidiary themes are three, the first also derived from

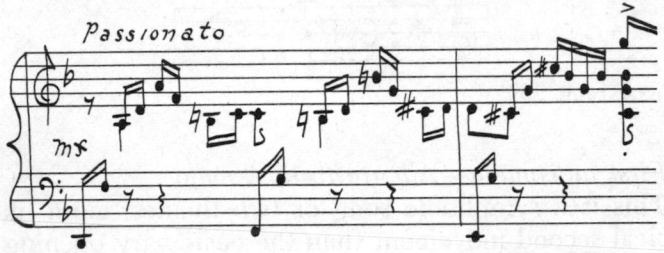

EXAMPLE 212.

Y, and the second and third lyric and impassioned melodies. In the development, the second (Example 213) of these melodies is combined with material derived from X after a recitativelike treatment of Y in its simplest form.

EXAMPLE 213.

The recapitulation follows the plan of the exposition and the animated coda deals with elements from X and Y.

Third movement—Recitativo—Fantasia, in D minor, F sharp minor

This movement is most unusual in that it has none of the character of minuet or scherzo, but serves as a reflective transition between the second movement and the finale. Also emphasizing its transitional character is the fact that it begins in one key and ends in another, paving the way for the tonality of the last movement. It is in three sections: the first section introduces several soliloquies on the violin based upon the theme X; the second section is an intense, lyric passage for violin accompanied by a simple arpeggio figure. First appears Y; than Z is introduced for the first time. A melodic fragment from this is then extended and

Z is repeated. The third section continues this broad melodic style with material from X and Z.

Fourth movement—Allegretto poco mosso in A major
The finale is a modified rondo with a refrain possibly originating in X but considerably changed in effect (Example 214). This refrain is always presented in canon on

EXAMPLE 214.

the octave between piano and violin. The effect of the canon is delightful, entirely unforced, and imposing no restrictions upon the tuneful, marchlike melody of the refrain. In between appearances of the refrain there are couplets in which Z, X, and Y form the basis of the material. The couplet after the third refrain is considerably extended in the manner of a development section. The fourth refrain, with changed ending, brings the work to a conclusion.

The Romantic Oratorio

One wonders at the reappearance from age to age of the baroque oratorio. In the Romantic period practically all traces of baroque conventions had disappeared. Instrumental music, as we have seen, had greatly changed in spirit and style long before, and now in the nineteenth century was undergoing further modifications. Opera was completely "modernized" and scarcely recognizable as an outgrowth of the earlier type. But the Handelian oratorio, complete with recitative, arias, and polyphonic choruses, continued to prosper—as, indeed, it still does, especially in England and America.

Naturally the audiences which support various kinds of music are not identical. There are separate audiences for opera, symphony, and chamber music, of widely differing tastes and musical receptivity. The oratorio audience, which with the Protestant church service keeps the oratorio in a flourishing state, is a very special group made up of the most conservative tastes and opinions. One suspects that it is recruited largely from friends and families of the singers. Now a stage full of happy and earnest oratorio singers must represent considerable potential ticket sales, and, if this is true, it does not make much difference what work the singers select to perform. Anyone who has ever sung in a chorus knows what fun it is to sing Handel. The music is easy to grasp, fits the voice well, and fine effects are achieved with a minimum of professional skill. The plan of the Handel oratorio is ideal for the ordinary amateur singing group. All the hard parts are taken by professional soloists, who can be imported for the occasion. Therefore the chorus can make a public appearance after long, leisurely preparation and add on at the last moment the final professional touches. Thus the never-ending vogue of the oratorio and its unchanging aspect must be attributed, at least partially, to the large number of amateur choral societies which are to be found in almost every community.

The fraternity of oratorio lovers discovered in Mendelssohn a composer after its own heart. His *Saint Paul* and *Elijah,* written in 1836 and 1846, respectively, were immediately accepted as worthy to stand beside the works of Handel and Haydn, and have never lost their popularity.

Other composers of the nineteenth century, among them Schubert, Spohr, Schumann (with a secular text, *Paradise and the Peri*, after Thomas Moore's *Lalla Rookh*), Liszt, Berlioz, Dvořák, Gounod, and Elgar, contributed to oratorio, but none of them achieved the same shattering success. Such works as Rossini's *Stabat Mater* and the *Requiems* of Brahms and Verdi, which are often sung by choral societies and are very popular, fall into different categories.

The English fondness for Mendelssohn is explained in interesting fashion by Dr. Ernest Walker in an article on oratorio in *Grove's Dictionary*. He says: "Mendelssohn's religious music gives the impression that he lived in untroubled unconsciousness of anything outside mid-19th century Protestantism. . . . He appealed directly and with absolute sincerity to a particular form of religious sentiment which, from early Victorian days, has lain deep in the heart of the average Englishman and Englishwoman; he is the only great artist, in words, or color, or music, who has ever touched this emotional spring, and he has had, and still has, his reward."

The music of Mendelssohn has had its ups and downs. The *Songs Without Words* for piano were played too much for their own good and became rather a nuisance. On the other hand, the incidental music to Shakespeare's *Midsummer Night's Dream* was equally popular but never seems to have lost its freshness and sparkle. The symphonies, particularly the brilliant *Italian Symphony in A major,* appear to be coming back into favor after a period of neglect. Among the concertos, the famous *Violin Concerto in E minor* has always been an indispensable part of the soloist's repertory. The chamber music, particularly the youthful string octet, is again being heard more often. Mendelssohn's success was so great during his lifetime that it was only natural for a reaction against him to come afterward. Now that this has come and gone we can see more clearly that, in spite of the superficial quality of some of his music, at its worst commonplace and trite, there is grace and beauty and remarkable skill and craftsmanship in his writing.

One of the things which makes us impatient with Mendelssohn, and it applies even to his fine oratorio *Elijah*, is that a great deal of the wishy-washy, palavering church music of the late nineteenth century and today is directly inspired by Mendelssohn's style. It is a far cry from the mystical beauty of the Renaissance motet and Mass and the forthright melodies of the Protestant chorale, this sentimental and sugary lyricism in which religious feeling is reduced to a comfortable expression of domestic virtues, sanctimonious and saccharine. This hypocritically pious attitude infected the music of Gounod and Franck and is present even in such a great work as Wagner's *Parsifal*. We should be grateful to such modern composers as Stravinsky and Hindemith, who in the *Symphonie de Psaumes* and *Mathis der Maler* have taken the chimes and the *vox humana* out of religious music.

MENDELSSOHN—*Elijah* (composed in 1846)

The book of *Elijah* is magnificently dramatic material. Mendelssohn, with the assistance of two friends, one a poet-diplomat, the other a churchman, compiled the libretto from the First Book of Kings and other Biblical passages, and it was prepared in translation for a first performance which the composer conducted at Birmingham. Various scenes from the life of the prophet are linked together: the prophecy of the drought, the raising of the widow's son, the competition with the priests of Baal and the coming of the rain in answer to Elijah's prayer, the persecution of Queen Jezebel, the sojourn in the desert when the Lord appears, not in the earthquake, nor the tempest, but in a still small voice, and finally Elijah's triumph and ascent to heaven in a fiery chariot.

These scenes are set with spirit by the composer in music

which is often vivid and exciting. One might wish for more force and color in some of the episodes dealing with the ungodly, and less prettiness in the music of Elijah and the angels, but there is no denying the effectiveness of the writing for both chorus and orchestra. Mendelssohn's enthusiasm for Bach's choral music (it was he who organized and conducted the performance of St. *Matthew Passion* in 1829, which led to the Bach revival) gave him an insight into baroque polyphonic style. Although his polyphony is less strong and independent than that of Brahms, the choruses of *Elijah* abound in imitative devices which indicate a mastery of contrapuntal technique unusual for the period. There is also a good example of instrumental fugue in the overture.

None of the choruses is at present available on recordings; hence our examples must be limited to some of the familiar solos and one double quartet, a rather inadequate expression of the dramatic quality of the work.

Part One. Air for Tenor—If with all your hearts (Obadiah)

Obadiah counsels the people, who are distressed at the continuation of the drought, to repent, forsake idolatry, and return to God, for Elijah has sealed the heavens because of their transgressions. This recitative is followed by a simple air in three sections, the first part of which is a consoling melody to the words of God: "If with all your hearts ye truly seek Me, ye shall surely find Me." The middle portion, set to different music, expresses a strong desire to find Him and come into His presence. This is followed gratefully by a return of the first melody of re-assurance.

Part One. Double Quartet of Angels—For He shall give His angels charge

Elijah is ordered by an angel to proceed to the brook of Cherith to drink its waters, and the Lord has commanded the ravens to feed him. This situation is followed by a setting of the Ninety-first Psalm in which a quartet of women's voices is alternated and blended with a male quartet with a charming antiphonal effect and the richness of harmony which comes from the eight separate parts. This is typical Mendelssohnian sweetness.

Part One. Air for Bass—Lord God of Abraham (Elijah)

This comes after a most dramatic scene in which the prophets of Baal call upon their God for a sign and are mocked by Elijah, who tells them to call him louder. There are several exciting choruses as the prophets are goaded to new efforts, but to no avail. Now Elijah calls the people together and makes his appeal to God, which is eventually answered by the fire descending from heaven. In this great moment Elijah's prayer, upon which so much depends, seems on the tuneful rather than the dramatic side. It is, however, dignified and vocally effective, a melody which has been widely known and loved. Mendelssohn has woven skillfully the motive of the refrain into the texture of the melody and the accompaniment.

Part Two. Soprano Aria—Hear ye, Israel

The second part of the oratorio begins with the principal soprano solo of the work, set to passages from *Isaiah*, an aria in two parts, an adagio in B minor linked by a short recitative to an allegro maestoso in B major. The first part, "Hear Ye, Israel. Hear what the Lord speaketh, 'O hadst thou heeded My commandments,' " is in the nature of a persistent lament, slightly Oriental in flavor, in which the motive to the words "Hear Ye Israel" appears frequently in both melody and accompaniment. The second part of the aria, which is concerned with words of reassurance—"I am He that comforteth: Be not afraid for I am thy God and will strengthen thee"—is a three-part, symmetrical air with an accompaniment of martial rhythm. Although effective, it has less personality than the first part of the aria.

Part Two. Bass Aria—It is enough (Elijah)

Persecuted by Jezebel, Elijah is warned by Obadiah that an attempt is to be made upon his life and that he must hasten into the wilderness. Discouraged at the sins of the people who have broken the covenants of the Lord and have slain His prophets and now, because of his zeal, are seeking his life, Elijah asks for release in death. This aria, one of the most famous solos ever written for bass, is in three parts, beginning with an expressive adagio melody based upon a descending minor chord, accompanied by a funereal rhythm. After a climax upon the words "My days are but vanity," the music changes into an animated middle section in major, in which the prophet is in a more militant mood. After another climax on the words "and they seek my life to take it away," the lamentation of the first part returns in abbreviated form for a conclusion of deep dejection.

The Romantic Opera

Three great operatic currents flowed in the nineteenth century, culminating in the dramatic works of the composers of Italy, Germany, and France. The traditional opera of the Italians was continued in unbroken succession, through the works of such composers as Rossini, Bellini, and Donizetti, to reach its fullest expression in the operas of Giuseppe Verdi. German Romantic opera, receiving its first impetus from the operas of Weber, was transformed by the unique gifts of Richard Wagner into a special type of opera, called by the composer "music drama." French opera, which for many years represented a struggle between the native vein of opéra comique and the somewhat hybrid and pretentious style of the Paris Grand Opera, was refreshed in the closing years of the century by the appearance of a genuinely national movement, represented by the lyric operas of Gounod, Massenet, and others. The unique dramatic opera *Carmen,* a work of Bizet, which made its appearance at this time, is far in advance of the general level of this movement and did not create a school of opera in France proper.

MUSIC DRAMA

Wagner is the ideal embodiment of the Romantic composer, an intellectual and artistic leader, a revolutionary with the strength not only to destroy but to build, whose musical gifts included a melodic and harmonic style of great expressive power and personality, mastery of the orchestra and of formal organization. He brings to the musical stage the German symphonic art as developed by Haydn, Mozart, and Beethoven. In Wagner's music dramas Romanticism reaches its fullest expression, and so great is his power that he is the dominating force in the latter half of the century.

Acknowledging the fashionable extramusical interests as of primary importance, Wagner is not content with Liszt's solution in the symphonic poem. Whatever is to be represented in music must, for him, be seen on the stage. Opera, however, with its patchwork of recitative and aria, and lack of musical or dramatic continuity, is not artistically satisfying. He conceives a music drama which is to unite the arts of drama, poetry, design, and music with complete expression for each. This drama must address the feeling rather than the understanding, and therefore its action must transcend the world of reality. For this reason the mythological is preferable to the customary historical subject, with its emphasis upon everyday detail. The unifying force is to be the orchestra, with its power of uttering the unspeakable. With this avowed artistic plan, Wagner wrote and composed his later operas, the *Nibelungen Ring, Tristan and Isolde,* and *Parsifal. The Mastersingers of Nuremberg,* although conceived as a comic opera, and therefore in a different category, has many features which resemble the music dramas.

WAGNER—*Tristan and Isolde* (composed in 1857–1859)

This work was regarded by Wagner as the fullest realization of his artistic aims. The subject is based upon a medieval legend. Tristan, knight of King Mark of Cornwall, is entrusted with the mission of bringing Isolde, princess of Ireland, as a bride for the elderly king. In a previous encounter Tristan has killed in battle Morold, betrothed of the princess, and, himself wounded, has been nursed back to health by Isolde, although she is aware of his identity. Now furious at his treachery in betraying her into a loveless marriage, she challenges him to drink a death potion with her. Her attendant Brangaena substitutes a love potion, and the love between Tristan and Isolde, which hitherto has been unacknowledged, now turns to a mad passion which sweeps away all scruples of honor and loyalty. Arrived in Cornwall, where Isolde is married to the king, the lovers are betrayed in a tryst and their illicit passion discovered. Tristan is wounded by the knight Melot and taken home to Brittany by his faithful servant Kurvenal. The latter hopes vainly that Isolde will follow and once again effect her magical cure. Meanwhile Brangaena has confessed her part in the affair and the king forgives and wishes to reunite the lovers. But the ship which finally brings Isolde to Tristan arrives too late and he dies in her arms. Isolde, believing that she will be reunited with Tristan in the love that can find its perfect expression only in death itself, sings the rapturous song of love death and dies in passionate transport.

Each scene in *Tristan and Isolde* has a musical as well as a dramatic unity, based upon themes stated in the orchestra and developed in accordance with symphonic procedure. These themes, also called "leitmotives," are often associated with dramatic ideas, and, as such, serve to recall events and situations from one scene to another. Each act is divided into a number of short scenes, new themes appearing in every scene as the main source of the music.

Prelude

Four principal themes, used throughout the opera, are introduced in the Prelude. The first, which may be divided

EXAMPLE 215.

melodically into two parts accompanied by a haunting succession of harmonies, suggests the underlying feeling of magic or enchantment in the drama (Example 215); it

EXAMPLE 216.

appears in nearly every scene. The second theme, associated with the lovers' glance, is an ascending melody of three sequences and descent (Example 216). The third and fourth themes are related to the love potion and de-

EXAMPLE 217.

EXAMPLE 218.

liverance by death (Examples 217 and 218). These themes, in extension and combination, with two great climaxes, provide the music of the Prelude.

Love music from Act II
This scene, the central portion of the second act, reveals the secret meeting of the lovers at night in the garden of the palace. The king has gone on a hunting expedition and Brangaena is watching on a tower above. The first part is a tender love duet, a hymn to the friendly night. The

EXAMPLE 219.

music is chiefly based upon a two-note succession, but is more of an organized melody than the balance of the scene, more dependent upon the singers' parts and less upon the orchestra (Example 219). Wagner has used this same music in a solo song outside the opera, *Träume*. A transition passage is furnished by the song of Brangaena from the tower. This music recalls the love duet and anticipates the next theme. One of the most hauntingly beautiful parts of the opera, it leads to the statement of a new theme of love by the orchestra and to a new section (Example 220). In this part the singers play only a subsidiary role in the music, which is a series of elaborations or variations of the new theme. The effect is not unlike the slow movement in variation form from a symphony.

EXAMPLE 220.

Isolde's love death

The final scene of the opera is the rapturous song which Isolde sings over the body of her lover. The music is a repetition of the end of the second act love scene, in which the lovers are surprised by the return of the king. There

EXAMPLE 221.

it suddenly breaks off at its climax, but now the climax, skillfully prepared by the composer, is reached with overwhelming effect as the opera ends. There are two themes which serve as the basis of this music, love death and

EXAMPLE 222.

rapture, both introduced in the previous act (Examples 221 and 222). Curiously enough, although the voice part is most effective it may be omitted and the accompaniment played alone, with almost equal impressiveness. As such, it often appears, following the Prelude, at orchestra concerts.

NINETEENTH-CENTURY ITALIAN OPERA

Opera is a natural form of musical expression in Italy, for the Italian language lends itself well to singing. Early in the seventeenth century it took hold of the popular imagination and became a great national art. But the immense popularity of opera was not limited to Italy; it was practically a world conquest. Italian opera troupes, composed of great operatic voices, dominated the musical stage all over Europe, even in Russia and England, and the influence extended to North and South America. Such famous German and Austrian composers as Handel, Gluck, and Mozart composed the majority of their operas, after the Italian model, to Italian libretti.

Giuseppe Verdi therefore had an old and satisfying tradition upon which to build. There was no urge to reform a medium which the public liked and which was a perfect vehicle for his talents. His operas were great successes both in Italy and abroad. It never occurred to him that he should be an artistic or intellectual leader, for he was content to function as a composer, ready to set in workmanlike fashion libretti, good and bad, as they came along.

Verdi was near the end of his life and his composing days were apparently over when the great Wagnerian success established Romantic music drama as a deadly European rival. Wagner's champions asserted that Italian opera was now an obsolete art, and Verdi was pounced upon as the chief victim of the attack. Whether it was the pressure of youthful Romanticists in Italy which made him restless, or merely that Boïto, who was both composer and poet, came along with an excellent libretto that called for a different type of setting, the fact is that at the mellow age of seventy-four he wrote a new opera in greatly modified style, *Otello*. This was followed, also with Boïto's collaboration, by *Falstaff*, composed when he was eighty. These two operas may be considered as the peak of Romanticism in Italy, and although they have never been as popular as Verdi's earlier works they are regarded today as his masterpieces.

In these operas the old division into aria and recitative practically disappears, and the form is arioso, a dramatic melodic style midway between the two, which allows for continuous dramatic action and greater theatrical plausibility. Formal songs, choruses, and duets occasionally appear, but are rarely in symmetrical patterns and are planned as a part of the action. The texture of the music continues to be melodic, not symphonic, and the leitmotive is not used to further musical or dramatic unity. The principal interest lies in the voice rather than in the orchestra, which, although treated imaginatively with additional dramatic effect, never robs the singer of rightful climax or forces him into a role of secondary importance. Verdi's great power lies in the vigor of his melody, often of passionate intensity, always effective in characterization. His characters are, above all, human, and in their singing they are eloquent of their essentially human feelings. One might claim that Verdi with his music has illumined and vivified the drama of Shakespeare. His interpretation may be Italian rather than English, but it is moving and absorbing in the theater, a collaboration between drama and music rarely achieved in the literature of the opera.

In the later style of Verdi, as represented by *Otello* and *Falstaff*, the music is so inseparably linked to the stage that excerpts from these operas suffer considerably in performance apart from the theater, particularly upon phonograph records. To gain an understanding of the remarkable dramatic power of this music, the listener must allow his imagination free play in re-creating the accompanying stage picture. Even then there is a great loss of the momentum and power of the works as they appear in their entirety in performance.

GIUSEPPE VERDI—*Otello* (composed in 1887)

Boïto's libretto follows the outline of Shakespeare's play but reduces it to four acts and somewhat simplifies the action. The essential features of the story and the principal characters are unchanged.

Act I—Inaffia l'ugola

Iago's plan to ruin Cassio is first to make him drunk, then to provoke him to combat and cause his arrest. This is a drinking song in which Iago is joined by the company of soldiers, sailors, and women. It is bluff, masculine music, giving a clear picture of honest John Iago and his friends making a night of it.

Act I—Duet—Scendean sulle mie tenebra

The rioters have been dispersed and Otello and Desdemona, alone upon the stage, sing of their love. The music follows the meaning of the words; the style is arioso rather than melody of formal design, a heightened musical speech of great intensity.

Act II—Desdemona rea

Iago has disturbed Otello's mind with insinuations about Cassio. Desdemona innocently pleads that he be released, and the jealous husband sends her away in a rage. Now he sings, in an outburst of suffering, of his betrayal and the death of his ambitions as a soldier. The first part is a dramatically accompanied recitative punctuated by Otello's cries and Iago's asides, then a passionate melody sung by Otello, which turns into an ironic martial air. It is expressive of uncontrolled passion and the heroic quality of Otello, the soldier.

Act II—Era la notte

This song is a masterly expression of the deceitful character of Iago. He is telling Otello of Cassio's dream of Desdemona, the unconscious words which reveal his guilty love. When this "proof" is accepted by Otello, Iago tells of the handkerchief seen in Cassio's possession which Otello had given to Desdemona. This provokes a fresh outburst of rage. The music of the dream is an unusual combination of attractive melody with an unpleasant underlying feeling, possibly contributed by the harmony and orchestration.

Act II—Ah mille vite

This duet continues the preceding scene. Otello, now livid with rage, swears revenge. Iago, pretending to be equally outraged, pledges his devotion to avenge Otello's honor. The music is in the traditional style of tenor and baritone duet so often followed by Verdi. It is in three verses with the same music repeated, the two voices combining for the last verse. Although more conventional than other scenes, this ending of the second act has great power, and the sonorous voices of the two men achieve a stunning dramatic climax.

Act IV—Mia madre

Desdemona, despairing now of convincing Otello of her innocence, has been savagely ordered to bed. As Emilia, her attendant, does her hair she sings the old willow song which her mother taught her. Verdi has caught the feeling of the old poem and the poignance of the situation. Mixed with its pathos, there is a quality of childlike innocence about the music. Just at the end, when Desdemona calls farewell to Emilia, her terror is vividly expressed.

Act IV—Niun mi tema

Otello has murdered Desdemona and the terrible deception of Iago has been revealed. Now at first numbed by the shock, then grief stricken as he sees Desdemona dead, he seizes a dagger, stabs himself, and kisses her farewell. The music ends with a recollection of the love duet from the first act. The style is arioso, melodramatic perhaps, but a moving expression of the scene.

FRENCH LYRIC OPERA

From the outset opera in France tended to diverge from the prevailing Italian style. The French language, not so well adapted to singing as the Italian, was at least partially responsible for the less opulent vocal tone of the French singer. As a result, French opera could not rely so completely upon the intoxicating sound of the human voice, which in Italy was sufficient to compensate for all manner of other shortcomings, dramatic and musical. French opera, on the other hand, stressed unity between text and music, quality of text, and dramatic plausibility. The virtuoso singing element of the Italian opera was replaced by the prodigality and technical virtuosity of the ballet, which were almost always present in French grand opera. The more modest opéra comique, the French counterpart of the German Singspiel and Italian opera buffa, paid little attention to virtuosity, but actually included spoken dialogue and emphasized the dramatic rather than the spectacular.

The operas of the late-nineteenth-century French composers are notable for their essentially lyric style, not the passionate melodic outpouring of Verdi, nor the ornamental vocalism of Rossini, but a direct, rather more discreet type of melody often of somewhat cloying sweetness. These operas do not reflect, except in the most superficial manner, the symphonic style of Wagner. They are seldom "through composed," and consist for the most part of separate airs and ensembles linked together either by recitative or by spoken dialogue.

BIZET—*Carmen* (composed in 1875)

Carmen cannot be classified as a typical French opera of the period because, musically and dramatically, it is more vivid and there is a far greater degree of unity between these elements. It is one of those rare operas which everyone finds irresistible because of its dramatic story, fascinating Spanish color, and, above all, abundance of lovely music. The libretto, based upon a short story of Prosper Mérimée, has as its central idea a love episode of savage brutality presented with all its realism. Carmen, a young gypsy worker in a cigarette factory in Seville, is arrested in the course of a fight with one of her companions. She is placed in charge of the corporal of dragoons, Don José, a respectable young man already betrothed to his village sweetheart, Micaela. Carmen extricates herself from this situation by exercising her wiles upon him and he lets her escape. From this point on the young man is marked for destruction. Infatuated by Carmen, he renounces his betrothed, takes arms against his superior officer, deserts, and joins the band of gypsy smugglers with which Carmen is associated. But she, heartless and fickle, has already transferred her affections to the toreador Escamillo, and Don José, helpless in his infatuation, ruined and bitter, finally stabs her to death as she waits outside the arena for her triumphant new lover.

The musical characterization of the opera is remarkable, particularly in the parts of the two women, Carmen and Micaela. Simple and direct, the melodic style is colored by the Spanish folk song and is invariably dramatic. The orchestration is transparent and discreet but notable for its variety of instrumental color. The purely instrumental parts, such as the prelude and interludes, are full of charm and are often performed separately in the concert hall. Intended to be spoken, the original dialogue often appears as musical recitative, especially at performances in this country.

Act I—Habanera (sung by Carmen)
It is the recess hour in the factory. Carmen, surrounded by admiring young men, has her eye on Don José, on guard

outside the factory. She sings this seductive song, which tells of the accessibility of her heart but of the danger involved for anyone upon whom she may fix her affections.

Act I—Seguidilla (sung by Carmen)
Carmen, now bound as a prisoner, flirts with Don José and invites him to meet her at the tavern of Lillas Pastias to dance and drink manzanilla if he will only let her go. She suggests that her heart, for the moment, is available for the asking. Don José attempts to silence the song but infatuation gradually overcomes his sense of duty and he looses the cord that binds her arms.

Act II—Gypsy song (sung by Carmen, Frasquita, Mercedes)
At Lillas Pastias' inn, Carmen and two gypsy companions are entertaining several officers, singing and dancing to the accompaniment of guitar and tambourine. The excitement of the music increases as the pace grows swifter and hotter.

Act II—Toreador song
The entrance of Escamillo, the self-assured and complacent hero of the bull ring, is too familiar to require comment. His sentiments describe the love conquests which invariably follow those over the bull.

Act II—Quintet (sung by Frasquita, Mercedes, Carmen, El Remendado, El Dancaïro)
This delightful concerted piece is sung by two of the gypsy smugglers in the act of persuading three of the girls to join them on an especially difficult undertaking. Two of them are quite willing, but Carmen, who is in love with Don José, would rather stay behind. The music is of a sparkling, mischievous quality, suggesting that smuggling has its lighter moments.

Act II—Je vais danser (sung by Carmen)
Carmen now completes the conquest of Don José by singing and dancing to the castanets. Her song gains vastly

by having no words. The melody is more suggestive without them. Don José is properly appreciative, but the music is interrupted by the sound of the bugle calling retreat from the distant garrison. Carmen mocks her lover's conscience. He cannot really love her if he allows himself to be distracted by anything so trivial.

Act II—La fleur que tu m'avais jetée (sung by Don José)

This is Don José's incandescent reply. There is no question of the extent and depth of his passion, which has conquered all his scruples and loyalties.

Entr'acte

The entr'acte between Acts II and III is an example of the exquisite instrumental style of Bizet, so economical in means and melodically so beguiling. It begins with a melody on the flute accompanied by harp. This is joined in polyphonic imitation by the clarinet, with soft, supporting string harmonies. Other instruments are added as the dialogue continues to the end.

Act III—Sextet and chorus

This concerted piece by six smugglers, now including both Carmen and Don José, accompanied by chorus and orchestra, gives the inside story of the life of a smuggler. They are encamped in the mountains, awaiting action. The music is sinister but not at all disturbing, a picturesque rather than a realistic treatment of the idea.

Act IV—Entrance of the Bullfighters—Les voici

This is an instrumental march of festive spirit, with a chorus shouting approval as the bullfighters pass by on their way to the arena. It is also used in the Prelude to the opera.

Act IV—Duet—Si tu m'aimes, Carmen (sung by Escamillo and Carmen)

At the end of the procession Escamillo arrives with great

acclaim and addresses himself to Carmen in this intense love song. She joins with him in a pledge of eternal devotion. A few moments later Don José, who is lurking near by, in a frenzy of despair kills her at the instant of Escamillo's victory in the arena.

6 *THE POST-ROMANTIC and MODERN PERIODS*

Introduction

WHEN we come to consider our own age many difficulties confront us. Is it really a separate and distinct period in the history of music and, if it is, when did it begin and what are its distinguishing characteristics? Doubtless in every age that we have considered there existed both the new and the continuation of the old, and only as perspective is afforded by the passing of the years does the line of demarcation clearly appear. There are new and important influences in the music of today which are apparent to every thoughtful person, but the conservative musician (and the large public is inclined to agree with him) usually dismisses them as eccentricities rather than as an indicated path for the future. He distinguishes between modern music, which means music dutifully observant of nineteenth-century tradition but written in this century, and modernistic music, which like totalitarianism and other contemporary ills is subversive of all that is fine in the past, and must be strongly opposed.

It is perfectly true that music does not have to be "different" in order to be good. Bach and Brahms do not seem any less great to us today because they were attacked by their contemporaries as reactionaries. But it is also true that artistic standards are continually shifting, and the ideals and conventions of one age gradually are modified so that each succeeding period presents a different aspect. The level may go up or down, but there is usually a period of change and unrest as the new wars upon the old, succeeded by a period of consolidation as the new discoveries are explored and turned to artistic profit. Thus, in spite of the musical die-hards who greet each new symphony with "it is not as great as Beethoven," or each contemporary opera with "it is far short of Wagner," we shall consider that the modern period, which begins shortly before the turn of the century, despite all its confusion and its many disappointing qualities, is slowly evolving new standards by which the music of our age will eventually be judged.

As Beethoven cast his shadow over the entire Romantic period, so Wagner may be said to have influenced the age succeeding him. There is this important difference, however, in the two situations. The Romanticists found in Beethoven a constant inspiration, frequently embarrassing because in spite of their best efforts they failed to measure up to his greatness, but they were not impelled to rebel against him. Post-Wagnerian composers, on the other hand, soon found that extension of the Wagner aesthetics and style led the art of music into nothing but grandiose and empty rhetoric. Wagner's musical personality was so individual and colorful that his imitators were driven to despair in attempting to establish a style of their own. There was nothing to do but to repudiate Romanticism, bag and baggage, and to find alternative paths for music to follow.

In the modern period we discover a number of trends, passionately defended with all manner of artistic and scientific theories, some of them aimed at destroying each other, but all united against Wagner, the common enemy. Many of these movements originated in Paris, to which the center of interest shifted at the turn of the century.

The first successful anti-Romantic movement was Impressionism, of which the leading exponent was Debussy. Impressionism in music was allied to a similar movement in painting and in literature. Opposed to intellectualism, overstatement, rhetoric, complexity, and the grand manner, it substituted a music of greater simplicity with more reliance upon purely sensuous effect, unpretentious in aim, and smaller in proportion. In the hands of a master like Debussy this style proved most effective, but no other composer was equally successful. Impressionism made a spirited stand against the enemy, but was soon itself the subject of attack from many quarters.

Directed against the sophistication of Impressionism came the Primitives. This movement was a persistence of the folk-song influence of late Romanticism. Emphasis changed, however, from melody to rhythm, and lyricism was displaced by a cultivation of the purely rhythmic, based upon patterns unfamiliar and outlandish. In this movement American dance music has exerted an obvious influence, but primitive music of all races and localities was sought after and was pressed into service. The culmination of this style came in Stravinsky's remarkable ballet *Le Sacre du Printemps.*

Another group in Paris, centering about Erik Satie, and also associated with parallel literary and art activities, was known as the Dadaist movement. Its aim appears to have been merely to deflate Romanticism and Impressionism by laughing at them. This music was simple and short, and by its grotesque malarrangement and conscious vulgarity it poked fun at everyone, including itself.

Meanwhile in Vienna Teutonic intellectualism was hard at work to find a substitute for defunct Romanticism. The extreme chromaticism of Wagner and Franck gradually obscured the tonal foundations of music so that they became practically nonexistent. Atonal music, or music completely emancipated from adherence to the diatonic scale and traditional chord sequence, came into being. This music was entirely free, but soon found its freedom rather irksome because it lacked direction. The public was anything but pleased at the result, which was often ugly and chaotic, although sometimes interesting in its new sonorities. A solution of the problem was offered by Arnold Schoenberg, who devised a new system based upon the chromatic scale, the "twelve tone row." This system has attracted the favorable notice of some talented composers, who have incorporated it into their works, but so far they have interested only a relatively small group in the musical results.

Finally there appeared the Neoclassic movement, an attempt to escape Romanticism by the deliberate cultivation of baroque and classic features of style. The spectacular conversion of Stravinsky, who repudiated the earlier style of his successful ballets, attracted attention to this movement, but it was probably merely a continuation of the sober strain of classicism that we have observed throughout the Romantic period, with some atonal features and devices of the baroque added to give it a modern cast of countenance. Paul Hindemith is one of the most successful composers of this type of music.

The modern period is therefore an age of experiment and unrest. There have been some composers who have gone calmly about their business, writing music of the traditional variety as if nothing had happened—Sibelius, for instance. Others have borrowed such discoveries of the innovators as have appealed to them, with equanimity and discretion. For the most part, however, the composer of the twentieth century has had a rather anxious time. He is aware of the public's preference for the music of the past and its dislike of the modern idiom, but he realizes that music is a changing art, now expanding, now contracting, but never standing still. So far there has been no composer of the new style sufficiently great in stature to lead the way. We can perhaps be comforted by the fact that each new age develops slowly, and the confusion of today may be the necessary prelude to a great new music of the future.

There must be some connection between the troubled modern spirit in art and the disordered and chaotic world conditions which are undermining many hitherto valid social conceptions. In music it is increasingly clear that patronage is shifting from the wealthy to the masses. We still have wealthy guarantors of opera and symphony concerts, but they are becoming fewer and less influential. In the totalitarian countries music, like everything else, is under the direct control and subvention of the governments. One would never have believed a few years ago that the United States government would ever concern itself with the arts, but we have seen the Works Program, with a well-coordinated relief plan for orchestral musicians, take a stand in support of American compositions—a stand which has exerted an important artistic influence upon the country as a whole. Recently, in New York City, festivals of American music have been conducted under the auspices of the municipal radio station. The government of Finland, by an annual allowance, has made possible the career of Sibelius. Commercial radio stations have appeared in the guise of music patrons by commissioning new works from contemporary composers. Music is probably understood and loved more widely than ever before in the history of the world. The spread of music education continues in schools, conservatories, and colleges, and the development of mechanical music via the radio and the phonograph is responsible for the constant growth of new audiences. Democratic patronage inclines to conservatism, but it also lays the basis for the cultivation of new music in opening new fields and uses for music which cannot always be supplied with the music of the past. The history of the art shows that musical composition flourishes best when the demand is the greatest.

It is difficult to generalize about the characteristics of

modern music because of the variety of styles. The most apparent feature of the new music is that it is more "dissonant." Dissonance, however, is a changing attribute. Our ears become accustomed to it rapidly. Its chief value is that when in juxtaposition with "consonance" it makes music move. The tendency today is away from the continuous dissonance of the period before 1930 toward a more judicious mixture. In post-Impressionistic music counterpoint plays a larger role than formerly and the colorful harmonies of the Romantic period are replaced by greater solidity of texture, resembling baroque style. Instrumental virtuosity has gone forward, especially on the wind and brass instruments, under the impetus of popular dance music. On the other hand, there is a greater demand for ensemble music which can be played by amateurs, and side by side with professional music of extreme difficulty may be found important modern compositions in a simpler style. The modern symphony orchestra required for the works of Strauss, Debussy, Stravinsky (in his ballets), and Ravel is larger than ever, but there is also a tendency toward a smaller "chamber orchestra" resembling the ensembles of the baroque and classic periods.

Practically all types of music of the past are being written today. Not only have the classic and Romantic symphonies, concertos, overtures, symphonic poems, suites, and chamber music interested the twentieth-century composer, but there has been a revival of earlier forms of the baroque, such as the fugue, the passacaglia, and the concerto grosso. The modern composer has discovered an important new field in the short ballet, thanks to the interest which dancers and choreographers have shown in contemporary music. Many of these ballets or ballet pantomimes, originating as stage pieces, have won a place in the concert repertory.

In the field of opera, particularly in this country, the modern composer has been less welcome. Although some of the Italians, among them Mascagni, Leoncavallo, and

Puccini, together with the operas of Richard Strauss, have been frequently performed, they seem to belong to an earlier age, and the only significant contemporary opera which has been universally accepted is Debussy's *Pelléas and Mélisande*.

Choral music, encouraged by the revival of interest in polyphony, has received more attention recently than in the past, particularly in England and America. As in the Romantic period, this activity is usually apart from the church, but there have been a number of successful choral works by contemporary composers, both sacred and secular, accompanied and *a cappella*.

The musical situation in the United States today is extremely interesting and full of promise. For many years we have had the benefit of the services of the greatest European artists, who have made our concerts the envy of the world. Recently these artists and a majority of the most important European composers have shifted their activities permanently to this country. A few years ago this would not have been an unmixed blessing, for the American public has been disinclined to welcome its own artists and composers, and such a deluge of talent might have discouraged native efforts. The public, however, has gradually discovered that American artists are not necessarily inferior to the European variety, and some of the most popular, particularly singers, are American. Our greatest lack at the moment is American conductors, but there is reason to believe that with so many conductors needed for symphony concerts and for radio the Americans will get a chance, if only through the law of supply and demand. The public is increasingly interested in the American composer, not because it has been told that it should be, although this must help, but because it has found that, if it must listen to contemporary music, the native brand is as acceptable as any other, and the American composer, much better educated than heretofore, seems to be making the most of his opportunity.

The preparation of a list of important composers of the modern period is even more difficult than in the case of the Romantics. The following are some of the well-known composers of the twentieth century. Some of them might well be classified as belated Romantics. In the case of the American composers the list is longer, but probably too long in places and too short in others because it is impossible to determine the eventual importance of the many American composers who are being performed today.

Some Composers of the Modern Period

German and Austrian

Richard Strauss, 1864–1949
Arnold Schoenberg, 1874–1951
Alban Berg, 1885–1935
Anton Webern, 1883–1945
Paul Hindemith, 1895–

French

Claude Debussy, 1862–1918
Erik Satie, 1866–1925
Maurice Ravel, 1875–1937
Darius Milhaud, 1892–
Arthur Honegger, 1892–1955

Russian

Nicholas Rimsky-Korsakov, 1844–1908
Sergei Rachmaninov, 1873–1943
Igor Stravinsky, 1882–
Sergei Prokofiev, 1891–1953
Dimitri Shostakovitch, 1906–

Hungarian
Béla Bartók, 1881–1945
Zoltán Kodály, 1882–

Finnish
Jean Sibelius, 1865–1957

English
Ralph Vaughan Williams, 1872–1958
William Walton, 1902–
Benjamin Britten, 1913–

American
Charles Ives, 1874–1954
Ernest Bloch, 1881–1959
Walter Piston, 1894–
Howard Hanson, 1896–
Roger Sessions, 1896–
Henry Cowell, 1897–
Roy Harris, 1898–
George Gershwin, 1898–1937
Aaron Copland, 1900–
Samuel Barber, 1910–
William Schuman, 1910–

The Symphonic Suite

The instrumental suite of the nineteenth and twentieth centuries, which has no relationship whatever with the dance suite of the baroque period, is made up of two types. The first is a product of late Romanticism and the second belongs more properly to the modern period. The Romantic suite is a concert assemblage of several pieces, from a stage work, opera, ballet, or incidental music to a play, and is therefore an afterthought or warming over of music originally intended for another purpose, and as such has only the artistic organization which can be added ex post facto. Suites of this variety appear more often on popular programs than on the regular symphonic bill of fare. Some frequently played examples are Grieg's *Peer Gynt Suite*, Bizet's suites from *Carmen* and *L'Arlésienne*, Tchaikovsky's *Nutcracker Suite*, all from the nineteenth century, and Stravinsky's *L'Oiseau de Feu* and *Petruchka* suites from the modern period. The second type of suite is a modern development of the divertimento or cassation of the classic period. These were really suites resembling the symphony, but the individual movements were shorter, less serious in content, and often more numerous.

The modern symphonic suite has the elements of both the symphony and the symphonic poem. There are usually descriptive titles, but the form of the pieces is less influenced by the program than in the case of the symphonic poem, and sometimes resembles the various movements of the symphony. Examples of symphonic suites are to be found in Holst's *The Planets*, Ravel's *Mother Goose* (transcribed from piano duet for orchestra) and Rimsky-Korsakov's *Scheherazade*.

RIMSKY-KORSAKOV—*Scheherazade* (composed in 1888)

Russian music has been enormously popular in this century and none of the Russians is better known than Rimsky-Korsakov, who started in life as a naval officer, became interested in composition, and ended up as benevolent artistic sponsor of the modern Russian school of composers. His music is more purely Russian than Tchaikovsky's, showing less influence of German Romanticism, but is definitely less vigorous and compelling. It is like a superior sauce, flavorsome and piquant, which may be spread over a commonplace entrée to make it seem better than it really is. A large part of the effectiveness of Rimsky-Korsakov's music comes from his use of the orchestra, which is transparent and glittering, with less doubling than the orchestra of Wagner and Strauss and with a fine sense of individual tone color.

Scheherazade is based upon the story of the *Arabian Nights*. The Sultan Schahriar is convinced of the perfidy of women and conceives the interesting plan of executing each of his brides after the wedding night. The Sultana, Scheherazade, being a resourceful young lady, postpones her unhappy fate from day to day by spinning out a series of tales which so completely fascinate the Sultan that he eventually gives up the idea entirely, and she becomes a permanent fixture of the palace.

For the suite, four tales are selected: the sea and Sinbad's ship, the story of Prince Kalander, the Prince and the Princess, and the festival at Bagdad, which also includes the wreck of the ship on a rock surmounted by a bronze warrior. There are four movements, linked together by various themes which have pictorial significance but which, according to Rimsky-Korsakov's statement in his memoirs, are chiefly of symphonic importance, and correspond each time to different images, actions, and pictures. He continues: "All I had desired was that the hearer, if he liked my piece as symphonic music, should carry away the impression that it is beyond doubt an Oriental narrative of some numerous and varied fairy-tale wonders, and not merely four pieces played one after the other and composed on the basis of themes common to all the four movements." He apparently, like Strauss, wished to have his cake and eat it, too. The music is descriptive but not descriptive, symphonic but not really symphonic. This artistic hedging on the part of the composer makes the function of the annotator rather perilous.

First movement—The Sea and Sinbad's Ship

Two principal themes are stated. The first one is a peremptory melodic fragment of heavily accented rhythm, supposedly the motive of the Sultan (Example 223). The second is a rhapsodic figure for solo violin—Scheherazade (Example 224). These serve as introduction. A moderate

EXAMPLE 223.

allegro with a constant rhythmical figure in the low strings, suggestive of the swell of the ocean, follows (Example 225). Over this the first theme is developed by transposition and

EXAMPLE 224.

occasional slight variation. The second theme appears and is similarly treated. The two themes are then combined in development over the supporting figure, the rhythm of

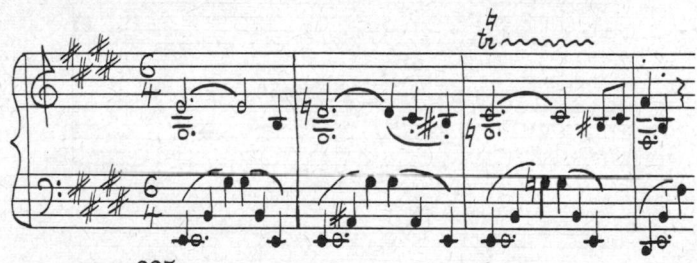

EXAMPLE 225.

which has been intensified. A tranquil coda concludes the movement.

Second movement—The Story of the Kalander Prince
The rhapsodic violin theme, Scheherazade, begins. Now

a new theme appears, a capricious dance melody of Russian folk flavor, on the bassoon and later the oboe (Example 226). It is repeated successively by the violins and

EXAMPLE 226.

the wood-wind ensemble. Then follows a set of fanfares on trombone and trumpet (Example 227). There is a short interlude of Scheherazade's motive elaborated on the clarinet. This is succeeded by development of the fanfares on various instruments and a stirring march based upon the fanfare motive. Another interlude brings Scheherazade's rhapsodic theme on the bassoon, and there follow several restatements of the principal theme of the movement to conclude.

EXAMPLE 227.

Third movement—The Young Prince and Princess

A most appealing melody, representing the Prince, perhaps, begins this movement (Example 228). It has an

EXAMPLE 228.

Oriental flavor which is marked particularly by a slithering
up-and-down scale figure appearing between phrases, first
on the clarinet and then on the strings. A second theme,
the Princess (Example 229), a graceful air, is introduced
on the clarinet (later the flute), accompanied by a tam-

EXAMPLE 229.

bourine rhythmic figure, which is transferred to the flute
and the strings as the melody goes on. Melody and accompaniment are shifted about in various orchestral colors.
There is a short interruption of the Scheherazade motive
on solo violin and the second half of the movement proceeds with restatements and an interweaving of the two
principal themes.

*Fourth movement—Festival at Bagdad, The Sea—The
Wreck, Conclusion*

The introduction is a dialogue between the themes of
the Sultan and Scheherazade from the first movement. The
Festival then gets under way and proceeds in brilliant fashion with two themes suggestive of an animated scene, the
first revealed on the flute (Example 230), the second on
the violins supported by winds (Example 231). The theme

of the Princess appears as contrast; there are also reflections of other themes from the second and third movements

EXAMPLE 230.

against the festive background, which becomes increasingly lively.

The first-movement motive of the sea, very broadly treated, arrives after a great climax and is maintained until the shipwreck occurs, marked by the fanfare from the sec-

EXAMPLE 231.

ond movement, fortissimo on the trumpets. A final dialogue between the now permanently established Sultana and her lord concludes the movement.

The Symphonic Poem

The modern symphonic poem differs from that of the Romantic period chiefly in its attitude toward realism. The Romanticists, as, for example, Liszt, regarded the representational powers of music as distinctly limited, and while a descriptive program might be preferred as a point of departure, or even as a form determinant of the music, the subjects taken were suggestive of interpretive rather than literal treatment. Also the Romantic composer was interested in ideas of noble or lofty character. He might flirt occasionally with the satanic, but, after all, Satan is a fallen angel and represents the aristocracy of evil. The modern composer, however, takes off his coat and plunges into life in its most unflattering aspects, apparently reveling in its ugliness, brutality, and drabness. All this is represented in the most literal fashion. We come upon tone pictures of a locomotive, of a rogue on the gallows, of a factory in full operation, of skeletons dancing in a graveyard, of a mosquito, or of the brutal realism of a battle. The composer is pleased with his ability to photograph, often forgetting that mere ingenuity of effect cannot create a music of any lasting value. There have been many poetical tone poems of great beauty by modern composers, such as Debussy's *Afternoon of a Faun* or Sibelius's *Tapiola,* but the seamy side of life has had a fascination for many of the most gifted artists. This may be part of the universal protest of art against the dreamy-eyed quality of Romanticism.

RICHARD STRAUSS—*Till Eulenspiegel* (composed in 1895)

Richard Strauss began his career as a composer with a series of symphonic poems which were regarded as extremely revolutionary. Part of the protest against them was because of their extensive use of dissonance. Today this dissonance has lost its sting, and the music of Strauss will shock no one by its sonorities, which are only a logical extension of the harmonic patterns of Wagner. A generation which has become accustomed to Stravinsky will receive Strauss without turning a hair, and may possibly find him rather tame. The other attack upon his music by the critics of the nineties is one that becomes increasingly valid. That is his somewhat naïve preoccupation with literal description, some of it autobiographical, and the fact that much of the music must be explained in advance in order to make sense to the listener. For instance, the bleating of the sheep in *Don Quixote* is the cleverest sort of orchestral effect, but, unless the audience is following a program guide, it will derive little satisfaction or understanding from this music. Strauss seems to have been aware of his precarious position because he apparently hoped that the title would be sufficient explanation of the music, and was compelled to add program details in the case of several of his pieces after it was seen that the music could not be understood without them.

The most disturbing thing about the music of Strauss is that after his early successes with such works as *Till Eulenspiegel, Don Juan,* and *Death and Transfiguration* the well seemed to run dry. It has been many years since he has written an orchestral work, and the last attempts have been entirely sterile. Perhaps his taste, along with that of other musicians of the period, has turned from the grandiose orchestral style, and, unlike some other contemporary composers, he has been unable to adjust himself to new musical trends. The orchestra for his early works is tremendous in size and power. The *Domestic Symphony,* written in 1904, calls for four flutes, two oboes, one oboe d'amore, four clarinets, one bass clarinet, four bassoons, one double bassoon, four saxophones, eight horns, four trumpets, three trombones, one bass tuba, four kettledrums, triangle, tambourine, glockenspiel, cymbals, and bass drum, two harps, besides an army of strings. This seems a formidable instrumental array to deal with such subjects as parental happiness, a child at play, and the family at breakfast.

It must not be understood that Strauss because of his preoccupation with photographic detail is an ineffective musical architect. He possesses the symphonic gift of the great German composers and is a master of development. One may quarrel with his choice of thematic material or his taste, which sometimes leads him to the overelaboration of ideas which are banal, however much dressed up, but, given good ideas and a subject which lends itself to musical treatment, he is a master craftsman.

Till Eulenspiegel's Merry Pranks, written in 1895, is generally regarded as Strauss's masterpiece. The program is a delightful one and sufficiently general in meaning to emancipate the listener who is not willing to study the program beforehand. One can enjoy this music as the embodiment of the mischievous spirit, as an extended scherzo filled with gay and sparkling development of two characteristic themes, easy to follow because of their definite personalities. Its program concerns a fourteenth-century legendary bad boy of Germany who actually existed; in a village near Lübeck his tombstone may be seen, or at least a tombstone with his name on it. After the first performance, when the public and musicians were mystified by the absence of a detailed program, Strauss made the following annotations on the score:

(1) Prologue "Once upon a time there was a rogue" (2) "Of the name of Till Eulenspiegel" (3) That was a mischievous sprite. (4) Away for new pranks. (5) Wait! you hypocrite! (6) Hop! on horseback through the midst of the market women! (7) With seven-league boots he makes off. (8) Hidden in a mousehole. (9) Disguised as a pastor he overflows with unction and morality (10) But the rogue peeps out from the great toe. (11) Before the end, however, a secret horror takes hold of him on account of the mockery of religion. (12) Till as cavalier exchanging ideas with pretty girls. (13) With one of them he has really fallen in love. (14) He proposes to her. (15) A polite refusal is also a refusal. (16) Turns away in rage. (17) Swears to take vengeance on the whole human race. (18) Philistine motive. (19) After proposing to the Philistines a couple of monstrous theses, he abandons the dumfounded ones to their fate! (20) Great grimace from afar. (21) Till's vulgar street song. (22) Watched by catch-poles and collared by the bailiff. (23) The judgment. (24) He whistles to himself with indifference. (25) Up the ladder! There he is swinging, his breath has gone out, a last quiver. All that is mortal of Till is ended. (26) Epilogue—What is immortal, his humor, remains.

All this may be found represented in the music, much of it easy to identify. There is, however, a long gap between

(21) and (22), in which there is a purely musical episode combining the two principal themes.

The first theme is stated after the few introductory bars, in which it is anticipated. It is a melody of three sequences and a descending arpeggio on solo French horn (Example 232). This is repeated and developed, leading to climax

EXAMPLE 232.

and pause. The second theme then appears on the clarinet in D, a melodic fragment of scherzolike rhythm (Example 233). From this point on the music is a continuous development of these two themes, either singly or in combination. There is especial music for the priest, for the

EXAMPLE 233.

philistines, the trial, and a snatch of a melody for the street song. For the rest, the music all stems from the two main themes, which are inexhaustible sources of new patterns. In paying too much attention to the program, there is danger of missing some of the charming, purely musical designs which Strauss has devised.

The Impressionism of Debussy

There is something revealing about Debussy's habit of adding to his signature the words *musicien français*. For it was on behalf of a French art that he labored, freed from the domination not only of Wagner but of all German theories and practices, which he regarded as incompatible with the true expression of French genius. From the early days at the National Conservatory of Music his iconoclasm had been noticed and deplored by official musical circles. The Symbolist poets Verlaine and Mallarmé and the Impressionist painters Monet and Pissarro, with their dislike of the overstatement and rhetoric of Romantic art, undoubtedly exerted a strong influence upon him, but in his attitude toward music he was for many years without the support of his fellow composers and his recognition came slowly and grudgingly.

The first evidences of Debussy's revolution in musical style were to be noticed in his harmony. He disliked the ordinary chord sequences based upon the major and minor scales and attempted to evade them by the introduction of strange and altered chords in the succession of harmonies. He made use of the whole tone scale as a basis of some of these harmonies, although he never allowed its neutralizing effect to destroy the sense of tonality, but merely to blur it. He had a fondness for successions of the open fourths and fifths, which had been banned from music since the Middle Ages. He treated some chords which had hitherto been regarded as dissonances as consonant, and went from one to another with no attempt at resolution.

In rhythm Debussy sought freedom from the recurrent accents of meter and found inspiration in the rhythmically vague patterns of the ancient Plain Chant. He was fond of irregular metrical arrangements and almost never wrote in a pattern of symmetrical phrases. In melody his restraint is always evident. Almost never do we find the sustained and organized melody of tradition. His melodic ideas are apt to be very short, mere snatches of tonal design which are seldom allowed to progress in unbroken line. He subjected many of his melodic ideas to modal influences as a further means of disguising the underlying tonal structure.

In Debussy's orchestral works there is little of conventional development, such as variation or contrapuntal device. His themes are simple patterns which are woven into a changing texture of harmony and orchestral effect in kaleidoscopic fashion. He inclines to the classic design of symmetrical sections, and the underlying tonal pattern, although obscured, is always present. His use of the orchestra is masterly. Its sound is luscious and sensuous, never strident or vulgar, but capable of great brilliance. He has an especial love for the instruments of the wood-wind family and for their individual colors. He often employs muted brass tone. His harp parts emerge clearly from the combination of sounds and are frequently of major importance. The strings more often accompany than lead in presentation of the ideas, and he obtains many effects of shimmering beauty in redividing the string sections, sometimes into as many as sixteen voices.

Debussy wrote no symphonies. His orchestral works, which might be called symphonic poems in one or more "movements," all have special titles of his own devising. For instance, *The Afternoon of a Faun* is a "prelude," *La Mer* is "three symphonic fragments," *Iberia* is one of several "images" for orchestra.

DEBUSSY—*Nocturnes* (composed in 1893–1899)

The three *Nocturnes* for orchestra all have poetic titles: *Clouds, Festivals,* and *Sirens.* The third is infrequently played because it demands a chorus of women's voices to supplement the orchestra. There is no text; the ladies simply sing "ah" or some other convenient syllable and are treated as instruments rather than as soloists. The first and second pieces have become two of the most dependable and popular modern compositions in the orchestral repertory.

No. I—Nuages (Clouds)

This is a most poetic tone picture of the night sky with vague, drifting clouds. Debussy once remarked that nature as usually reflected in music was as little like the real thing as the cardboard rocks in the scenery at the opera. His own treatment of nature is imaginative and subtle, the

EXAMPLE 234.

evocation of a mood rather than an attempt at literal description. A rather neutral pattern of a series of fifths and thirds on clarinets and bassoons, which is the background of the entire piece, is introduced in the opening bars (Example 234). This is followed by a short melodic idea on the English horn, the main theme of the piece (Example

EXAMPLE 235.

235). In the second part a new melodic design is introduced over divided strings on the flute and the harp. This is all the material upon which the piece is based. It never reaches a climax or a forte, but, with all its vagueness and mistiness, it carries the interest forward to the end.

No. II—Fêtes (Festivals)

This piece is a brilliant contrast to the first. From the start the mood is lively and gay. An exciting rhythmic figure begins on the violins, and above this rises an irregular curve of melody on the clarinets and the English horn (Example 236), suggestive of the happy confusion of a fes-

EXAMPLE 236.

tival crowd. Again there is no attempt at realism, as in the fair scene in Stravinsky's *Petruchka,* where the milling of the crowd is earthy and vivid. Debussy's picture gives one the feeling he might have about a festival if he were two thousand feet above it and saw only the lights and the animated pattern of its motion. The rhythm is sometimes ir-

EXAMPLE 237.

regular, sometimes suggestive of dancing, and a charming little tune emerges above it on the winds and later the strings as the piece goes on (Example 237). Suddenly there is a break in the music and a march rhythm appears on strings, tympani, and harp. Evidently a procession is coming past. There is a new melody, harmonized in thirds and sixths, on muted trumpets, then on wood winds, and finally in a brilliant climax on the full orchestra, as the gay procession comes nearer (Example 238). The last part is similar

EXAMPLE 238.

to the first as the procession disappears, and the two original rhythms are tossed about in a varied pattern of tonal and color combination.

No. III—Sirènes (Sirens)

This is evidently a poetical interpretation of those Homeric ladies who played havoc with the sailors of antiquity. The composition begins by establishing an orchestral background suggesting the movement of the sea. The women's

EXAMPLE 239.

voices are heard in a chord formation, rather like a beckoning call. An expressive accompanying figure on the English horn is added to the sea music, which becomes more active as the effect of the call is noted, and then the sirens begin their song. Like the usual Debussy theme, it is a simple pattern, a few adjacent tones in a provocative rhythmic arrangement (Example 239). The theme is the source of the rest of the music, sometimes merely transposed and repeated, sometimes heard in fragments. Against this theme the accompanying sea music weaves an agitated pattern which reaches a climax and then fades into a soft echo at the conclusion.

Piano Music of Impressionism

Even better adapted to the characteristics of Impressionistic style than the varied and subtle colors of the large orchestra was the piano, with its shimmering arpeggios, range of expressive dynamics, tonal shading and blurring, made possible by the damper and *una corda* pedals. The piano is essentially a chordal rather than a melodic instrument, and, since the favorite device of the Impressionists was harmonic color, it lent itself admirably to the expression of their music.

Late Romanticism added little to the development of piano style as perfected by Schumann, Chopin, and Liszt. In spite of the contributions of Brahms, both numerous and significant, piano music was a less active force in the expansion and enrichment of the literature than it had been earlier in the century. It appeared that the golden age of the piano was drawing to a close. Performers were quite content with the rich repertory bequeathed to them by the earlier masters, and recital programs were a reflection of this attitude. The piano music of Debussy and Ravel, however, proved that there were fresh and exciting sonorities and effects still to come, and that Impressionistic style was to afford an important new literature to the piano repertory.

The great difference between Impressionistic and Romantic piano style is in form and content. The virtuoso technical devices are not as different as the way in which they are employed. In the music of Chopin and Liszt there is always a developing melody and logical harmonic sequence as a framework upon which to display the ornamentation. Particularly in the case of Debussy, the fundamental idea is a poetic mood; melodic fragments and shifting harmonies are used to adorn rather than to direct the course of the music. The various effects of harmony, rhythm, and melody already noted in his orchestral music give the piano compositions a distinctive and original sound. There is the same sensuous beauty, vague outline, and subtlety of expression. Ravel, whose early piano compositions greatly resemble those of Debussy, and even may have influenced the older composer, was at heart a classicist, less of a poet in imagination, in warmth, and, as his later career was to prove, a composer whose invention could not keep pace with his technical development. His later piano music tends more and more to resemble the compact, objective style of the old French harpsichordists, Couperin in particular.

COMPOSITIONS OF DEBUSSY

Reflets dans l'eau (*Reflections in the Water*) from *Images* (composed in 1905)

This composition is a lovely evocation of a mood, suggested by the title. We seem to feel the hypnotic spell of the water surface, now tranquil and reflecting the images of the sky and the trees, now indistinct and blurred as a movement of the current effaces them. There are two melodic fragments and several chord patterns which are repeated in the design, but the traditional idea of symmetrical construction is evidenced only by the underlying plan of tonality, which is present as a unifying force, moving subtly from D flat major to a pause on E flat major and returning at the conclusion to the same key.

Golliwog's Cake Walk from *The Children's Corner* (composed in 1906–1908)

This is possibly the first influence of American Negro minstrel music, ancestor of our ragtime and jazz, to be noted in European music. The Golliwog was a frizzly-haired, colored doll, companion of two little girl dolls, appearing in one of those series for children so popular around 1900. Debussy has pictured him doing the cake walk to a melody very much like an American popular song of the period. The middle section is a suggestion of a shuffling step which is amusingly linked up with a mischievous quotation of a love theme from *Tristan and Isolde*. This piece is in simple, three-part design and, apart from its originality of color, traditional in organization.

La cathédrale engloutie (*The sunken cathedral*) from *Préludes, Book I* (composed in 1910)

The two volumes of *Preludes*, which are among the later compositions of Debussy, are perhaps the finest examples of his poetic imagination and mastery of expression. The descriptive titles, serving to indicate the underlying poetic idea, are put at the end of each piece, perhaps in the hope that the music will not be considered as merely pictorial but as existing independently. Each piece is indeed a perfect musical design, but to know the titles beforehand is an aid to understanding them more fully.

This prelude is in a mood of nostalgic mystery, showing the imaginative influence of Edgar Allan Poe, a great favorite of the composer. The bare chord patterns of the beginning suggest the sound of medieval church music, as if the old harmonies were arising mistily from the depths of the sea. These patterns, variously presented, are the musical basis of the whole composition.

La fille aux cheveux de lin (*The flaxen-haired girl*) from *Préludes, Book I*

This is one of a few examples of developed melody in

Debussy, who generally prefers to suggest rather than to state the implications of a melodic idea. It is in several phrases, with a modulation from G flat to E flat major and return. The mood is one of simple and almost naïve lyricism, full of charm and sweetness.

La puerta del vino from *Préludes, Book II* (composed in 1913)

This is in Spanish vein, a color always fascinating to Debussy. It is the picture of the crowded quarter of a Spanish town, with mule drivers loitering about and clapping their hands to the rhythm of a dancing girl. There is an ostinato rhythm in the bass, continuing throughout, and embroideries of melodic fragments above.

COMPOSITIONS OF RAVEL

Ondine from *Gaspard de la nuit* (composed in 1908)

An acompanying prose excerpt furnishes the program of this composition. Ondine, the princess of the wave, appears seductively and begs the poet to wear her ring and visit her palace to become king of the lakes. When he replies that he loves a mortal, she weeps and then bursts into laughter as she vanishes into the foam.

The plan of the music shows that Ravel, in conception of form, is closer to the style of Liszt than to that of Debussy. There is a definitely controlled melodic idea, varied and expanded, which is present at all times, and upon this is woven the elaborate pictorial ornamentation suggestive of the sea and of the magic of the night. At the end it appears briefly, alone, before the surging arpeggios of the concluding bass.

Le tombeau de Couperin (composed in 1914–1917)

This suite of six pieces, composed as an offering to the memory of the great François Couperin, shows the essentially classic spirit of Ravel, who at this point appears to reject the sensuous and imaginative features of Impressionistic style in favor of the precise, objective designs of early keyboard music, with here and there a touch of his own particular flavor of ironic wit.

I—Prélude
The prelude is pattern music based upon a figuration of triplets which progresses in binary form from E minor to G major, pauses and returns somewhat obviously to the original key.

II—Fugue
The second movement is a short and graceful three-voiced fugue in E minor, with the subject entering in traditional fashion, the voices in descending order. There are short episodes, inversions of the subject, and a stretto pattern between the theme and its inversion.

III—Forlane
This is an acid little dance in six-eight time, in three parts, with a contrasting middle section. The dissonance of the piece gives it a highly spiced quality, amusingly at variance with its classic spirit. The origin of this dance was in Italian instrumental music of the early eighteenth century.

IV—Rigaudon
The rigaudon is a lively two-four dance with a characteristic jumping step often found in the old dance suites. Ravel has employed this rhythmic idea as a central motive. There is a quiet middle section of less rapid motion.

V—Menuet
The minuet is a charming alliance between the old dance style and Ravel's individual harmonic style of piquant dissonance. There is a musette (a dance often associated with the bagpipe) for a second section in which triad chords slip about the diatonic and chromatic scales over a reiterated G and D in the bass.

VI—Toccata

The finale is a virtuoso figuration piece on a constant rhythmic pattern, moving through various keys from E minor to E major.

The Ballet or Ballet Pantomime

The ballet was originally an offshoot of the opera. Especially in France, no opera could expect success with the public unless there was a substantial portion of the evening devoted to dancing, and ballet dancers were an important part of the opera personnel. During the latter part of the nineteenth century full-length ballets made their appearance and proved popular. The music of the ballet was seldom of much importance, and the dancing itself was stereotyped and, while often of great technical skill, lacking in variety.

During the present century the ballet and ballet music have become vital artistic influences, representative of the modern point of view about stage performance. Thus twentieth-century ballet is vitally different from the old conception of formal ballet with set dances, as found in grand opera. Really more of a pantomime with a narrative choreography, often of genuine dramatic interest, the ballet now exists independently as a popular form of entertainment, and is seldom included at all in contemporary opera. Ballet organizations, usually with large orchestras, travel about the country giving performances which compete in popularity with the theatrical companies and opera troupes. But, since this type of ballet is relatively new, the repertory includes a great many modern compositions, in contradistinction to that of the opera companies which, as we have mentioned before, resolutely devote themselves to opera masterpieces of the eighteenth and nineteenth centuries.

Much credit for the emphasis upon serious music in the

ballet must be given to the American dancer Isadora Duncan, who started the vogue of adapting the dance to instrumental masterpieces and abandoned the tinseled charms of the typical ballet compositions. But the great artistic leader of the movement was Diaghilev, a Russian impresario who, from 1909 to his death in 1929, gave ballet performances which enlisted the services of such expert choreographers as Fokine, Massine, and Nijinsky, the best of the modern painters for décors, and a talented group of young composers to write original scores and make arrangements of suitable music of the past. Diaghilev originated the idea of an evening of short ballets, usually three, which is still the usual practice. As a result of this exciting new opportunity for theater music, many young composers were inspired to renounce the opera and to write ballets. Several of them owe their success directly to the Diaghilev venture. Of these the best known is Igor Stravinsky, whose most frequently played compositions are ballets.

Stravinsky's style developed rapidly from 1910, when he wrote the fairy-tale ballet *The Fire Bird*, a charming work, but still under the influence of his teacher, Rimsky-Korsakov; through *Petruchka* in 1911, which showed greater individuality; to the *Rites of Spring*, first produced in 1913, which established him immediately as the most original and vital force in modern music. Since the first World War, however, Stravinsky has devoted himself almost entirely to abstract music, in the form of chamber music, concertos, the symphony, and oratorio. He has even asserted that his early ballets are not really representational music, but should be regarded as symphonies. However regarded, they continue to hold their place on the stage, recently even on the screen, and in orchestral programs. They are works of vitality and freshness, which are widely imitated by other composers, and have reached a popularity difficult for Stravinsky to recapture in his more recent abstract compositions.

The première of the *Rites of Spring* in 1913 shook Paris to its artistic foundations. Enough was known of Stravinsky so that a noisy and dissonant work was expected, but from the very outset this music outraged the audience to such an extent that its violent expressions of disfavor almost drowned out the orchestra. Today the work still sounds harsh and dissonant, but the public has come to like it, because of its barbaric strength and continuous excitement. The only reason that it is not more frequently played is that it requires many additional players, and the expense of producing it is a deterrent.

STRAVINSKY—*Le sacre du printemps* (composed in 1913)

Stravinsky is responsible for the plan of action as well as the music. He is quoted as saying that the theme "was conceived in a strong, brutal manner." He goes on: "I took as a pretext for developments, for the evocation of this music, the Russian prehistoric epoch, since I am Russian." (He became a French citizen after the Revolution.) It is concerned with the adoration of spring, the impulse of fertility as represented by ancient pagan rites.

The work is divided into two parts, "The Fertility of the Earth" and "The Sacrifice." Each section or dance is a separate unit, representing a definite ritual, culminating in the sacrificial dance, when the chosen virgin dances herself to death. The outstanding characteristic of the music is the rhythm which, always striking and making frequent use of the ostinato, is sometimes of great complexity because of the combination of two different rhythms with cross-accents, or, as a result of metrical schemes of continuously changing pattern. There are several Russian folk melodies in the score and one or two melodies of Stravinsky's invention, but the work can hardly be called melodious. The texture is harmonic rather than contrapuntal and moves in blocks of chords which are often very dissonant. The orchestra, huge in size, generally proceeds in tone masses in the different choirs, and there is little of Impressionistic or symphonic device.

Part 1—Introduction
A high bassoon melody introduces a section evocative of the mystery of spring before the curtain rises (Example 240).

EXAMPLE 240.

Dance of the youths and maidens
This consists of heavy stamping rhythm (Example 241) with snatches of melodic fragments occasionally appearing over massed chords.

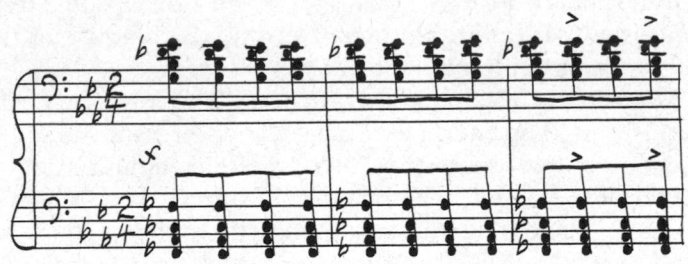

EXAMPLE 241.

Mock abduction
A free rhythm of changing meter is linked to the preceding section.

Spring rounds
This begins with a clarinet melody suggestive of the freshness of spring (Example 242), is followed by a heavily

EXAMPLE 242.

accented melody on the strings, already outlined in the first dance, and is concluded with the clarinet melody.

Games of the rival towns
This is based upon a simple tune introduced on the horns (Example 243).

EXAMPLE 243.

Entrance of the celebrant
The tubas have a broad melody against a varied rhythmic background (Example 244).

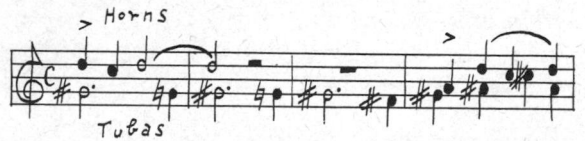

EXAMPLE 244.

The kiss to the earth and dance of the earth
After four preliminary bars, a rapid dance commences, of combined rhythms and almost complete absence of melody.

Part 2—Introduction pagan night
The only part of the ballet which might be called Im-

pressionistic, this is a mood piece with a melodic fragment suggestive of Debussy (Example 245).

EXAMPLE 245.

Mystic circle of adolescents
After a short introduction a folk theme, which is the basis of the movement, is introduced on the flute against divided tremolo strings (Example 246).

EXAMPLE 246.

Dance to the elected victim
This is a dance of uneven ostinato rhythms, very dynamic and entirely unmelodic.

Evocation of ancestors
Heavy and ponderous rhythms of uneven design are used to evoke the ancestors.

Ritual performance of the ancestors
This is a slow dance of ostinato figures with a fragment of folk song appearing first on the trumpets (Example 247).

EXAMPLE 247.

Sacrificial dance

This is probably the most complicated rhythm ever devised, as the time signature changes constantly from bar to bar. Although extremely difficult to play, its effect is vivid and striking.

The Modern Concerto

The concerto in the nineteenth century was often a display piece calculated to astonish audiences with the virtuosity of the performer. In this featuring of the performer, the orchestra was sometimes neglected and merely served to furnish a background. There might be interludes when the soloist was given a chance to cool off, but the real center of attention was the performer and his brilliant technique. However, in speaking this way of the Romantic concerto, two exceptions should be noted. Brahms wrote symphonies with obbligato piano (or violin) and Liszt wrote symphonic poems for piano and orchestra. But in the average Romantic concerto—Tchaikovsky, Rubinstein, Grieg, etc.—the old idea of antiphonal relationship and equality of importance had practically disappeared.

The modern concerto tends to re-establish the orchestra as the artistic equal of the soloist. One factor responsible for this is that the modern orchestra has become so much of a virtuoso itself that audiences are not content to see it relegated to an inferior role by any soloist. In fact, for a time it looked as if the concerto were about to disappear entirely from orchestra programs because of the rise of the virtuoso conductor, who has become so much of a leading attraction that all but a few ultraglamorous figures among soloists pale before his much-advertised splendor. Since audiences come to see him and hear his interpretations, why bother to engage soloists, and without soloists one cannot have concertos. But the concerto has recently shown signs of a return to popular favor. This may be because the repertory for large orchestras has been played so much that it threatens to go stale, and there are not enough modern works which appeal to the public to keep it fresh. Thus, to keep things going and to provide "novelties," conductors have turned again to the concerto literature, not so much to attract audiences as to keep them happy and satisfied.

A large number of concertos have been written by performer composers of today and by composers who have been commissioned by performers. Among the Europeans there have been Ravel, Stravinsky, Rachmaninov, Sibelius, Berg, Bartók, and Prokofiev. Americans who have succeeded in the form are Piston, Copland, Sessions, Gershwin, and Barber.

PROKOFIEV—*Concerto no. 3 in C major* (composed in 1917–1921)

Prokofiev is one of the most successful of modern composers. He manages to write in contemporary style without unduly disturbing the public, which is very much on its guard against experimental composers. The reason for Prokofiev's popularity is probably that his music is surprisingly tuneful and has a humor and gaiety which are very attractive. Unlike some twentieth-century composers, his humor is not in distortion or in the use of conscious banality, but is inherent in his musical style, which is entirely spontaneous. There is a certain kinship with the musical wit of Haydn, as found in the finales to his symphonies. Prokofiev's music is festive and good natured, and a good antidote to the stern intellectuality of some contemporary music. He is less successful in his expressive melodies, which usually lack the distinction of his jaunty allegro themes. Prokofiev was an excellent solo pianist and wrote five concertos for piano and orchestra, as well as two for violin and one for violoncello with orchestra.

The third concerto for piano was begun in Leningrad in

1917 (unlike Stravinsky, Prokofiev eventually returned to Russia and was accepted by the Soviet government) but was not completed until 1921 in France. In this concerto he has kept a nice balance between orchestra and solo instrument. He uses the piano as a foil to the more sustained and varied tone of the orchestra, allowing the percussive and staccato effects of the instrument full play. Themes alternate between the two mediums, and there is dialogue between them and exchange of characteristic comment which give a certain baroque quality to the music. His forms are clear and easily related to classic designs.

First movement—Andante-Allegro in C major
There is a slow introduction upon a lyric theme of Romantic flavor (Example 248), announced by the clarinet

EXAMPLE 248.

and taken up by the violins, which is succeeded by a rapid rhythmic figuration as the allegro commences. Against this background the piano makes its appearance with a sprightly pattern more rhythmic than melodic (Example

EXAMPLE 249.

249). This is succeeded by a second theme on the oboe, accompanied by pizzicato strings (Example 250). There is a decided element of fun in this spicy and somewhat perverse idea, which the piano develops at some length.

EXAMPLE 250.

The development is mostly concerned with the lyric theme of the introduction, to which is now added dynamic treatment by the piano. There is a recapitulation of both the principal themes of the allegro with especial emphasis on the second, now considerably extended. The orchestra and piano both contribute to a lively conclusion.

Second movement—Andantino—Tema con variazioni in E minor

The second movement is a theme and variations of somewhat unconventional conception although clearly outlined in its main divisions. The theme is a crisp little melody, like an old dance, but piquant in its melodic turns and modern in its harmony (Example 251). There is a plagal cadence at the end of the theme which is repeated in the variations,

EXAMPLE 251.

and serves to mark them off. The first variation is a much elaborated version of the theme featuring the piano, the second and third are of dazzling virtuosity, the fourth is quiet and meditative, but the fifth resumes the virtuoso and dashing mood of the others. At the conclusion of this the theme in repeated, with added commentary on the part of the piano.

Third movement—Allegro ma non troppo in C major

The finale is in three sections, arranged in a modified ABA pattern. The first theme is a staccato pattern in the bass (Example 252), stated by the orchestra and soon in-

EXAMPLE 252.

terrupted by the piano, which proceeds to development in combination with the orchestra. The middle section is devoted to a romantic melody (Example 253) stated on the

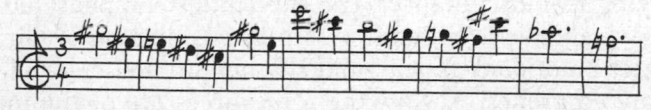

EXAMPLE 253.

wood winds, of which the piano evidently disapproves, for it superimposes upon it a cynical little figure entirely out of the mood of the other (Example 254). The lyricism persists, however, and the piano decides to collaborate, and leads to an expressive climax. After this, the staccato theme of the beginning returns and is developed at some length.

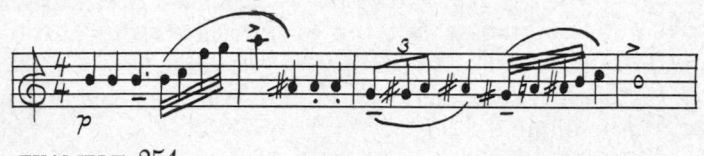

EXAMPLE 254.

The conclusion, with the piano and orchestra vying in sonorities, is exciting and brilliant.

The Modern Symphony

If the Romantic composers were embarrassed by what to do with the symphony, the modern composers are in an even more confused state. The public regards the symphony as the supreme instrumental achievement; no other type of composition can compete with it in prestige, and a symphony concert is unusual without it. The classic symphonies of Haydn, Mozart, and Beethoven, plus the Romantic additions of Schubert, Brahms, Tchaikovsky, Franck, and Dvořák, are still the backbone of orchestra programs. But how adapt the symphony's characteristic form to changing styles and the new harmonic idiom, so as to keep it fresh and contemporary in spirit without destroying its individuality? The Romantics compensated for their weakened architecture with intensification of climax, greater emotional appeal, and the heightened color of the expanded orchestra. Now these resources are beginning to lose their potency. After Wagner and Tchaikovsky what can be added in the way of climax or in emotional force? The public is glutted with sensation along these lines, and is inclined to be cynical toward new works that try to go further. What can be added to the glittering orchestra of Rimsky-Korsakov, Debussy, or Ravel that will sound interesting and novel? Some new factor must be found to give the modern symphony an excuse for existing.

Certainly it cannot be the obscured tonality which has featured so many modern works, for the very essence of the symphony is tonal logic, and, if the succession of tonalities is not clear, it loses its momentum and balance: an atonal symphony would be like an opera without a plot. An attempt has been made by some modern composers to restore the symphony more nearly to classic proportions, reducing the size of the orchestra, making it more objective and less emotional, and infusing it with some of the baroque spirit by a greater use of counterpoint and the formal devices of the age of Bach. The public, however, is not especially sympathetic to this chastened and denatured manifestation of the form, and seems to prefer the grand manner of the nineteenth century.

Many famous modern composers have evaded the issue by not writing symphonies, at least after their period of incubation, and others have followed the nineteenth-century model, hoping the modern revolution will blow over and leave musical style relatively undisturbed. Gustave Mahler at the beginning of the century wrote symphonies in expanded nineteenth-century vein, derivative in thematic material, but beautifully orchestrated and impressive in bulk. Rachmaninov wrote three symphonies in lyric vein, less successful than his concertos, but frequently played. D'Indy and Roussel in France, Vaughan Williams in England, Daniel Gregory Mason and Howard Hanson in America, all have written symphonies which, although eclectic in style, have met with some measure of success. Shostakovitch, the young Russian composer, has attracted attention with his symphonies because of their lusty vulgarity and good showmanship. More experimental symphonies along the new Neoclassic lines have been written by Stravinsky (a choral symphony, the most striking of his postwar compositions), Prokofiev (the *Classical Sym-*

phony, an avowed imitation, or perhaps even satire, of eighteenth-century style), and in America by such composers as Roy Harris, Aaron Copland, Walter Piston, and Roger Sessions.

One man, however, outdistanced all the others in popularity, and wrote symphonies which, in America at least, have been placed beside the great works of the past as standard compositions: the Finnish composer, Jean Sibelius. Opinion is divided as to the eventual importance of the Sibelius symphonies. His supporters rank him with the best, his detractors say that he is merely a fad. There is no doubt that Sibelius has a distinctive musical style. Although at times eclectic, his personality is readily recognizable after a few bars of his music. This is partly because of his use of the orchestra, which abounds in brassy climaxes, cold and dark wood-wind effects, and tremolo strings. His harmony is often dissonant, but the tonal foundations are clearly indicated. His use of melody varies from little fragments of folk-song figures to great emotional outpourings in the manner of Tchaikovsky.

Sibelius is perhaps most original in his conception of symphonic form. Many of the movements are based upon a collection of fragmentary ideas which fuse and coalesce as the music proceeds. This, to the uninitiate, gives them a somewhat chaotic effect. The line is broken, the music is rather desultory, the style seems pictorial and descriptive rather than symphonic. To members of the Sibelius cult, however, these are the manifestations of his subtle genius, and, once understood, are the patterns of a master mind. It is an interesting problem for the musical amateur to decide for himself at which point between these two conflicting opinions the truth may lie.

SIBELIUS—*Symphony No. 5 in E flat* (composed in 1915)

First movement—Tempo molto moderato in E flat major
This is a complex movement in typical Sibelius vein.
It has some relationship to sonata form in its contrast of

EXAMPLE 255.

tonalities E flat to G and return, but is unconventional
in that the first half is in a compound meter of twelve-
eight, which in the second is reduced to an allegro in three-

EXAMPLE 256.

quarter time. There are six principal divisions. In the first
two, four short motives are presented and restated. The
first motive appears on the horn, a sort of hunting call fea-

EXAMPLE 257.

turing a skip of a fourth (Example 255). The second is on
flutes, oboes, and clarinet over tremolo strings, and begins
with a downward skip (Example 256). The other two mo-

tives are subsidiary and consist of a rhythmic pattern of thirds (Examples 257 and 258). The third section is a development of the second motive. There is a slow-paced transition on the first motive which leads in accelerated

EXAMPLE 258.

tempo to the fourth, fifth, and sixth sections in the new meter of three quarters. In these sections the two principal motives are restated and developed with increasing clarity, somewhat after the fashion of a scherzo.

Second movement—Andante mosso, Quasi allegretto in G major

This movement is more traditional than the first and is easy to understand. It consists of variations on a theme

EXAMPLE 259.

stated in alternation on staccato flutes and pizzicato strings over sustained wind harmonies. The theme is diatonic and simple, like a folk melody (Example 259). There are four variations of formal arrangement in which the theme is rhythmically altered and changed in instrumental coloring. A fairly long coda based on fragments of the theme begins after the fourth variation.

Third movement—Allegro molto in E flat major

The finale is the climax of the symphony in power and effectiveness. It is a good example of the driving assault upon the emotions which Sibelius, borrowing the ostinato technique of the Russian composers, manages so skillfully. The movement begins with a chattering of staccato strings

EXAMPLE 260.

from which emerges, first on the viola and then on the first violin, the outline of a scherzolike melody (Example 260). As this dies away a very behemoth of a theme, harmonized in thirds, appears on horns and strings (Example 261). It

EXAMPLE 261.

is even in rhythm but irresistible in its progress. Against this appears a triumphant theme on the wood winds (Example 262). This is developed to a climax and is succeeded by the first theme on the wood winds, and then, *misterioso,*

EXAMPLE 262.

on the strings. This stirs up the ponderous second theme, which appears on the strings with its countertheme in the wood winds. There is a broad lyric section devoted to the countertheme. Then the second theme starts as an ostinato on the trumpets and continues devastatingly, with increasing dissonance and force, to a conclusion. The end is a series of sharp, brutal chords for full orchestra.

The Chamber Orchestra

While the great symphony orchestra has gone its majestic way as emperor of the realm of music, full of prestige and glory, there have been signs of trouble lying ahead. For one thing it is very expensive to maintain, and deficits are not as easy to meet as they once were. Few symphony orchestras are self-supporting and, although the public is probably larger than ever before, it is difficult to organize its enthusiasm into the kind of support which will replace the vanishing wealthy patron. Meanwhile composers have shown considerable interest in the old chamber ensemble, a small body of strings with a few wood winds and brasses thrown in for good measure. This may be the tacit recognition of an economic situation and provision for a musical future when the large orchestra will become a rarity, or it may be merely that contemporary taste is turning away from the tonal splendors and mass effects of the large orchestra. From the point of view of a music which prefers clarity of line and sobriety of effect to harmonic and instrumental color and thrilling climaxes, the smaller orchestra has much to recommend it. Many modern compositions reflect this point of view, and it is only natural that the modern sympathy with baroque and classic forms should bring with it the smaller performing mediums of these periods.

Today there are a number of organizations in the concert hall and on the radio calling themselves sinfoniettas and devoting their programs to baroque, early classic, and modern works. There is no dearth of compositions for these programs. The concertos and suites of Bach, Handel, and

Corelli and the inexhaustible supply of Haydn and Mozart symphonies provide good standard fare, greatly in vogue at the present time. Composers like Stravinsky, Bartók, Schoenberg, Hindemith, Bloch, and many young Americans have written interesting works for this type of ensemble.

For one such organization, the chamber orchestra of Basel, the Hungarian composer Béla Bartók wrote his *Music For String Instruments, Percussion, and Celesta.*

Bartók, as did the young Stravinsky, found his inspiration in the folk music of his native country. Together with his friend Kodály he made an extensive study of Hungarian folk songs. He had discovered that the so-called Hungarian melodies used by Liszt and Brahms were in reality not Magyar but gypsy in origin. His subsequent compositions, beginning with arrangements of Balkan melodies, show a strong folk song influence although his mature musical style, dissonant, percussive, contrapuntal, and highly concentrated in design often conceals its derivation.

There is however a fundamental lyricism and folk spirit underlying the Bartók music and this, combined with his gift for brilliant and fresh instrumental sounds, has made his music increasingly understandable and enjoyable.

BÉLA BARTÓK—*Music for String Instruments, Percussion, and Celesta* (1937)

Bartók wrote a number of concertos but no symphonies. This four-movement work, completed a few years before he came to stay in the United States, has some of the elements of the twentieth-century symphony which, of course, was far from being standardized. It is written for two antiphonal groups of strings; violins, violas, cellos, and basses contrasted with drums, cymbals, tam tam, timpani, xylophone, harp, and pianoforte.

First movement—Andante tranquillo is an extended fugue with a chromatic subject ranging within a fifth from A to E. This has a driving intensity in its upward striving and exerts a basic influence upon all four movements of the composition.

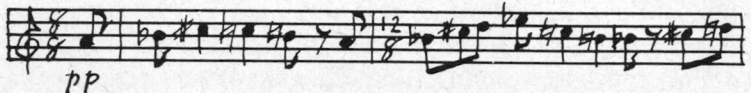

EXAMPLE 262A.*

The first movement consists entirely of successive entrances of this subject in various keys until a climax on E-flat, emphasized by timpani and cymbals, is reached. The subject is then inverted and the harmonic ground is retraced with the addition of an arabesque figure on the celesta.

Second movement—Allegro

The mood of poignancy is dispelled by a dynamic sonata allegro which has a principal theme derived from the fugue subject of the first movement. Here we have music of impetuosity and forward sweep with many contrasting rhythms.

Third movement—Adagio

This is a reflective, somber piece, the mood of which is heralded by a reiterated high *F* which sounds mysteriously on the xylophone. The thematic material is entirely derived from motives contained in the original fugue subject. There are six sections, the first and sixth resembling each other, and the melancholy feeling is reaffirmed by the returning high xylophone notes at the end.

Fourth movement

The finale, a rondo with a dancelike refrain, also derived from the fugue subject, reveals the kinship of Bartók's complex musical style to the spirit of folk music. There are several couplets which bring in new material and a return to the original fugue subject which is then spaced out to eliminate the extreme chromaticism of the idea. The dance refrain furnishes material for the coda. In this movement the tragic implications of the earlier movements are dispelled by a mood of reckless gaiety.

Another significant development in the contemporary scene is the appearance of functional music (called in Germany *Gebrauchsmusik*). This music is calculated to respond to the demand for compositions suitable for amateurs to play, or for educational purposes. During the early part of this century there was an alarming abyss between the modern composer and the musical public. He was so preoccupied with being modern and different that he suddenly discovered that he had left the public behind, and his compositions were of interest chiefly to his fellow composers, whose professional approbation meant little in the spread and popularity of his music. Meanwhile the great body of student musicians in schools, conservatories, and colleges, if performing any new music at all, had to rely upon a derivative and perfunctory literature written by hacks. And so Mahomet has come to the mountain, and today many of our most expert and successful composers are writing what they are pleased to call functional music.

ERNEST BLOCH—*Concerto Grosso for string orchestra with piano obbligato* (composed in 1925)

Ernest Bloch, born in Switzerland, lived for many years in America and became an American citizen. The *Concerto Grosso* was written in 1925 when he was director of the Cleveland Institute of Music, and was expressly intended for the student orchestra of that school.

It proved to be of such interest, however, that, although of moderate technical difficulty, it has been played by almost all our professional orchestras, both large and small.

Bloch first attracted attention because of the Jewish character of his music. As a general rule, Jewish composers —Mendelssohn, Meyerbeer, and Mahler, for instance— have shown little influence of their Hebrew ancestry and have written a music totally devoid of racial feeling. Bloch, in such works as his *Israel Symphony, Schelomo,* and *Jewish Poems,* has filled them with the fervor, exaltation, and deep dejection of the Old Testament. His music is vehe-

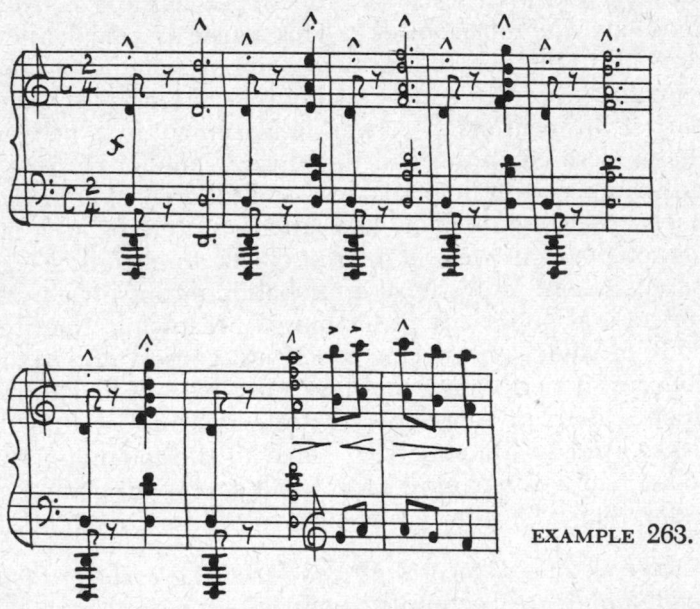

EXAMPLE 263.

ment and passionate, now introspective with wailing dissonance, now savagely rhythmical. These elements are controlled by a fine sense of musical architecture and a discipline usually lacking in the ardent Romantic.

In the *Concerto Grosso* he attempts to write in the objective vein of Handel, with emphasis on line rather than on color, and in the rich contrapuntal texture of the baroque style. He replaces the harpsichord with the piano, but the function of the instrument is much the same as in the old concerto grosso: to support and fuse the music of the strings rather than to play a solo role. The writing for the strings differs from the old concerto in that there is frequent use of the higher register of the violins, and variety of color effects is secured by subdividing the strings.

First movement—Prelude—Allegro energico e pesante in D minor

This is a spirited and intense piece in which an irregular metrical scheme of four-four and two-four is used to give an unusual rhythmical effect (Example 263). This rhythm serves as a central motive of driving force that carries forward the music. There is a brief lyrical interlude for contrast. Despite the fact that the harmony used is simple, and for the most part diatonic, the result is fresh and modern in feeling.

Second movement—Dirge—Andante moderato in C sharp minor

The character of this piece is somewhat like a sarabande, but the underlying emotional feeling is romantic and there is an admixture of the Jewish strain characteristic of Bloch's music. The design is a modified song form. The first and third sections are based upon the opening theme, a heavily accented, grief-laden melody (Example 264). The contrasting section unfolds an expressive melody in long phrases with arpeggio accompaniment, interrupted occasionally by the rhythm of the first theme.

EXAMPLE 264.

Third movement—Pastorale and rustic dances—Assai lento—allegro giocoso in F major

This movement is intended to follow without pause. It is an alternation in mood and design between a reflective

EXAMPLE 265.

pastorale music (Example 265) with sustained accompaniment, and lively dance tunes, one of which suggests the French folk song *En passant par Lorraine*. In the dance section there is contrapuntal interest in the combination of themes and fragments of these, in imitation between the voices. The movement contains brief suggestions of the melody of the Dirge.

Fourth movement—Fugue—Allegro in D minor

The last movement is a fugue based upon a lively diatonic theme (Example 266). The exposition is in the traditional pattern, with the four voices entering separately. There is a contrasting episode (Example 267) appearing several times, an exposition in major, inversions and augmentations of the subject, and near the end a reminiscence of the rhythmic figure of the first movement appears to lead to a triumphant conclusion in the major mode.

EXAMPLE 266.

EXAMPLE 267.

Modern Chamber Music—The String Quartet

Chamber music has always been rather like the Supreme Court. Dignified and aloof, it is supported by the aristocracy of the intellect, and is not easily swayed by the pressure of popular art movements. It changes with the times, but slowly and carefully, and it is a bulwark against sensationalism. During the Romantic period chamber music inclined toward classicism, and such features of the Romantic idiom that it adopted were modified to fit in with its tradition of sobriety. The revolutionary Romanticists, Liszt, Berlioz, and Wagner, gave the string quartet a wide berth, but those with classic tendencies, Schubert, Schumann, Mendelssohn, and Brahms, found it a most congenial medium. In the modern period, to the dismay of the traditionalists, the revolutionary composers have seized upon the field of chamber music as an ideal place in which to conduct their experiments. This is explainable because the modern Neoclassic movement in music is an intellectual one, a deliberate attempt to reinterpret the tonal values of music as a means of establishing a new idiom. The best chance for understanding and appreciation lies with the chamber-music audience, which is accustomed to regard music as a vehicle of thought as well as feeling.

A great deal of modern music has been written according to the atonal principle. This means that key relationships are abandoned and the chromatic scale of twelve equal semitones is substituted for the diatonic major and minor scales, with their orderly progression of triads forming the basis of the harmony. Since practically all traditional musical designs are based upon successions of keys, atonal music has to look elsewhere for some sort of unity and logic. Repetition and contrapuntal combination of rhythmic patterns have been the chief resources of the atonalists. These must be clear to be understood at all, and composers of this tendency turn naturally to chamber music, and especially to the string quartet, as the most transparent medium.

Since all atonal music must be dissonant or run the risk of suggesting triad harmony, dissonance is no longer a driving force as it is when alternated with consonance. Atonal music has a tendency to sound static, and composers rarely succeed in anything but short forms. Thus atonality today seems to be losing ground. Schoenberg's system of the twelve tone row has been mentioned previously. It was designed to afford new laws of construction, but in some of his later works he seems to have abandoned it. Composers once regarded as inclining to atonality, like Hindemith and Bartók, profess that their music is constructed upon a tonal basis, with modified emphasis. This is not a great departure from the idiom of Wagner, who wrote the Prelude to *Tristan* using the signature of C major (A minor) without once employing the C major or A minor chord. For a short time radical composers were interested in the idea of subdividing the half tones into quarter tones and thus bringing about new effects. Quarter-tone pianos were tried out, and string quartets were written which incorporated these smaller divisions. However, audiences, who have never been very enthusiastic about atonal music, cared even less for quarter-tone experiments, and they have been appearing less frequently in recent years.

Modern composers of more or less traditional chamber music have been Reger in Germany; Debussy, Fauré, Ravel, and others in France; and many British and American composers less well known. The more radical chamber music composers have been Schoenberg, Berg, Webern, and Hindemith in Germany and Austria; Bartók in Hungary; Milhaud in France; and Sessions in America.

HINDEMITH—*Quartet no. 3, opus 22* (composed in 1922)

This quartet, although more atonal in style than recent works of Hindemith, has proved to be one of the most successful and widely known modern works. It is written without key signatures or metrical indications, and is entirely free in these respects, but the style is melodious, the form is clear, and the themes have so much personality that they make a very definite impression upon the listener's musical consciousness, even at a single hearing.

First movement—Fugato—Sehr langsame viertel (*Very slow quarter-note rhythm*)

The movement begins with a fugue theme of uncertain tonality but of very melodious and expressive quality, on the first violin (Example 268). Second and third entrances

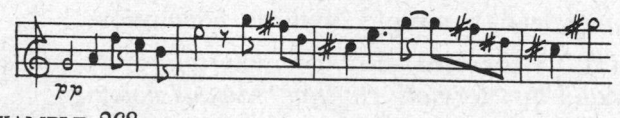

EXAMPLE 268.

are made on the viola and cello, but the second violin appears simultaneously with the cello in free counterpoint and does not play the subject until several bars later. There is an accelerando leading to a rapid dynamic passage, which serves as middle section. The expressive mood then returns with three more entrances of the subject and related episodes.

Second movement—Schnelle achtel—Sehr energisch (Rapid eighth-note rhythm. Very energetic)

This is rather like a scherzo with a primitive rhythm of five heavily accented eighth notes alternating with twelve

EXAMPLE 269.

sixteenth notes (Example 269) and a barbaric melody on the violins following after (Example 270). The savage humors of this music are succeeded by a graceful, lyric second section. As this dies away, there is a stirring of the original

EXAMPLE 270.

rhythm, which then returns with added intensity. A second appearance of the contrasting music, simplified in accompaniment, leads to a rapid rhythmic conclusion.

Third movement—Ruhige viertel—Stets fliessend (Tranquil quarter-note rhythm. Always flowing)

This attractive slow movement has a mysterious, rather Oriental flavor. Against an even rhythm of pizzicato chords on the viola and cello a tuneful melody (apparently unrelated in tonality to the accompaniment) makes its appearance (Example 271). This enters fragmentarily in one or

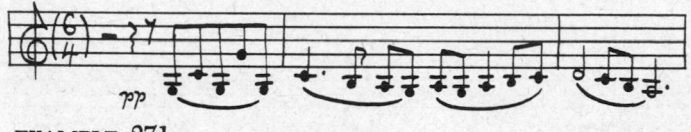

EXAMPLE 271.

another of the upper voices. There is a transition melody (Example 272) in the first violin and then a new theme is heard in the viola, also with pizzicato accompaniment (Ex-

EXAMPLE 272.

ample 273). The transition theme leads to a reappearance on the cello of the first melody and a return of the first design. There is a coda with appearances of transition, second theme, and first theme to conclude.

EXAMPLE 273.

Fourth movement—Mässig schnelle viertel (Moderately rapid quarter-note rhythm)

This is a short rhythmic movement based upon a pattern of accented rhythmic figures without definite thematic or melodic organization.

Fifth movement—Rondo—Gemächlich und mit Grazie (Easily and gracefully)

The final rondo is capricious and gay with a refrain surprisingly tuneful in view of its tonal ambiguity (Example 274). The first couplet is a saucy figure moving up and

EXAMPLE 274.

down on the first violin (Example 275). The refrain reappears on the viola and again on the first violin. After this there is a second couplet in more lyric vein (Example

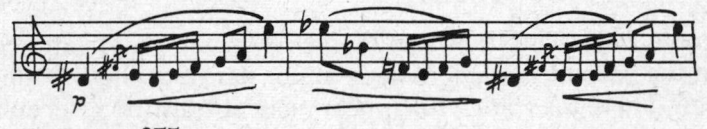

EXAMPLE 275.

276). The first couplet theme returns to lead to a final section in which the refrain, after two joyful appearances, bogs down and loses its high spirits. This is only momen-

EXAMPLE 276.

tary, however, and it returns softly at its original tempo with a surprise fortissimo at the very end.

Modern Choral Music

From the baroque to the present day, instruments have more or less dominated the musical scene and music for the voice has been forced into a secondary role. The victory was not won overnight. Baroque opera and oratorio were certainly as important as any instrumental music of the period, but in both these types instruments played an increasingly large part. Even the Mass, buttressed by years of traditional hostility to instrumental music on the part of the church, capitulated to the orchestra, and all the great Masses of Bach, Mozart, Haydn, Beethoven, Berlioz, and Brahms were composed with elaborate orchestral accompaniments. The ultimate victory came in the Wagnerian music drama, when the orchestra was placed above the voice in musical emphasis.

Meanwhile instrumental style as opposed to choral style penetrated all music. One has only to compare the nature and resources of the voice with various instruments to realize what this means. The voice is limited in range, in dynamics, and in sustaining power. It appears to best advantage when singing a melody which makes musical sense to the singer, because the singer is entirely dependent upon his ear to keep to the pitch. Extreme dissonance is possible with a chorus if every part is separately logical, but, even in this case, consonance between voices gives a feeling of confidence to the singer, and best results are obtained when all the singers of a chorus are confident. The voice has a natural inclination to the intervals of the diatonic scale, finds chromatic progressions difficult, and dislikes wide leaps from tone to tone if they occur too frequently. Instruments excel in range, in dynamics, in rhythmical effects, in rapid passagework, and do not care if their music is diatonic or chromatic. They will tolerate and perform capably a completely incoherent succession of tones, if given time to adjust themselves to the difficulties involved.

Nineteenth-century music, which depends so much upon chromatic harmony and instrumental effects, is the logical result of the long journey away from the pure choral style of the Renaissance. The twentieth-century composer turns naturally again to the voice in his attempt to re-establish the contrapuntal style as an alternative path for music to follow. He will not, of course, write in the consonant vein of Palestrina and Lassus—too much water has gone under the bridge for that—and he will seek, as always, new sonorities and combinations, but he does try to write for voices with an understanding of their potentialities, and does not treat them as if they were instruments. This is merely a tendency to be noted and not by any means a universal rule.

There are many fine choral works by modern composers, both accompanied and *a cappella*. Debussy and Ravel led the way, each with a set of three *a cappella* choruses which showed the possibility of a fusion of the *a cappella* style with the modern idiom. Stravinsky has written an oratorio, *Oedipus Rex*, and a choral symphony, the *Symphonie de Psaumes*, two of his best works since his early ballets. The British composers Vaughan Williams, Holst, and Walton have brought about a genuine renaissance of choral music in England, with many excellent sacred and secular choral pieces. In America choral music is a natural part of the contemporary scene. Randall Thompson has written an extended work for voices *a cappella, The Peaceable Kingdom,* in addition to many excellent short pieces in similar vein.

ARTHUR HONEGGER—*King David* (symphonic psalm composed in 1923)

One of the most widely known modern choral works, *King David*, is by the Swiss composer Arthur Honegger. Honegger first attracted attention as a member of the French "group of six," a widely publicized band of young composers who appeared in Paris around 1920. All that the group appeared to have in common was the desire for the limelight, but from its ranks emerged two composers who established solid reputations during the twenties and thirties, Milhaud and Honegger.

Honegger has an unquestioned flair for the dramatic and the pictorial. His tone poem about a locomotive, *Pacific 231*, an ingenious piece of musical photography, and *King David* did much to establish his reputation. The latter work was originally written as incidental music to a play of René Morax, but was later revised for concert performance. It is a collection of solos, choruses, and instrumental interludes, giving the effect of a dramatic oratorio. Many of the choruses are settings of the Psalms. The writing for the chorus is extremely effective and a good example of modern choral composition, with emphasis on melodious treatment of the voice. The style of the work is, however, eclectic and at times embarrassingly derivative. One chorus in Handelian vein is succeeded by something that sounds like Gounod, and then a harsh, self-consciously modern interlude may appear. One suspects that the unevenness of the work will militate against its eventual survival.

No. 3. Psalm—Loué soit le Seigneur (All praise to Him, the Lord of glory)

A unison chorus, this psalm has a melody and accompaniment almost completely in the style of Handel.

No. 7. Psalm—Ah si j'avais des ailes de colombe (Oh, had I wings like a dove)

This is a solo song for soprano in two verses, with instrumental interlude and postlude. The voice has a simple melody which is set against a somewhat irrelevant and dissonant background, suggesting the distress indicated in the poem. The instrumental parts are gently and persuasively tuneful.

No. 17. Cantique—De mon coeur jaillit un cantique (Now my voice in song upsoaring)

A unison chorus of three verses, in which the music is repeated, this is a song in praise of the glory of David, a humble shepherd, chosen by the Lord to be king. The musical elements are simple in essence, a diatonic melody with ostinato accompaniment rather like a fanfare. The modernity comes from the clash between chorus and accompaniment, and by sudden shifts in the key.

No. 19. Penitential Psalm—Misericorde, O Dieu, pitie (Pity me, God)

This is a two-part chorus for men's and women's voices. After a bar of accompaniment the tenors and basses enter with an appealing melody expressive of the feeling of the text. Sopranos and altos take up this melody at the sixth bar and the two parts are antiphonally combined. There is an interesting rhythmical clash between voices, which move in a fundamental beat of three against an ostinato block chord grouping of two in the accompaniment.

No. 23. Marche des Hébreux (March of the Hebrews)

Depicting a procession of the Hebrew warriors before King David, it starts with a strident brass fanfare and follows with a diatonic march melody against a persistent rhythmic figure in the accompaniment.

No. 24. Psalm—Je t'aimerai, Seigneur, d'un amour tendre (Thee will I love, O Lord)

This is a mixed chorus. The words are an expression of contentment and faith, which are reflected in the serenity of melody and accompaniment. In the central section to the words "When waves of death encompassed me, and snares of men made me afraid," the massing of the voices in chromatic figures dispels the mood of serenity in a momentary harshness, but this mood returns again to conclude.

Nos. 27–28. La mort de David (The death of David)

The finale to the oratorio sees David happy in the acclamation of the people at the crowning as king of his son, Solomon, and he dies in beatific vision of the fulfillment of this promise of the Lord. After a richly harmonic introduction, the women's voices enter with a simple melodic phrase, punctuated by the men's voices singing softly "Alleluia." Now the chorus takes up this word in an ornate melodic line, with increasing richness of polyphonic texture which builds into a sonorous and moving conclusion.

Modern Opera

The most frequently produced operas of the twentieth century have been those of Puccini and Strauss, post-romantic and leaning heavily upon well established models of Verdi and Wagner. Debussy's *Pelléas and Mélisande*, also in the familiar repertory, is unique as an example of Impressionism. For his libretto Debussy chose a play of Maurice Maeterlinck and set it verbatim in a quasi recitative style with a pictorial orchestral accompaniment of great subtlety and beauty.

A number of composers, distinguished in other fields, among them Schoenberg, Stravinsky, Bartók, and Hindemith have written operas in the modern idiom without winning a place in the traditional repertory. In England Benjamin Britten and in America Gian Carlo Menotti have written more traditional operas which have been widely performed both at home and abroad.

ALBAN BERG—*Wozzeck* (1923)

Among the composers of the atonal school Alban Berg, pupil of Arnold Schoenberg, has been most warmly received by the public. His opera *Wozzeck* is generally regarded as a twentieth-century masterpiece.

Following the example of Debussy, Berg selected a play as the basis of his opera, the work of a nineteenth-century

German, Georg Büchner (1813–1837). The story concerns itself with the tragic career of Wozzeck, an infantry man. He is stupid, stolid, and a mark for injustice and persecution. He is mocked by his superiors, bullied by his captain, cheated by his mistress who is the mother of his child. He ends up by murdering her and taking his own life. The sordid sequence of events is transfigured by the eloquence and splendor of Berg's musical setting.

The melodic style is angular in familiar atonal style. Occasionally tone speech, a strange combination of singing and speaking invented by Schoenberg, is used for dramatic emphasis. The harmony is naturally unrelieved in its dissonance but yet often strikingly effective. It is however in the orchestral accompaniment that the work achieves its expressive power. The scenes are organized by various symphonic designs such as variations, sonata, rondo, passacaglia etc. The structural aspects of the work do not however intrude, and many of the scenes convey an overwhelmingly emotional effect.

Scene from Act 2

Marie, mistress of Wozzeck, who has been unfaithful to him, is reading the Bible. She is moved by the story of the woman taken in adultery. She alternately reads and exclaims as the text stirs her to grief over her own situation. She concludes with an outburst; "Lord you had pity on her; have pity on me also."

Act 3 End of 4th scene, interlude, and end of the opera.

Wozzeck wades into the pond where he has cast the body of his murdered mistress. The waters gradually cover him. The moon rises and there is stillness. The scene changes and a group of children are playing in the street. They discuss the death of the woman. Marie's child, who is among them riding a hobby horse, is apparently unmoved and continues to call "Hop, hop."

DICTIONARY OF MUSICAL TERMS

Note: The definitions given below are confined to the technical meaning of each term as it is employed in the text. Supplementary meanings are not included.

A cappella—Music for chorus without instrumental accompaniment.

Accompaniment—In vocal music, the parts written for instruments. In instrumental music, the harmonic background furnished by one or more instruments to the principal melody or melodies.

Adagio—A tempo indication meaning very slow.

Agnus Dei—A portion of the Mass to the words beginning "Lamb of God."

Allegretto—A tempo indication meaning a little fast.

Allegro—A tempo indication meaning fast.

Allemande—The characteristic first movement of the baroque instrumental suite. A dance in duple rhythm.

Amplification—A device of development in which the theme or motive is expanded with additional notes.

Anacrusis—When a melody does not begin with a strong beat, the notes which precede the first strong beat are called a rhythmic anacrusis.

Andante—A tempo indication meaning moderately slow.

Answer—A term used in the fugue for the subject when transposed to the dominant. Subject and answer alternate in the exposition of the fugue.

Antiphony—The setting-off of one choral or instrumental group against another, with effects of imitation and alternation.

Aria—The formalized solo song used in the opera. The standard form is a design of ABA.

Arioso—A type of song used in the opera midway between recitative and aria, with the melodious style but without the set pattern of the latter.

Arpeggio—A broken chord—that is, the notes are played in succession rather than simultaneously.

Atonal—A term to characterize harmony which is not derived from either the major or minor scale and therefore does not follow the laws of tonality.

Augmentation—The magnifying (usually doubling) of the time values of each note of a theme, motive, or melody.

Ballad—A dance-song with instrumental accompaniment found in the music of the Middle Ages. Later used to indicate a narrative song with a number of verses.

Ballade—A piano piece of the Romantic period.

Bar—The short metrical division used in music notation indicated by bar lines.

Bass—A. The low register of the male voice. B. The string bass or bass viol used in the string section of the orchestra.

Bassoon—The double-reed instrument which serves as bass in the wood-wind section of the orchestra.

Benedictus—A portion of the Mass beginning with the words "Blessed is he that cometh in the Name of the Lord."

Berceuse—A lullaby or cradle song.

Binary form—A two-part design used in the baroque instrumental suite. The first section modulates to the dominant (in minor to the relative major). The second section, somewhat longer, brings about a return to the original key. Each section is repeated.

Bourrée—A dance in duple rhythm resembling the gavotte used in the baroque instrumental suite.

Branle—An old round dance in duple time in which the dancers, in couples, follow the leader.

Bridge—A modulatory passage in first-movement sonata form found in the exposition section and serving to link the principal theme with subsidiary themes. Often itself of thematic importance.

Cadence—A rhythmic pause or point of repose at the end of

a phrase. Its effect is partially controlled by melodic and harmonic features of the music.

Cadenza—A device for virtuoso display by the soloist in which the accompaniment is silent. Originally cadenzas were improvised by the performer, but today they are generally written out. The cadenza is a standard feature of the first movement of the concerto, appearing generally shortly before the end.

Canon—The literal imitation of one melody, instrumental or vocal, by another at a specific time interval.

Canonic imitation—The imitation, not necessarily literal, of the features of one melody by another.

Cantata—A choral type, sacred or secular, found in the baroque. Polyphonic choruses are employed as well as recitatives, arias, and various solo ensembles. It is usually a short piece, but at times assumes ample proportions.

Canzone—Instrumental piece found in the Renaissance, generally a transcribed madrigal or chanson.

Capriccio—An instrumental piece of polyphonic texture resembling the fantasia and ricercar.

Cassation—Another name for the classic serenade or divertimento.

Chamber music—Ensemble music designed for a small-audience room. The chief types are sonatas, trios, quartets, quintets, etc.

Chanson—Choral type found in the Renaissance. The French counterpart of the madrigal. Generally in four voices. Instruments are sometimes used to supplant one or more of the voices.

Chorale—A hymn of the Lutheran Reformation.

Chorale prelude—A short instrumental piece based on a Lutheran chorale.

Choral music—Music for an ensemble of voices with or without instrumental accompaniment.

Chord—Three or more tones of different pitch occurring simultaneously.

Chordal style—As opposed to polyphonic style indicating a harmonic texture based on successions of chords rather than combined melodies.

Chromatic—Music under the influence either melodically or harmonically of the chromatic scale, a scale composed of twelve equal semitones and their octave duplications.

Clarinet—A single-reed instrument of the wood-wind family.

Clavichord—An early type of keyboard instrument in which the depression of the keys causes metal tangents not only to excite the sounding strings but also to divide them into the required pitch length.

Clavier—The baroque term meaning the keyboard of the organ, clavichord, or harpsichord, but often restricted to the last two.

Closing theme—In first-movement sonata form, a subsidiary theme with the feeling of close that comes near the end of the exposition.

Coda—A section appended to a given design to serve as an ending. It may be either short or long. In the symphony and sonata it is sometimes of great importance, serving as an additional development section.

Concertino—In the concerto grosso the group of solo instruments as opposed to the accompanying ensemble, the tutti, or concerto.

Concerto—An ensemble instrumental piece in which a soloist or group of soloists is accompanied by an ensemble of instruments. Generally in three movements.

Concerto Grosso—A type of concerto found in the baroque.

Consonance—Literally, sounds which blend or sound together as opposed to dissonance, sounds which tend to draw apart and clash. Ideas of consonance and dissonance are variable, but, according to laws of acoustics, the lower the vibration ratio, the greater degree of fusion between tones.

Continuo—A type of accompaniment used in all baroque ensemble music. The bass part is doubled by a keyboard instrument (harpsichord or organ). Over this part figures indicate the supporting harmonies which are to be played by the performer. Also called figured bass or thorough bass.

Contrapuntal—Pertaining to counterpoint.

Counterpoint—The combination of two or more independent melodies heard simultaneously. In contrapuntal music the resultant harmonies are by-products of the melodic combination.

Countersubject—A subsidiary subject sometimes appearing in the fugue. It is usually presented in counterpoint with the answer.

Couplet—In the rondo the sections which alternate with the refrain are called couplets.

Courante—The traditional second movement of the baroque instrumental suite. A dance piece, generally polyphonic in texture, in triple rhythm and rapid motion.

Credo—A portion of the Mass beginning with the words "I believe in One God, Maker of Heaven and Earth."

Crescendo—The gradual increase of sonority from soft to loud.

Cross-accent—When two melodies are combined so that the accents are not parallel but oppose each other.

Cyclic form—In symphonic compositions where thematic material is an interinfluence between movements, the design is said to be cyclic.

Da capo—Indicates that the music is to be repeated from the beginning.

Damper pedal—Commonly known as the "loud" pedal. It raises all the felts, allowing the strings of the piano to vibrate at will.

Deceptive cadence—The last chord of the final cadence substitutes another (generally the triad of the sixth degree of the scale) instead of the expected tonic.

Development—Repetition, with variation of some of its essential elements, of a melody, theme, or motive. The development section of first-movement sonata form constitutes the middle part of the design and it is here that the material of the exposition is varied and extended.

Diatonic scale—In major, an ascending series of adjacent white notes (on the piano) from C to C. In minor, a descending series of white notes from A to A. It is composed of a series of whole and half tones which may be reproduced in any key by the use of the black notes.

Diminution—A device of development in which the time values of each note are diminished, usually halved.

Discant—A type of medieval polyphony in which independent melodies are combined.

Disintegration—A device of development, used especially by Beethoven, in which essential features of the theme disappear progressively, leaving only scattered fragments.

Dissonance—*See* Consonance.

Divertimento—Also known as serenade or cassation. A type of instrumental suite somewhat resembling the design of the symphony but lighter in texture. Often played at outdoor entertainments. Found in the classic period.

Dominant—The fifth note of the diatonic scale. The key of the dominant means that the music is related to a diatonic scale with this degree serving as tonic or key note. The dominant chord, or triad, is the closest relative of the tonic chord.

Dotted note—The addition of a dot to a written note means that the time value is extended by one half. This is usually borrowed from the succeeding note, which is therefore shorter. A dotted-note rhythm is one in which a number of such alternate long and short notes are combined with uneven effect.

Double bassoon—Also called contrabassoon. A double-reed, wood-wind instrument resembling the bassoon but larger and an octave lower in pitch.

Double stopping—The violin ordinarily sounds only one string at a time. When two tones are played simultaneously, two strings are used and the effect is called double stopping. Triple and quadruple stopping are used less often.

Duple rhythm—A fundamental beat of two as the basis of the rhythm.

Dynamics—Gradations of tonal volume such as forte, piano, crescendo, diminuendo, etc.

English horn—A double-reed instrument similar to the oboe but pitched a fifth lower.

Episode—A portion of the fugue in which neither the subject nor answer appears in any one of the voices.

Etude—A technical study for the piano. Some études, such as those of Chopin, are performed as recital pieces.

Exposition—In first-movement sonata form the initial section in which the principal theme, bridge, and subsidiary themes are stated.

Fantasia—An instrumental composition of unpredictable design, sometimes polyphonic, sometimes free, often used to indicate an improvisation. The term "fantasia" is sometimes applied to a portion of a composition in which the themes are freely treated.

Fauxbourdon—A device used in medieval polyphony.

Figuration—A rhythmic arrangement lacking the melodic personality or compact quality of a fugue subject, theme, or motive, often used as the basis of baroque instrumental music.

Figured bass—*See* Continuo.

Flat—A device placed before a written note to indicate that its pitch is to be lowered by a half tone.

Flute—A wood-wind instrument used as the top voice in the wood-wind section of the orchestra. In the present day made of metal.

Forte—An indication that the volume of the sound is to be loud. Fortissimo means very loud.

Fugal style—In instrumental music when a theme enters successively in each voice, with the effect of subject and answer, the style is said to be fugal.

Fugue—A polyphonic design based upon a central subject. Several independent voices, each entering separately with the subject or answer (subject transposed), are the identifying characteristic of the type.

Gaillarde—An old dance, generally in triple rhythm and rapid in tempo, which was often combined with the stately pavane.

Gavotte—A French dance in duple rhythm beginning with an upbeat, often used in the early instrumental suite.

Gigue—Like the English jig, in some form of triple rhythm. Generally serves as last movement of the early instrumental suite.

Glockenspiel—Steel bars struck with hammers. Used in the percussion section of the orchestra.

Gloria—A portion of the Mass beginning with the words "Glory to God in the Highest."

Grave—A tempo indication meaning very slow.

Gregorian Chant—Also called Plain Chant. The unison and solo chants forming from the early Middle Ages the chief liturgical music of the Roman Catholic Church.

Harmony—The science of chord combination and chord succession. The harmonic background of a composition refers to its chord color.

Harpsichord—A keyboard instrument of the Renaissance and baroque in which the action of the keys induces quills to pluck the strings. Sometimes more than one set of keys (manuals) is used. Various color effects can be obtained by varying the position and type of quill. Other similar types are the virginal, spinet, cembalo, and clavecin.

Homophonic—Single-voiced as opposed to polyphonic or many-voiced music. Homophonic style means that the music consists of a single line of melody supported by blocks of chords.

Horn—The French horn, an orchestral descendant of the old hunting horn.

Improvisation—The music is made up on the spot by the performer.

Instrumental suite—A collection of short movements of dance types, found in the baroque, for small ensemble or keyboard instruments.

Invention—A short, polphonic instrumental composition found in the baroque.

Inversion—Every interval of a theme is replaced by its ascending or descending opposite.

Key—When music has the feeling of centering about a given tone, it is said to be in the key of that tone, which is called its keynote or tonic.

Kyrie—A portion of the Mass beginning with the words "Lord have Mercy."

Largo—A tempo indication meaning very slow.

Legato—The tones are linked together or slurred so that there is no break between them.

Leitmotives—The use of recurring themes in Wagnerian operas to indicate characters or incidents and to recall them from one scene to another.

Lied—Literally "song," but used to distinguish the art song from the folk song.

Loure—A dance in triple rhythm somewhat like the sarabande, used in the early instrumental suite.

Lute—Pear-shaped instrument with fretted fingerboard, played by plucking. Very popular in the Renaissance.

Madrigal—Secular polyphonic choral song of the Renaissance.

Mass—The basic part of the Roman Catholic liturgy, certain portions of which are set to music in polyphonic style.

Mazurka—A Polish national dance generally in triple rhythm with an accent on the third beat.

Melismatic—When several notes of music are used for a single word syllable as opposed to *syllabic,* one note for each syllable.

Melodic style—As opposed to symphonic style, melodic style is organized in regular phrase lengths with little polyphony or development.

Melody—A succession of related tones organized by rhythm.

Meter—The system by which the rhythm of music is indicated in measured notation.

Minuet—An old court dance of triple rhythm used in the early instrumental suite and the classic symphony and chamber music.

Modal—The modes were tone series somewhat like modern scale patterns, used in the music of antiquity, the Middle Ages, and the Renaissance. Since they are different in organization, harmony based upon them has a different sound from ordinary chordal design, which is based upon the major and minor scales. Melodies may also be found which show their influence.

Modulation—The transference from one key center, or tonic, to another as the basis for the organization of the music.

Motet—A Latin, polyphonic, sacred choral song of the Renaissance.

Motive—A compact musical idea appearing in a theme or melody which is susceptible of varied repetition or development.

Music drama—A form of opera found in the works of Richard Wagner.

Natural scale—A series of tones, the result of acoustic phenomena, which has served as the basis for the development of all Western music.

Notation—The system of recording a musical design on a staff by means of clefs and notes.

Oboe—A double-reed instrument used in the wood-wind section of the orchestra.

Oboe d'amore—Baroque instrument, similar to the oboe but pitched a third lower.

Octave—The duplication of a tone in a pitch either higher or lower. The vibration rate between a tone and its octave above is one to two.

Open fifth—The fifth degree of the diatonic scale sounded together with the first, or tonic.

Opera buffa—Classical Italian comic opera.

Opéra comique—French comic opera with spoken dialogue.

Opera seria—The old form of baroque opera as it existed before the reforms of Gluck.

Oratorio—See page 84.

Orchestration—The orchestral setting of a piece of music.

Organum—The oldest form of polyphony as it existed in the Middle Ages.

Osanna—A portion of the Mass beginning with the words "Hosanna in the Highest."

Ostinato, i. e., "obstinate"—The persistence of a given musical device, such as a rhythm or a melodic fragment.

Overtones—The partial tones caused by the tendency of a sounding surface to divide into smaller segments, each with its sound related to the fundamental tone. The overtone series plays a large part in the laws of harmony and in the determination of tone color.

Overture—Originally the instrumental piece played before the rise of the curtain in the opera. Later used independently as a specific instrumental form.

Partita—Another name for the baroque instrumental suite.

Passacaglia—An instrumental composition in which a short bass theme is repeated in a number of sections of equal length, each time with varied counterpoint in the upper voices.

Passion—A setting in oratorio form of the Gospel story of the New Testament.

Pastorale—An instrumental composition of rural flavor, generally indicated by the rhythm.

Pavane—A stately processional dance generally in duple rhythm, ancient in origin.

Pedal—On the piano, pedals are used to raise the string dampers, to soften the tone, and to allow a single tone to continue to vibrate after the others are dampened. On the organ there is a supplementary pedal keyboard on which the low notes of the bass are generally played. A pedal point in harmony is a single tone in the bass over which the harmony moves freely.

Phrase—A portion of a melody set apart from the rest by a rhythmic cadence or point of repose. Sometimes subdivisions are found in a single phrase.

Piano—An indication that the volume of the sound is to be soft. Pianissimo means very soft. The instrument known as the piano is also called pianoforte because of its wide range of dynamics.

Pizzicato—Plucking the strings of a bowed instrument to produce the tone.

Plagal cadence—The most ordinary form of harmonic cadence, known as the authentic cadence, consists of the chord based on the fifth degree of the scale (the dominant) followed by the tonic chord. The plagal cadence is less strong. It consists of the chord based on the fourth degree of the scale (the subdominant) followed by the tonic. The usual Amen sung in hymn tunes is a plagal cadence.

Plain Chant—*See* Gregorian Chant.

Polonaise—A Polish court dance in triple rhythm but moving only moderately fast, as in a processional.

Polyphonic—Music is called polyphonic when its texture is composed of independent melodies rather than successions of chords.

Polyphony—Literally many-voiced, but used to indicate music composed on a contrapuntal or combined melody plan.

Prelude—A short instrumental piece generally preceding something else, but sometimes appearing independently. Variable in design.

Program music—Music in which the design is determined, or at least appreciably influenced, by a program or story.

Quarter tones—The smallest tone division recognized in our system is the semitone or half tone. These tones again divided in half produce the quarter tone. Experiments in the use of these intervals have been made in the twentieth century.

Recapitulation—The third section of first-movement sonata form in which the material of the exposition reappears with such changes as may be necessary because of the key plan or tonality.

Recitative—A device used in dramatic music, opera, oratorio, or cantata in which the vocal line follows the plan of speech or is declaimed rather than subjected to the design of a melody. The accompaniment is simple and consists of occasional chords marking the important accents with now and then a cadence. It may also be accompanied by animated orchestral figuration.

Recorder—A mouthpiece flute widely used in the Renaissance.

Refrain—In a rondo the refrain is a simple melody in several phrases which recurs in alternate sections of the design.

Relative major—The major scale or key which uses the same tones and signature as a given minor.

Relative minor—The minor scale or key which uses the same tones and signature as a given major.

Requiem Mass—A Mass for the dead.

Rhythm—The organization in time of music. The fundamental rhythm is the underlying plan of grouping by two (duple rhythm) or by three (triple rhythm). Rhythm also is concerned with the duration of tones, their spacing in the design, their relationship in accentuation, and their division into phrases.

Ricercar—An instrumental form found in the Renaissance, polyphonic in style. Often the transcription of a motet.

Rigaudon—A dance used in the early instrumental suite. In duple rhythm with a characteristic jumping step.

Rondo—An instrumental form found in the sonata and the symphony and also existing independently, in which a refrain is alternated with contrasting sections known as couplets.

Round—An old device of popular music in which each performer or group of performers sings or plays a different phrase of the song at the same time. This is achieved by a succession of delayed starts, one phrase apart. When the end is reached they all go back to the beginning. Stopping is more or less an informal matter.

Sanctus—A portion of the Mass beginning with the words "Holy, Holy, Holy, Lord God of Hosts."

Sarabande—A slow, expressive movement in triple rhythm, derived from an old Spanish dance, regularly used in the early instrumental suite.

Scale—An ascending or descending series of tones used in Western music as the traditional basis for melody and harmony since the time of the Renaissance. *See also* Diatonic scale.

Scherzo—A form resembling the minuet in design, used in the sonata and the symphony but sometimes appearing independently. Generally in triple rhythm and humorous or bold in character.

Serenade—*See* Divertimento.

Shake—Another name for trill.

Sharp—A device placed before a written note to indicate that its pitch is to be raised by a half tone.

Signature—The indication at the beginning of each line of musical notation of the tones to be used. Flats and sharps are here specified. If none are indicated, the tones to be used are the white tones on the keyboard which are used in the key of C major and its relative, A minor.

Sinfonia—The Italian name for symphony. It is often used to indicate the instrumental prelude to a baroque opera or cantata.

Singspiel—The German form of comic opera with spoken dialogue.

Sixths—Two tones of the scale six degrees apart sounded together constitute a sixth, as for instance 1 and 6, 2 and 7, etc. After the third, the sixth is second in popularity, although these intervals from an acoustical point of view are less consonant than the octave, the fourth, and the fifth.

Solo concerto—An outgrowth of the baroque concerto grosso, in which the concertino is replaced by a single soloist.

Sonata—An instrumental composition in several movements of varying design, to be played by one or two performers.

Sonata da camera—The chamber sonata of the baroque period, resembling the instrumental suite. *See* page 56.

Sonata da chiesa—The church sonata of the baroque period. *See* page 56.

Sonata form—The characteristic design found in the first movement (occasionally in any of the other movements) of the classic sonata and symphony. In three sections, exposition, development, and recapitulation, to which may be added an introduction and a coda.

Song form—An instrumental design of three sections, the first and last of which are similar, the middle one of contrasting material.

Staccato—The notes are detached, short, and percussive.

Stepwise—When a melody moves to one or another adjacent tone of the scale, it is called a stepwise progression.

Stretto—More than one entrance of a fugue subject, occurring not in the orderly fashion of the exposition but dramatically crowding one upon the other. Term is also used for similar treatment of a symphonic theme.

String quartet—An ensemble of two violins, viola, and cello used in chamber music. Also used to indicate a composition in several movements of the design of the sonata for such an ensemble.

Strophic pattern—When the same music is used for the differing verses of a song, the pattern is said to be strophic.

Subject (of a fugue)—A concentrated musical idea which serves as the basis of the design of the fugue.

Subsidiary theme—In sonata form, besides the principal theme, which usually occurs first, there are various additional themes called subsidiary themes usually of lesser importance.

Symphonic poem—A one-movement symphonic form in which the design is influenced by the program or story.

Symphonic style—Symphonic style as opposed to melodic style is not organized in simple melodic phrases, but makes use of themes, motives, and development. The texture, especially in development sections, is frequently polyphonic.

Symphony—The most common meaning of this term, which is used variously, is that of a composition in several movements for orchestra. Several designs are found in the symphony, but the first movement is traditionally in sonata form.

Syncopation—The strong accentuation of a metrical beat, normally weak.

Tarantella—An instrumental composition in fast, triple rhythm based on a persistent figure.

Tempered scale—An artificial division of the octave into twelve equal semitones which changes slightly the pitch of several of the tones of the natural scale, but which makes possible the modern tuning of keyboard instruments.

Tempo—The rate of speed at which a given rhythm is to proceed.

Theme—A melody used symphonically, that is, susceptible of development and having no independent melodic entity apart from the texture of the movement.

Theme and variations—A musical design in several sections of approximately equal length, in which the initial melody is progressively varied in each section.

Theme metamorphosis—A theme presented in differing guise but retaining some of its original character. A device used by Liszt in his symphonic poems.

Thirds—Two alternate notes of the scale when sounded together constitute a third, as for instance 1 and 3, 2 and 4, etc.

Through-composed—A song is said to be "through-composed" when the music of the various verses does not repeat but changes with the meaning and mood of the poem.

Toccata—In early music a general name for keyboard piece. In modern times a piece characterized by rapidly moving figuration.

Tonality—The general plan of key succession in a composition. There is a central tonality or key, various contrasting keys, and a return to the original point of departure.

Tonic—The first note of a given scale is the key note and is also called the tonic.

Transcription—The arrangement of music for a different performing medium from that originally indicated by the composer.

Transposition—The change in tonal level of a melody, a chord, or any portion or the whole of a musical composition. If this change involves modulation it means also change of key, but a fragment of a melody may be transposed without necessarily involving modulation.

Tremolo—In string music the rapid repetition of a note or chord by moving the bow up and down. In keyboard music the effect can best be obtained by the rapid alternation of divisions of a chord or the tones of the octave. The tremolo in the voice is a slight (unfortunately often excessive) wavering of pitch. In the violin this slight wavering of pitch is sought after to give color to the tone, but is known as vibrato.

Triad harmony—The first, third, and fifth tones of the scale form what is known as the tonic triad, or common chord. A triad can be formed upon each degree of the scale by adding the third and fifth tones above. These triads are the basis of simple harmony. When a composition confines itself to these chords, which in fact can provide great variety, it is said to be composed of triad harmony.

Trill—The rapid oscillation of a tone with its upper neighbor.

Trio—A. A chamber-music ensemble of three instruments, or a piece for such a group. B. The contrasting section of a minuet or scherzo in the sonata and the symphony.

Trio sonata—An instrumental composition of the baroque, generally for two violins, gamba, and harpsichord. Each part was frequently played by several performers, giving the effect of a sizable ensemble.

Triple rhythm—A fundamental beat of three as the basis of the rhythm.

Triplet—Three notes to be played in the time supposedly allotted in the metrical scheme to two—share and share alike. Triplet rhythm would indicate movement in groups of threes.

Trombone—A brass instrument of the orchestra in which each position of the slide provides for a number of tones of the overtone series. It is used in the lower register of the brass choir.

Trumpet—A brass instrument used in the orchestra. It forms the higher register of the brass choir.

Tuba—A large brass instrument used for the lowest tones of the brass choir of the orchestra.

Tutti—In the concerto grosso the tutti is the body of accompanying instruments as distinguished from the concertino, the solo group.

Twelve tone row—A system of harmony based upon the chromatic scale used by Schoenberg and other modern composers.

Tympani—Kettledrums, with definite pitch, used in the orchestra.

Una corda pedal—The "soft" pedal of the piano. It moves the hammers so that they strike only one of the two or three strings which are tuned to each pitch degree, and thereby produce a tone of less volume.

336 Dictionary of Musical Terms

Vibrato—See Tremolo.

Viol—The family of instruments which preceded the violin family. They were thicker, had more strings, a flat back, sloping shoulders, and produced a softer tone than the violin type. They were also played without vibrato.

Viola da gamba (knee viol)—The prototype of the violoncello in the viol family.

Virginal—An instrument of the harpsichord type used in England in the Renaissance.

Virtuoso—A performer of exceptional technical ability.

Vivace—A tempo indication meaning very fast.

Vox humana—An organ stop which gives a tremolo effect supposed to sound like the human voice.

Whole-tone scale—A series of tones in which 'every tone is a whole tone apart. Since the diatonic scale is composed of whole and half tones, the whole-tone scale, like the chromatic scale, has no variety and is artificial; but it is useful for its color.

BIBLIOGRAPHY

BIOGRAPHICAL REFERENCE

Nicolas Slonimsky, ed. *Baker's Biographical Dictionary of Musicians*, 5th ed. New York, Schirmer.

MUSICAL TERMS

Willi Apel. *Harvard Dictionary of Music*. Cambridge, Harvard.

INTRODUCTORY MUSIC BOOKS

David D. Boyden. *An Introduction to Music*. New York, Knopf. (The elements of music and a survey of its development.)

Joseph Machlis. *The Enjoyment of Music*. New York, Norton. (An elementary introduction to music, including history and appreciation.)

Douglas Moore. *Listening to Music*. New York, Norton. (The materials of music explained for the layman.)

GENERAL HISTORY BOOKS

Donald Jay Grout. *A History of Western Music*. New York, Norton. (A history of musical style from ancient times to the present.)

Paul Henry Lang. *Music in Western Civilization*. New York, Norton. (A complete history of music as related to the development of Western culture.)

Alfred Einstein. *A Short History of Music*. New York, Knopf.

Karl Nef. *Outline of the History of Music*. New York, Columbia.

Curt Sachs. *Our Musical Heritage*. Englewood Cliffs, N. J., Prentice-Hall.

    (The last three items are compact surveys.)

HISTORICAL PERIODS

Note: The books in this section by Bukofzer, Einstein, Reese, and Sachs are advanced studies in their respective subjects.

Gerald Abraham. *A Hundred Years of Music.* New York, Macmillan. (A discussion of musical style in the century after the death of Beethoven.)

Manfred Bukofzer. *Music in the Baroque Era.* New York, Norton.

Archibald T. Davidson and Willi Apel, eds. *Harvard Anthology of Music.* Cambridge, Harvard. (Selected musical compositions: Vol. I, Oriental, Medieval, and Renaissance Music; Vol. II, Baroque, Rococo, and pre-Classical Music.)

Alfred Einstein. *Music in the Romantic Era.* New York, Norton.

John Tasker Howard. *Our Contemporary Composers.* New York, Crowell. (American music in the twentieth century.)

Joseph Machlis. *Introduction to Contemporary Music.* New York, Norton. (A guide to the understanding of twentieth-century music.)

Carl Parrish and John F. Ohl. *Masterpieces of Music Before 1750.* New York, Norton. (An anthology of musical examples from Gregorian Chant to Bach. All the examples are also available on three long-playing records.)

Carl Parrish. *A Treasury of Early Music.* New York, Norton. (An anthology of masterworks of the Middle Ages, Renaissance, and Baroque. These works are also available on long-playing records.)

Gustave Reese. *Music in the Middle Ages.* New York, Norton.
———. *Music in the Renaissance.* New York, Norton.

Curt Sachs. *The Rise of Music in the Ancient World.* New York, Norton.

TYPES AND FORMS: HISTORICAL OR ANALYTICAL

Cobbett's Cyclopedic Survey of Chamber Music. New York, Oxford. (A standard reference work.)

Edward J. Dent. *Opera.* Baltimore, Penguin. (A popular survey of opera from early beginnings to the twentieth century.)

Donald Jay Grout. *A Short History of Opera.* New York, Columbia. (A detailed study of the development of opera.)

A. J. B. Hutchings. *The Baroque Concerto.* New York, Norton. (The evolution of the concerto to the middle of the eighteenth century.)

Alfred Mann. *The Study of Fugue.* New Brunswick, N. J., Rutgers. (A historical outline and excerpts from classic texts.)

William S. Newman. *The Sonata in the Baroque Era.* Chapel Hill, N. C., U. of North Carolina. (A comprehensive study of the earliest works called "sonata.")

Denis Stevens, ed. *A History of Song.* New York, Norton. (Essays on the history of the art song in various countries.)

Robert Stevenson. *Patterns of Protestant Church Music.* Durham, N. C., Duke. (The musical traditions in the various Protestant denominations.)

Sir Donald F. Tovey. *Essays in Musical Analysis.* Seven volumes. New York, Oxford. (An analysis of various types and forms of instrumental, vocal, and chamber music.)

INSTRUMENTS

Anthony Baines. *Woodwind Instruments and Their History.* New York, Norton.

Anthony Baines, ed. *Musical Instruments Through the Ages.* Baltimore, Penguin. (Historical studies by various authors.)

Cecil Forsyth. *Orchestration.* New York, Macmillan. (A technical description of the instruments of the orchestra.)

Kent Kennan. *The Technique of Orchestration.* Englewood Cliffs, N. J., Prentice-Hall. (A textbook.)

Walter Piston. *Orchestration.* New York, Norton. (Analysis of the procedures of many masters.)

Gardner Read. *Thesaurus of Orchestral Devices.* New York, Pitman. (A compendium of instrumental effects and lists of works, mostly contemporary, in which they are found.)

Bernard Rogers. *The Art of Orchestration.* New York, Appleton-Century-Crofts. (Principles of tone color in modern scoring.)

Curt Sachs. *The History of Musical Instruments.* New York, Norton. (An authoritative historical presentation.)

THE COMPOSER AS CRITIC AND AUTHOR

Hector Berlioz. *Evenings in the Orchestra*. New York, Knopf. (A composer's notes on the Romantic scene.)

Sam Morgenstern, ed. *Composers on Music*. New York, Pantheon. (An anthology of composers' writings from Palestrina to Copland.)

INDEX

Compositions marked with an asterisk (*) are analyzed and described in detail.

342 Index

344 Index

THE NORTON LIBRARY

FREUD in the New STRACHEY Standard Edition

An Autobiographical Study N146
The Ego and the Id N142
Jokes and Their Relation to the Unconscious N145
On Dreams N144
An Outline of Psychoanalysis N147
Totem and Taboo N143
